LIGHT TRAVELER
Adventure Series

Book Two

Silver Hawk's Revenge

LIGHT TRAVELER ADVENTURE SERIES

My Body Fell Off!

Silver Hawk's Revenge

Missing Children

LIGHT TRAVELER
Adventure Series

Book Two

Silver Hawk's Revenge

a novel

BJ ROWLEY

GoldenWings

This is a work of fiction, and the events in this book are not intended as doctrinal statements or beliefs. The views expressed herein are the sole responsibility of the author. Likewise, characters, places, and incidents are either the product of the author's imagination or are represented fictitiously, and any resemblance to actual persons, living or dead, or actual events or locales, is entirely coincidental.

Silver Hawk's Revenge

Published by Golden Wings Enterprises
P.O. Box 468, Orem, Utah 84059-0468

First Printing, 1998
Completely Revised, 2000

ISBN 0-9700103-2-X

Printed in the United States of America
Year of first printing, current edition: 2000

10 9 8 7 6 5 4 3 2 1

This book is dedicated to Ann, Lisa, Emily, Cherie, Shaylynn, and all the other wonderful people who have done such a terrific job of promoting my books. You're the greatest!

Special thanks to Monte Burke, attorney at law, for his invaluable input and technical expertise.

Also to my younger children, for finding and correcting more loose ends than I thought possible in one book.

Dearly beloved, avenge not yourselves,
but rather give place unto wrath:
for it is written, Vengeance is mine;
I will repay, saith the Lord.

Romans 12:19

PROLOGUE

Samuel Taylor Clawson had been a prominent and successful businessman in the Utah Valley area. He was known as a hard-working, enterprising entrepreneur, a sharp dresser and sharp talker. He was respected by his associates and admired by his peers. After many long years of dogged determination, he had finally made it in life and lived a comfortable and coveted existence in a plush mansion in Woodland Hills.

But comfortable was not enough for "The Man." Wealthy was not enough. Respectable was not enough. Mr. Clawson yearned to be filthy rich and invincibly powerful. He was possessed and consumed by hunger and thirst for more. Nothing was going to stop him from feeding his endless lust.

And so he devised a scheme—a fantastic, ingenious, and almost foolproof scheme: Invisible Blackmail.

To achieve his objectives, Mr. Clawson employed the able assistance of two extremely talented individuals. Derek Monroe, his faithful bodyguard, standing 6' 9" and weighing in at 305 pounds of solid muscle—an outcast mercenary and expert in electronics, explosives, small arms, espionage and subterfuge; and Silver Hawk, an aging Indian medicine man, banished from his tribe for the corrupt use of his "magic"—his ability to see into people's lives and observe firsthand their most intimate and secret affairs, their dishonest business dealings, and their deepest, darkest, most closely guarded secrets.

Together they orchestrated an intricate plan of virtually invisible spying and blackmailing, which quickly proved to be an exhilarating and challenging undertaking—and a remarkably lucrative one. Gone unchecked, they could easily have become some of the most devious and notorious white-collar criminals of the twentieth century. They were ruthless, unscrupulous, and murderous. There was absolutely no way of detecting their presence; no escaping their demands; no one on earth who could stop them.

Until God evened the odds by granting a certain rare and precious gift to an innocent and unsuspecting teenager. Within a few short months, all their grandiose plans for fortune and supremacy came tumbling down. All their cunning ploys were uncovered, all their shrewd and crafty works destroyed.

In the end, they were convicted by the Fourth District Court and imprisoned for life in the Utah State Penitentiary for first degree murder in the brutal death of Mr. Clawson's own step-daughter, Tiffany Short; for masterminding the kidnapping of a seventeen-year-old Provo girl named Andrea Fenton and holding her for a $3 million ransom; for blackmailing several local businessmen for a total of nearly $1 million; for the kidnapping and aggravated assault and battery of Cindy Davenport, a Payson High School cheerleader; for the deliberate destruction of private property in a bombing at the Provo Airport; for the illegal use of firearms and explosives (same incident); for a second count of first degree murder in the death of Adam Carmichael, Provo police officer (also same incident); and for the attempted murder of four Payson youth, namely: Cindy Davenport, Paul Bishop, Roshayne Pennini, and myself—Bart Elderberry.

I was that unsuspecting youth. The unusual gift granted to me, for reasons I've never altogether understood, was the unique ability to astral project—to separate my spirit self from my physical body at will. That was the unpredictable wild card against Mr. Clawson and his cronies. None of them ever considered the possibility that someone else might actually be able to duplicate Silver Hawk's so-called magic—to see THEIR dishonest business dealings, THEIR criminal activities, and THEIR deepest, darkest, most closely guarded secrets.

With the help of my friends, we brought them down. We won the battle. We put them away—for life.

Or so we thought. In reality, the war was far from over. Little did we know that for the year and a half that they were incarcerated at the state prison, Mr. Clawson and his henchmen had exactly three things on their evil minds:

Get out.

Get rich.

Get revenge.

Chapter 1

- Camp-out -

"Hey, Bart! Top this!"

At the sound of my name, I looked upstream and saw Gary, one of my fellow campers, standing in the middle of the river, grinning from ear to ear. He raised his arm, proudly displaying his latest catch—a beautiful, shiny rainbow trout that had to be at least fifteen inches long.

"Shoots and ladders," I cussed under my breath as I started reeling in my line.

"Guess that about does it," Joe called from a few yards downriver. "Time's up. That should be plenty for supper, anyway."

"Sure is," added Michael, already cleaning his fish behind us on the bank. "And it looks like Bart drew KP duty tonight."

KP—alias kitchen patrol—meant I got stuck with cleaning up after supper. By losing the contest, I inherited the dubious privilege of tidying up the cooking and eating area and washing all the dishes, pots, and pans while the rest played in their tents or sat around the campfire. That wouldn't have been so bad if we'd at least had a Coleman stove to heat water on. Mr. Allred, our leader, had decided that we were going to really rough it. We had spent the whole first day of camp lashing together makeshift picnic tables, cooking tripods, and all the basics. The second day we had built a rope bridge across the river. That was fun enough. By the third day, we were finally settled into fishing, hiking, and having a regular good time. Things went fine until I made a hasty bet with the guys about how good a fisherman I was—being a California native and all. I didn't realize there was so much difference between fresh-water fishing and the deep-sea stuff I grew up with.

I gathered up my gear, retrieved my one and only skinny six-inch fish, and headed for camp.

"Hey, Bart," Karl teased. "Is that the five-foot tuna fish you promised? Or is it a shark?"

"Yeah, yeah, yeah," I grimaced. "Go ahead, rub it in."

Once we had arrived back at camp and properly cleaned our fish, Mr. McLean, our assistant advisor, kindly reminded us of the dreaded second part of the bet—the Marine-style fish decapitation. Delbert McLean was a celebrated, decorated—and anything but humble—ex-marine, and had been making a big deal all week about the way a "real man" takes care of a fish.

So we had made a wager: In addition to KP duty, the one who caught the shortest fish got to try out Mr. McLean's technique.

"Okay, Elderberry," he said, grabbing Gary's record-setting fish off the table, "choose your weapon."

I checked out the array of disgusting-looking fish, made a sour face, and tried to duck out of camp. The guys caught me from behind. "Oh, no you don't," one of them said. "We've been waiting all day for this."

Reluctantly, I picked up my own scrawny fish gingerly by the gills. Everybody gathered around in a tight circle.

"Now watch closely," Mr. McLean said with obvious delight. "Here's the way it's done. First you grab the fish firmly with both hands." He grabbed his fish and squeezed so hard I thought it would pop. I grabbed mine firmly, too. "It's a lot more fun when they're still wiggling around," he laughed. "Then you stick it in your mouth . . ." He stuck the fish's head in his mouth and, with one quick, bone-chilling crunch, he bit down hard and twisted the fish vigorously. ". . . and bite off the head," he said, after pulling the severed fish head out of his mouth with two fingers.

The guys all hooted and hollered. "Okay, Bart!" "Yeah!" "Go for it!" "Be a man!"

I looked around in panic. *Surely they don't really expect me to do this,* I thought desperately. The looks on everyone's faces convinced me that I was doomed. I had no choice.

"You can do it, Bart," Mr. McLean encouraged. "Nothing to it."

Tentatively, I brought the fish up to eye level. The smell just about brought up my lunch.

I hesitated. My hands started shaking, and my knees suddenly felt weak.

"What's the matter?" one of the guys taunted in a sissy voice. "Can't handle it?"

That did it. I took a deep breath and closed my eyes. *The sooner I start, the sooner I finish,* I decided. Then, in one quick motion, I stuck the fish two inches into my mouth and bit down as fast and as hard as I could, crunching through bones and scales and everything. My gag reflexes kicked in immediately, and I spat the whole mess out into the fire. Everybody laughed as I wiped my sour mouth with my sleeve.

Mr. McLean looked real disappointed. "Oh, man, Bart. You let the head fall in the fire."

"So?"

"So, now you can't finish the job."

"What job?" I asked nervously.

"You're supposed to . . . " He stuck his fish head back in his mouth. His cheeks collapsed and puckered and his eyes squeezed shut as he made a tremendous sucking noise. Then he removed the head and swallowed, very big and exaggerated. " . . . suck out the eyeballs!" he announced triumphantly, smacking his lips.

Even some of the more aggressive of the bunch looked a little green around the gills after that.

I was a basket case for the next couple of hours. I hardly noticed the KP duty, and, needless to say, I did NOT eat any fish for supper.

Just as I was storing away the last of the kitchen gear, it began to rain, and I beat a trail for the tent. Actually, it wasn't a tent at all. It was a huge teepee, made of authentic buckskins. It was so big that eight of us could sleep in it with plenty of room for our gear. Mr. McLean owned two of them, and the other seven members of our Explorer post slept with him in the other one. Gratefully, I had been assigned to Mr. Allred's teepee, so I didn't have to endure the endless military stories and the horrendous singing Mr. McLean treated everybody to.

We had set up our camp in a really nice meadow near Silver Lake, at an altitude of somewhere around ten thousand feet. The teepees were too big to put up close to the trees, so they sat right in the middle of the meadow, about thirty feet apart, where they soaked up every ray of sunshine. As it turned out, though, that wasn't so bad. Since it was barely the first week of June, it was plenty chilly up there. On the north side of the hills in the shade there was still snow on the ground—a perfect place to refrigerate our perishable food.

As I stepped through the small, round opening, I saw that the nightly card games were well underway. I flopped down on my sleeping bag next to Curtis.

He was busy reading a book by flashlight, as usual—a practice that had earned him relentless harassment from the rest of the group. They couldn't understand why anyone would want to even touch a book a mere two weeks after being released from the prison of the school system. Summer was short enough as it was.

But none of them were really good friends with Curtis, anyway; they were all too interested in girls and partying. Curtis was just too serious all the time. It didn't help that his dad made his living as a mortician. Curtis' house was actually the back half of the mortuary—not exactly a cool place for guys and girls to hang out and have fun.

But I liked Curtis, and we got along pretty well. He was much more capable of carrying on a meaningful, intelligent conversation than any of the others, and was the closest friend I had in my Orem neighborhood.

Not as close a friend, though, as Paul Bishop had been when I lived in Payson. Paul and I had become the best of friends from practically the first day of school, after my family moved up from California, and I was a regular in his group in no time. But Payson was too far away to carry on any kind of ongoing friendship, and after my family moved to Orem at the end of that year, we only saw each other on rare occasions.

On the other hand, after being in Orem for a whole year, I was still treated as the newcomer by most everybody. That was why they all got so much satisfaction out of seeing me get stuck with Mr. McLean's fish head business.

"What are you reading?" I asked quietly.

"He better be studying up on how to win at cards," laughed one of the guys. "We just cleaned him out." They all laughed and resumed their noisy game.

"Sorry," I whispered sympathetically.

"Sorry about the fish," he whispered back. "That was the grossest thing I've ever seen in my life. I can't believe you did that."

"I didn't really have much choice, did I?" I replied.

"I would have hiked all the way home before I ever did anything like that."

"Well, believe me, I thought about it. But it wasn't all that bad."

Curtis went back to his reading.

I lay back on my pillow and stared at the steep, sloping sides of the teepee and listened to the rain. I wondered what it must have been like being an Indian and living in teepees every day of their lives—hunting for food and braving the weather. I'd only been gone three days, and I already missed the TVs and VCRs, telephones and CD players, and, of course, Mom's meals.

Nothing like a little camping trip to make a guy appreciate the little things, I thought to myself. I smiled and closed my eyes.

Suddenly, without any warning at all, the entire teepee lit up in a blinding flash of brilliant white light, accompanied, not even a millisecond later, by a deafening, earsplitting explosion that lasted several seconds. Cards and flashlights flew in all directions, and we all yelled and scrambled around going nowhere.

The whole teepee bulged inward from the air shock, and we sensed more than heard the crackling and snapping and sizzling of millions of volts of electricity being discharged into the air all around us, causing the hair on our arms and heads to stand straight up.

Finally, a big heat wave rushed through like a blast in the face from a freshly opened oven door. Lyle screamed and yanked the metal chain from around his neck, and Ricky pulled his pocketknife from his pocket and dropped it like a hot potato on the ground, blowing on his burned fingers.

As fast as it came, it was over, and the thunder rolled slowly away over the mountains. As if on cue, the rain came down with a vengeance. We all lay sprawled out on our sleeping bags like flattened bowling pins, hearts pounding, not daring to breathe.

"What in the heck was that?!" someone finally asked.

"We've been hit by lightning!" someone else whispered hoarsely.

"That wasn't lightning! That was a bomb! We're being attacked!"

"Get out of town."

"You guys okay?" someone yelled from the other teepee.

"Yeah, we're fine," we yelled back.

Nobody bothered gathering up the cards. We all just lay there propped up on our elbows and stared at the poles and skins of the teepee, wondering if we were going to get hit again.

"We're sitting ducks out here in the middle of this meadow," someone observed after a minute.

"Come on," another said, faking bravery. "Lightning never strikes the same place twice."

"That's what YOU think," Curtis answered.

"That's what he HOPES," I corrected.

Just then the tent lit up again, and we were jolted by another tremendous explosion, slightly after the lightning and ever so slightly less intense than the first one.

"Holy schmoly!" I yelled amidst everyone else's expletives.

Twenty seconds later the third one hit, followed by another and another, approximately every ten or fifteen seconds. Each one was slightly farther away than the last, until finally they were distant enough that we could count a whole two seconds between lightning and thunder. After another ten minutes, the rain let up to a light drizzle.

"I'm going out and look around," one of the guys said, grabbing a lantern. "You girls can stay here if you want." Nothing like a little peer pressure to get everyone going. We all started looking for shoes and jackets. I donned my plastic rain jacket, grabbed my mini-mag flashlight, and joined them outside.

The first ones out went straight to the kitchen area. "Everything looks okay over here," they yelled back.

Mr. Allred and his son, Jimmy, who had been in the other teepee, dashed directly to the vehicles. "Thank goodness," Jimmy said with relief.

"Good heck! Take a look at this!"

We all gathered around where Kyle and Gary were shining their lights, and stared in disbelief. There, exactly centered between the two teepees, not thirty feet from where we had been sitting, was a big black circle about ten feet in diameter. Every single leaf, twig, or blade of grass that had ever been there was vaporized, and the rocks and dirt were burnt pitch black several inches deep. If it hadn't been for the pouring rain immediately afterwards, we would have had a raging brush fire on our hands.

"We could've been killed," someone observed in a hushed voice. "It's a miracle we didn't get killed."

As we were standing there around the circle, contemplating our close call, we heard a truck's engine approaching and soon saw lights coming up through the trees. Before we hardly had time to take notice, a mini-van raced past on the muddy road across the meadow and continued helter-skelter up the mountain.

"What an idiot—driving like that in this weather," someone remarked.

Then we heard another engine and sprinted toward the road to see who was coming. Before we got there, a white Blazer dashed by, bouncing wildly on the pitted road. We were just able to make out the star on the mud-splattered door.

"That looked like a sheriff," Kyle said. "You think he's chasing the other guy?"

A pickup truck and another four-wheel drive, both pulling trailers, came racing by not far behind.

"Those are Search and Rescue guys," Curtis said excitedly. "I wonder what's going on."

We had finally reached the road and flagged down the last truck by jumping around like crazy people in the middle of the road. Visibility was so poor that he just about ran us over.

"What's the problem?" he yelled angrily, rolling down his window.

"Nothing. We're fine," Mr. McLean answered. "We just wondered what in the heck's going on."

"There's a little girl lost in the hills somewhere up by the lake," he explained. "Her family's been looking for her for hours."

"You're kidding," Michael said. "In this storm?"

"Is there anything we can do?" asked Mr. Allred.

"I don't think—"

"We're an Explorer post . . . from Orem," Joe cut in. "We've been camping up here for years. Most of us know these hills better than our own backyards."

"We can help search," piped in someone.

"Yeah," we all agreed.

He considered this for a minute. "Okay," he said, looking back and forth from Mr. McLean to Mr. Allred. "Bring your guys up to the lake as soon as you can get them ready. Dress warm and dry . . . and bring plenty of lights and spare batteries. It could be a long night."

We all smiled in the darkness. Some of the guys high-fived each other.

"Just remember," he said to our leaders, "you're responsible for these guys." He rolled up the window and spun off up the road.

"You heard him, men," barked Mr. McLean, suddenly all Marine. "Fall out! Move it! Move it!"

As we were running back to camp, we heard another vehicle approaching and turned in time to see a white Suburban whip past with the word SHERIFF painted on the side.

"Now THAT one was a real sheriff," Curtis informed us.

Back in the teepee, I peeled off the rain slick, put on my coat, and pulled the jacket back over. I added another pair of socks, but didn't have any waterproof boots to wear, so I put my hiking boots back on. Then I grabbed a set of spare AA batteries and shoved them in my pocket. I wished I had some gloves, but I didn't know it was going to be so cold when I packed for camp. By the time I got out to the trucks, most of the guys were there already. Mr. Allred was busy unhooking the trailer from his Jeep Cherokee, and Mr. McLean had his Montero running and ready.

"Come on, you guys," he yelled from the driver's seat. "Get a move on!" The last ones finally came running.

The drive up to the lake was only about five miles from our camp, but it took us nearly thirty minutes to get there. The road was slick and muddy, and Mr. Allred slid off it after only a couple of minutes. Since we didn't have a chain or a towrope, we had to push it out the hard way, leaving us all splattered with mud and nearly soaked through.

Chapter 2

- Becky -

The Search and Rescue guys were just about ready to hit the trail when we finally pulled up. They all had on bright yellow raincoats and rain pants, and big packs on their backs. None of them seemed the least bit anxious or hurried, but the girl's parents were practically beside themselves with panic. One of the guys, who turned out to be the real sheriff, came and introduced himself as Lieutenant Sykes.

"I understand you guys want to help," he said to our group.

"That's right."

"All right. I have five guys ready to go," he told us. "We've already worked out a search grid, based on what the parents have told us. Since you don't have radios, I'm going to assign two of you to each of my guys. You'll work alongside them, one on each side. You need to spread out as much as you can, but still stay in voice contact. The best way to do that is to keep calling the girl's name—Becky. She could be injured and immobile, or even unconscious, so sweep your flashlights back and forth in wide arcs as you go, and keep your eyes peeled."

"Can you tell us about the girl?" Mr. McLean asked.

"She's ten years old, wearing a blue-jean jumpsuit with a red sweatshirt underneath, and white tennis shoes. No coat, though. She wandered away from camp just before dusk. She told her parents she was going to pick flowers, and headed east into the trees. The parents and her two brothers did a fair amount of looking before the older boy drove down and called us."

I figured he must have been the first one we saw drive by in the mini-van.

Lt. Sykes called his men over and assigned ten of our guys to go with them, and they all took off. Mr. McLean, Mr. Allred, myself, Curtis, and two others were left over. “I’m sorry I can’t send you all,” he apologized, “but I just can’t afford to have people out searching in the dark without radios. There might be a couple more guys up here shortly, so just hang around.”

Lt. Sykes took his place in his Suburban, and we hung around the outside where we could hear the radio. At first there was quite a bit of chatter, then it thinned out as the guys concentrated on their patterns.

“How cold is it supposed to get tonight?” I asked.

“Cold,” he answered. “Especially with this storm front passing through.”

“Can she stay warm enough . . . ? I mean, is it possible she could . . . you know . . . ”

“Depends on where she is. If she snuggles up under a pine tree or somewhere where she can stay fairly dry, well then . . . maybe she’ll be okay. Very cold, but okay.”

Mr. Allred had been walking around and noticed that there were three all-terrain four-wheelers on one of the trailers.

“Can’t you use those to find her faster?” he asked.

“Not in the dark like this. Too dangerous for us and her—and too noisy.”

“Then why did you bring them?” he asked impatiently.

“And what about that other thing?” Mr. McLean asked, pointing to the other trailer.

Lt. Sykes paused a moment. “There’s a good chance we won’t be done before daybreak,” he answered. “That other thing is a hover-craft—in case we have to look elsewhere tomorrow morning.” Seeing the blank looks on our faces, he glanced at the lake out to our left. My heart tightened up inside.

“You think—?” Curtis started.

“Let’s hope not,” he answered. “And whatever you do, don’t mention that possibility with the parents around—although I’m sure they’ve thought of it already. Maybe we’ll get lucky early.”

We were interrupted by a radio call. “Lieutenant, this is Three, over,” a voice squawked from the speaker.

“Go ahead, Three.”

"We've reached the summit. No sign. We're starting down the next grid line."

"Roger, Three."

The rain started to pick up again, and the lieutenant invited us inside the Suburban where we could stay warm and dry.

For the next couple of hours, we listened with growing anxiety as each of the units called in and reported. About every fifteen minutes, Becky's mother came over wanting an update. Lt. Sykes tried his best to reassure her and keep her optimistic. He was gentle and diplomatic, but it was evident that she was losing it.

After studying his maps for a few minutes, he turned to us in the back. "It looks like my other guys aren't going to make it," he said. "You guys say you know this area?"

"Pretty well," Michael answered.

"Okay. Take a look at this map." We all strained to see. "My men are climbing through an area from here to approximately here." He circled the area with his finger. "If we come up dry by the time we cover that, I'll move some farther south down here, and the others north. In the meantime, I'm thinking I could start you guys around the perimeter of the lake, and maybe a ways up into this valley over here."

"All right!" Kyle exclaimed.

"Plan on being back here within ninety minutes, no matter what. That means you turn around and head back in forty-five minutes. Then we can regroup. If we find her in the meantime, we'll signal you with my siren. Any questions?"

"What do we do if WE find her?" asked Mr. McLean.

Lt. Sykes extracted a funny-looking pistol from a box on the floor and handed it to Mr. McLean. "This is a flare gun. If you find her, shoot this out over the lake. I'll call in my troops and send them to you."

We quickly piled out of the Suburban and zipped up our coats. As one, we broke off and headed across the meadow. Mr. McLean paired up with Michael, and Mr. Allred with Kyle. The four of them headed north and west around the lake. Curtis and I elected to cover the near side and headed around to the south.

We were just about to the lake when I stopped and spun around, causing Curtis to run into me. I turned off my flashlight.

"What's the deal?" he asked, annoyed. "Get moving!"

"Curtis," I said, grabbing him by the shoulders. "We've got to do this different. We don't have time for this. Becky could be soaking wet and freezing to death."

"What do you mean, we don't have time? This what?"

"There's a better way." I grabbed him by the arm and headed him back toward the base area. "But I need your help."

"Bart, what are you talking about?!" he yelled at me, refusing to move.

"I need go Inviz," I answered quickly. "I can look a lot faster that way. But I need to lie down somewhere. Come on. I'll explain later." I took off at a run. Curtis stared after me for a couple of seconds, then ran to catch up. "Turn off your light," I called back softly.

As we neared base, I slowed down and swung around where I could keep vehicles between the lieutenant and us. Not that it mattered; he was pretty busy studying his maps and watching the mountainside. Signaling Curtis to keep quiet, I opened the door of Mr. Allred's Jeep, and we climbed in. Then I eased the door closed carefully until it caught.

"What do you think you're doing?" Curtis whispered, very annoyed. "We should be out looking—"

"Listen, Curtis," I interrupted, "I'm going to let you in on a secret. You have to promise me that you'll KEEP it a secret. Okay?"

"I don't know what you're—"

"Promise?"

"Okay, already. I promise," he whispered angrily. "What?"

I looked him dead in the eye and got serious. "Curtis, I can astral project. Do you know what that means?"

He shook his head slightly, his eyes still narrow and glaring.

"It means I can get out of my body—invisible. I can separate myself from my physical body."

"Get out of your body?" he smirked. "Right. What a laugh."

"I'm serious."

Curtis stared at me for a long moment. "You're putting me on, right?"

"No, I'm not. I'm dead serious."

"You're saying you can become like a ghost and float around invisible?" he asked dryly.

"Exactly. That's why I call it 'Going Inviz'—for invisible," I explained.

"Yeah, right. And then what?"

"Then I can search about a hundred times faster, and I can see and hear about a hundred times better."

He saw the determined look in my eye. "What am I supposed to do while you're . . . invisible?" he said, a little more seriously.

"You just sit here and keep watch. It'll look like I'm sleeping—very soundly. Keep your head down so no one sees you, but if someone heads toward the Jeep, like they're going to get in, you shake me as hard as you can until you wake me up."

"What do you mean 'wake you up'? I thought—"

"I'm not really sleeping. It just looks like it. But if my body gets disturbed enough, it signals me to come back. Can you do that?"

"This is extremely weird, Bart."

I just stared at him hard again.

"Okay, fine," he agreed finally. "But if anybody finds us in here, you get to come up with the excuses. It'll sure make us look like a couple of real wimps."

We crawled over into the backseat, and I lay down across the bench. Curtis squatted down on the floor where he could see out the windows.

My challenge at that point was to relax—completely. No easy task, with all the pressure and excitement going on. It took me a good four or five minutes before I could finally get my mind and body to cooperate. Then the expected vibrations finally came, coursing through my body like painless mild electricity. Seconds later, I lifted free. With the body and its physical abilities detached, my mind was in complete control.

Up, I mentally commanded myself. Just like that, I rose straight up out of my body, still in the prone position. I rolled over and straightened up. I wasn't really interested in seeing myself—I had done that so many times that it was old hat long ago. But I did want to get a good look at Curtis. He was staring very intently at me—at my body, that is—and looked extremely nervous. *I hope he doesn't blow it,* I thought.

There was nothing else I could do, since he couldn't see or hear me, so I floated up through the roof of the Jeep and took a look around. I was relieved to have my out-of-body night vision. Everything was clearly visible, even though it was pretty dark. It was like having military infrared, but without the weird greenish color.

Okay, now I'm out, where do I start?

I tried to remember what the lieutenant had said about the search patterns as I gazed at the hillsides. I had never been involved in a search before, and the grids were not entirely clear to me. I drifted over to the edge of the trees and started moving back and forth up the mountainside.

This is no good, I thought after a minute. *Even though I can go tons faster, I don't have a clue where to start or where to look.*

I rose up into the air about a hundred feet or so and had another look around. The trees seemed to stretch endlessly in all directions.

God, I prayed quickly, *I need some help here. I know you gave me this gift to bless people. I want to find this little girl. She's in real trouble. Please tell me where to look.*

The thought suddenly came to me, "Think like a ten-year-old."

Think like a ten-year-old? I floated back over the family's campsite and looked over the area. *Lt. Sykes said she went to pick flowers.* I studied the immediate area by the trees. *That's funny. There aren't any flowers here to pick.* I looked around some more. *If I were Becky, where would I go to find flowers?* I looked towards the trees, where everyone had assumed she went. *She probably wouldn't head straight into the trees. That would be plenty scary for a little girl around sunset.* To the north, the grass was fairly high and thick. *Not likely,* I thought. To the south, the meadow was more barren. I headed in that direction, staying high in the air.

At the far end of the meadow, the ground gradually dropped off for about fifty feet and opened out into another small meadow full of flowers. *Bingo!* I thought. Near the tree line, I found a small creek wandering lazily through the undergrowth. *She probably wouldn't try to cross that, with so many flowers to choose from on this side.* I kept going south. Gradually the creek re-entered a wooded area. At the same time, I found several different trails that headed both into the woods and across the meadow.

I stopped. *Now what?* I looked in all directions again, but couldn't find any clues. There were flowers everywhere. I rose several hundred feet higher to get a broader view. The higher I went, the more impossible it looked. The mountainside was endless.

Then my attention was drawn by a sound. I looked around.

What did I hear? Whenever I went Inviz, I was able to hear lots of things from great distances that couldn't be heard in-body—sometimes sounds from miles away. All kinds of things from everywhere, all joined together creating a subdued background noise in my ears. It was like being in a busy mall, with every imaginable sound competing with each other. I had been out-of-body so many times that I had become accustomed to it and didn't usually pay much attention.

I concentrated on the different sounds. Every sound was crystal clear, if I paid enough attention and focused. I mentally began taking inventory. I could hear the gentle rain falling on the ground and the creek gurgling softly, barely making any noise at all. I detected a few animal sounds, but not many.

Then I heard the squawk of a radio and some voices. Turning slightly, I directed my attention to the mountainside.

"Base, this is Five, over." There was some static I didn't catch. "Okay, we'll head that direction, over."

I was straining to hear the reply from base when another sound penetrated my consciousness. It was a soft cry, like a whimpering puppy.

A little girl crying! I realized excitedly. *It must be Becky!*

I focused intensely on the source and allowed my subconscious to draw me down toward the sound. As I neared the ground, I made out the roof of a small cabin, maybe fifteen feet square, nestled among the trees. The cabin sat in the upper end of a small draw and was almost completely overgrown with vines and trees. From ground level, it was almost completely hidden from view. One would have had to pass within three or four yards to even see it, which was unlikely, seeing that the draw went nowhere but straight up the steep mountainside. There was little chance for anyone to get close, even during a search.

I came down to ground level in front of the only door, which was partly opened and hanging crooked from one hinge. Without further hesitation, I passed through it and entered the cabin.

There on the floor in the far corner sat little Becky. She had her knees drawn up to her chest, with her arms wrapped around them. Her forehead was resting on her kneecaps, and she was crying softly. As I looked closer, I noticed that she was shivering from the cold.

Thank goodness she's alive, I thought with a sigh of relief. *She must be scared to death. It's almost pitch black in here.* The only window was completely covered by the surrounding foliage.

I've got to go for help! I shot back up through the ceiling into the sky and looked around. *I've got to be sure where she is, so I can tell the lieutenant.* I slowly scanned the area, making mental notes of the prominent landmarks.

Then a thought occurred to me. *How am I going to explain to him how I know where she is? He'll never believe me. I'm supposed to be looking around the lake with the others.* I sank dejectedly back down into the cabin. *I should have thought of that before. Now I have no choice. I'm going to have to get her out myself.*

Positioning myself in the middle of the room, I closed my eyes and concentrated all my mental strength on creating light. I knew once I did that, I could materialize and make myself visible. It was difficult to do and required a great deal of effort. Slowly the room began to light up, until it was about the equivalent of a couple of gas lanterns. Becky was too lost in her misery to notice.

"Becky," I said softly. She didn't seem to hear me. "Becky," I said louder. The crying stopped. "Becky, look at me," I said as gently as I could. She slowly raised her head and wiped the tears from her eyes.

"Can you see me?" I asked. She nodded slightly and wiped her eyes again. "Listen to me very carefully. I'm going to help you find your parents, but I need you to be brave. Can you do that?"

She nodded again.

"Can you walk?"

"Yes," she managed.

"Okay, stand up. You need to follow me. I'm going to lead you down the mountain, okay?"

She climbed to her feet and brushed off her pants.

"Ready?" I asked.

"Can't you carry me, please?" she pleaded, her eyes tired and sad. "I'm scared."

I looked at her compassionately. "No, Becky, I can't."

"Why not?"

"Because . . . because I'm just a spirit," I said softly. "I can't pick you up."

She studied me intently, realizing I was standing a foot or so above the floor. "Are you an angel?" she whispered.

I hesitated again. "Well, sort of, I guess."

"Neat," she said with a big smile.

I wonder if I'll get in trouble for impersonating an angel.

"Let's go," I urged, "before your mother has a fit."

I moved out the door, trying to make it look like I was squeezing through the narrow opening and not going through solid wood. She followed quickly without noticing, and we were soon working our way down the hill. I was unable to clear the path or hold limbs out of her way, and she had a hard time following without stumbling and falling every so often. The going was painstakingly slow, and in a matter of minutes she was soaking wet.

"We need to hurry," I coaxed.

"I'm trying," she replied bravely.

After about twenty minutes or so, I detected some radio noise again. I stopped to listen.

"What's the matter?" she asked, practically walking right through me before she stopped.

"Shh," I said. "I need to listen." I rose up into the air about fifty feet and faced the mountain. Becky followed me intently with her eyes.

"Base, this is Five, come in." The sound was much louder to me than before.

"Base here. Go ahead Five."

"We're down on the—" There was a prolonged pause. "Whoa! Lieutenant, you're not going to believe this."

"What?" came Lt. Sykes' voice over the radio.

"There's a . . . bright white light hovering over the trees, about three hundred yards south-east of us."

I spun around to face the opposite direction and spotted three guys in a small clearing looking straight at me.

"Say again?" Lt. Sykes demanded.

Shoot! I'm still visible.

"It . . . it looks like a man . . . floating—"

I thought "darkness" and immediately became invisible.

"Wait! Now it's gone. I could have sworn . . ."

Back down on the ground, I appeared to Becky again. She was a little scared after watching me disappear.

"Becky, listen. There are three men just up ahead a ways, waiting for you." She looked anxiously down the trail into the darkness. "I'm going to leave now. You need to be real brave and keep walking down this little trail, and they'll find you."

"But I can't see anything without you with me," she said, trying hard not to cry.

"Just go real slow," I answered encouragingly, "and call out to them. Two of them are named Gary and Joe. Yell their names real loud, and they'll hear you."

By that time I could hear footsteps approaching through the trees, even though they were still a good distance away. I faded from her view with the biggest, most loving and reassuring smile on my face that I could manage.

For a few seconds she just stood there, frozen with fear. Then slowly and cautiously, she started moving forward.

Call out their names, I thought. *Call their names.*

As if she read my mind, she mustered up a squeaky, "Gary? Joe?" Encouraged by the sound of her own voice, she called again, much louder. "Gary? Joe?" She called again, and again.

Within moments, Gary, Joe, and Five came crashing through the brush, flashlights blinding her eyes. I watched with overflowing emotions as Five squatted down on the ground in front of her and gathered her up in his arms.

"Are you all right?" he asked hoarsely.

"I think so."

"Base? Five," he said into the radio. "We found her! We found her! She's okay!"

"Thank goodness," came Lt. Sykes' voice.

I followed, floating a few feet above and behind, as they forged their way back through the thick woods toward the road. Over the radio, I could hear Lt. Sykes announcing to the rest of the crew that the search was over. I could also hear the excited voices of Becky's family in the background.

Then I heard the shrill, faraway sound of a police siren from the direction of the base as Lt. Sykes signaled the guys around the lake.

The guys around the lake! I realized suddenly. *Holy schmoly!*

Just about that time, I felt the urgent tugging of the invisible elastic-like cord that bound my spirit to my body, and I knew Curtis was trying to raise me.

Back to body! I commanded myself.

Instantly, I was yanked back into my body. I sat up quickly, and Curtis gasped and jumped back.

"Heck, Bart! You scared me to death."

"Sorry," I said lamely.

"The search is over," he said, dropping to a whisper. "They found her."

"I know," I said, smiling.

"You mean—?"

"Let's get out of here. Hurry."

We climbed out of the Jeep in the nick of time, just as Mr. Allred and Kyle came running across the far side of the meadow. Lt. Sykes and Becky's family were already in their vehicles and pulling away to go meet the rescuers. We just managed to stop them long enough to hitch a ride.

A teary and joyful reunion soon followed as we found the guys standing by the road, with Becky standing tall and proud in front of them. Becky hugged everybody, including the lieutenant. Her parents did the same. Everybody started talking at once, prying Becky with questions and trying to learn what had happened to her.

After the commotion had died down a little, Gary spoke up. "Becky?" he asked with a puzzled look on his face, "how did you know our names?"

"What?" she asked.

"You were calling my name and Joe's," he said, "just before we found you."

Becky's parents and the lieutenant stopped talking and looked questioningly at them and at each other. I pulled my hat down low over my eyes.

She looked Gary squarely in the eye and answered simply, "The angel told me."

"The ang—?"

"Can we get in the van now?" she said, cutting him off. "I'm cold." She grabbed her parents' hands and led them away.

Gary and Joe looked like they'd seen a ghost . . . which, I guess, they really had. Five was busy telling the lieutenant "I told you so." Curtis just stood there staring holes in me, his eyes and mouth wide open.

I just grinned and winked.

Chapter 3

- Another Rescue -

The next morning we woke up to six inches of snow on the ground and temperatures near freezing, but we didn't mind. I shuddered to think what it might have been like all night for Becky, though. Talk of the rescue was incessant, and the story of the angel became greatly embellished by Gary and Joe with each telling. Curtis tried several times to corner me for more information, but there were always too many guys around. Finally the week was over, and we struck camp and returned home on Saturday afternoon as planned.

Sunday afternoon Curtis came over, and we retired to my bedroom.

"Okay, Bart," he said before I even closed the door. "I want to know everything."

"You sure?" I asked.

"Everything," he insisted as he stretched out on my bed and got comfortable.

"Okay. You asked for it."

I spent the better part of the afternoon relating to him everything I could think of, starting with the automobile accident up Payson Canyon in tenth grade, and what we had thought was a near-death experience, and all the details regarding Tiffany Short's murder and Andrea Fenton's kidnapping. And, finally, about Paul and Roshayne and Cindy, and our narrow escape from the airport hangar and the bomb.

He was particularly keen on the fact that Silver Hawk could also get out of his body. "He could still be doing that from prison, you know," he observed.

"I've thought of that. In fact, I've felt him hanging around a few times, but that was several months ago. I think he finally decided I'm not worth the bother."

"You hope," he said.

Just the thought of Hawk watching me made a shiver run down my spine, and I imagined for a second that he was there in the room.

Don't be ridiculous, I scolded myself. *You're just being paranoid.*

Before I could contemplate the issue much further, we were interrupted by a loud knocking on the door. "You have a phone call," Mom said.

I picked up the extension on my desk. "Hello?"

"Bart? This is George. How you doing?"

George was a year or so younger than me and had been working overtime at becoming my bosom buddy, though I wasn't sure why.

"Hi, George," I answered, pulling a face at Curtis. He just smiled. "What's up?"

"Hey, I got these three free tickets to the Buzz game this Saturday. I was wondering if you'd like to go with me."

Minor league baseball was not my favorite thing to do, but it sounded a lot better than doing chores around the house. "Who else is going?" I asked.

"I was thinking of asking Curtis. What do you think?"

"He's right here. Wait a sec, and I'll ask him." I covered the phone and relayed the good news to Curtis.

He thought about it for a second. "You're right," he said. "Sounds better than being stuck at home. Sure. Why not?"

"Okay," I said to George. "Sounds fun. You want me to drive?" I figured that was one of the reasons he was calling.

"Hey, could you?" he said excitedly. "That'd be great. I don't have a car, you know."

"Yeah, I know."

"Game starts at four. If we hit the freeway by two-thirty, we can get there a bit early."

"Two-thirty it is."

When I hung up the phone, I got that funny feeling again that Silver Hawk was in the room. It was creepy. *Forget it, Bart,* I told myself. *He's in prison. He's harmless.*

A few days later, I was wandering around the house, being generally bored with summer and wondering what I could do. Miraculously, the house was quiet. My younger brother Darin and my two little sisters, Charlene and Cynthia, were apparently all at friends' houses, and my mom was shopping.

This looks like a good time to do some exploring, I thought. Of course, my definition of "exploring" was a tiny bit different from most people's.

After closing my curtains, I locked my bedroom door and lay down on my bed. I assumed what I had come to call the "coffin position"—face up, flat on my back, and my hands on my stomach. I consciously tensed and relaxed all my muscles, starting with my toes and working my way upward until I felt calm and relaxed. Then I did a minute or two of deep breathing. Finally, I concentrated on seeing and thinking blackness and nothingness, pushing all other thoughts out of my mind. Right on schedule, the vibrations began, pulsing gently up and down my body. When that happened, I knew I was being turned loose. All I had to do then was think *UP,* and my spirit body separated from my phyzbod—my acronym for "physical body"—and I was free.

Usually, when I lifted out, I already had in mind where I wanted to go or who I wanted to visit. I had learned that if I didn't, my subconscious mind would make the decision for me, sometimes leading to interesting and unexpected situations. I had also learned that my spirit super-conscious had a unique way of tracking people. It was like some sort of high-level, spiritual homing device that sensed brain waves . . . or something. If I thought about someone I knew, it didn't matter how far away that person was, I could almost always find them.

Not always, though. There were still a few things about the whole astral projecting business that I hadn't quite figured out. It wasn't very consistent.

I hovered in the air for a couple of seconds, trying to decide what to do.

I've never been to George's house, I thought.

That was all I needed, and my subconscious kicked in. At the speed of thought—barely the blink of an eye—I was transported five blocks away and found myself floating in the air over George's backyard. He was jumping on his trampoline with his sister. Their little dog was barking and yapping at them, chasing around and around. I rose up into the air a few more feet to see where I was in the neighborhood. I felt a little guilty to think I didn't even know where George lived. He was always so intent on following me around that I hadn't bothered to find out.

From my prime perspective in the air, I could see the whole neighborhood, and I enjoyed just floating there and watching people. I got a great deal of satisfaction from knowing I could watch everybody, and no one could see me doing the watching.

Of course I had to be careful not to invade people's privacy, although it usually wasn't a problem in the afternoons. I had promised God I wouldn't do that. I almost lost my gift once, after inadvertently transporting myself into the girls' showers at the high school. It was like I was being punished or something. What a disaster. There was no way I was EVER going to do that again, if I could help it.

After several minutes, I suddenly felt the need to return to my body. I had long since learned not to ignore that kind of prompting. It could be something as simple as when Curtis was trying to wake me up on the camping trip, or it could be something much more desperate.

Back to body, I commanded myself.

As always, I felt the jerk of the cord, but instead of the usual split-second return, I seemed to move in slow motion, like I was being dragged through molasses. Finally I felt my body underneath me, and I slid in headfirst, like going down a slippery slide. Very unusual.

Before I could even open my eyes, I began to gag and cough uncontrollably. The air around me was burning hot, and it was hard to breathe.

I looked around. Instead of being on my bed, staring at the ceiling, I was face down on the floor. The room was darker than it should have been. *What's going on?* I thought. *How did I get dumped on the floor?*

I pushed myself up onto my elbows and became aware of a loud, crackling sound and an intense heat around my face. My eyes stung from the effects of smoke.

The house is on fire! I realized suddenly. *I've got to get out of here!*

I was about to jump to my feet when I remembered all the drills in school, and caught myself in the nick of time. Crawling around on all fours, I tried to get my bearings.

Where's my bed? Where's the door? I've got to get downstairs!

The smoke was so thick and dark that I could hardly see, and I had an increasingly hard time breathing. I decided to pull off my T-shirt and hold it over my mouth to try to filter out some of the smoke. I grabbed the bottom of my shirt and tried to pull it over my head.

This isn't a T-shirt, I realized. *What gives? I'm sure I was wearing a T-shirt.*

Too desperate to analyze anything, I quickly unbuttoned and removed the shirt and use it to cover my mouth. I started crawling with my free hand, sure that I would find a wall quickly and discover where I was. After fifteen or twenty feet, I was still totally surrounded by thick, black, swirling smoke.

I know my room isn't this big, I thought. Then I realized that the floor was not carpeted, as my bedroom should have been. It was hardwood. Nowhere in our house did we have a hardwood floor.

Real panic set in. *Where in the heck am I?*

I stopped and forced myself to think, in spite of the searing heat burning at my face and my bare upper body. My eyes watering, I rotated around slowly, trying to determine where the most heat was. Sensing that there might be one direction slightly less hot than the rest, I set out crawling in that direction.

I had barely gone four feet when I stumbled over something big on the floor and fell over it onto my face. I looked back and was shocked to discover the body of a young girl face down, unconscious on the floor. Quickly I rolled her onto her back, grabbed her by one wrist, and began pulling her across the floor, still totally unsure about where I was going.

Progress was painfully slow as I pulled her along, mere inches at a time. Somewhere, I lost the shirt. Without the benefit of filtered air to breathe, my strength ebbed quickly, and it became more and more difficult to pull the girl.

During a brief rest, I leaned over to look closely at her face and received the shock of a lifetime.

It's Charlene! My sister!

"Charlene!" I yelled, shaking her shoulders. Her head shook back and forth, but she did not respond. My eyes flooded instantly with tears, and my heart felt like it was going to explode. "Charlene!" I yelled again. "Don't die! I'll get you out!"

Desperately I grabbed her by both wrists and began crawling backward on my knees through the smoke. Breathing became more and more painful. Every breath was like a searing blast furnace blowing into my lungs. I smelled a horrible, acrid odor and realized that the hair on my arms was beginning to smolder. Although I still had not seen any flames, I could hear them, and I knew they were rapidly closing in on us.

Drawing one last burning gulp of air, I yanked on Charlene's arms and crawled backward as fast as my weakened condition would allow. After a couple of minutes, my progress was stopped. I had run into a step-up. Quickly, I pulled Charlene up and found that we were on a hard, carpeted floor. After a few more feet, the heat seemed lower by a few degrees. I pulled her another several feet, then stopped, collapsing to the floor and breathing heavily.

Although I couldn't see around me, I sensed I was in a hallway or a small room, maybe by the way the sound had changed. The majority of the fire was behind me. I rolled over on my back and struggled to find some oxygen to relieve my aching lungs. My eyes felt like they were bathed in acid, and no amount of blinking seemed to bring any relief. How easy it would have been to just quit right there. My arms and legs felt like rubber and ached from the effort of sliding and pulling. My chest heaved, and I coughed repeatedly. My strength was being sucked out by the oven-like heat.

Dear God, I prayed, *please don't let us die! Give me strength! At least help me save my sister!*

At that moment, I felt a surge of energy coursing through my body, starting at my head and spreading to my fingers and toes. Feeling the heat closing in again, I decided that the time factor had become more dangerous than the risk of breathing hot or toxic air. Taking the chance, I stood slowly, testing the air. Then I scooped Charlene's limp body up into my arms and staggered through the thick fumes in the direction I could only hope was an exit. One step after another, I forced myself onward.

My arms began to tremble and quiver from the weight of Charlene's body. Twice my legs buckled, and I dropped painfully to my knees. Both times I summoned every fiber of strength and determination I could muster, and rose again. Finally, after what seemed an eternity, I saw a dim light through the smoke and sensed that I was nearing an entrance.

Just before I stepped through the opening, I was hit full in the face by a tremendous gush of water that knocked me backward to the floor. Charlene collapsed in a heap on top of me. The relief of the drenching water was overwhelming and gave me the vital burst of last-minute determination I needed. After gasping for breath, I pushed Charlene off and pulled myself to my knees. I slid my arms again under her neck and legs and heaved myself upward with one last burst of willpower. The veins in my neck bulged almost to the bursting point, and my face was contorted in pain. Slowly I rose, inch by inch, my legs quivering and shaking like sticks of rubber, my whole body pouring with sweat. After an eternity of sheer Herculean effort, I felt my knees lock and knew I was upright again.

I had to command my feet to move forward one step at a time. *One. Two. Three.* I gasped for air and felt like my lungs were going to explode. *Four. Five.* The light grew steadily bigger through the haze, and everything started to spin. I felt my consciousness slipping. *Six. Seven.*

Suddenly, I was through a doorway and stumbling off the edge of a sidewalk, trying desperately to keep my legs under me so I wouldn't drop my sister.

"There comes somebody!" I heard someone shout. "Quick! Bring a stretcher!"

"It's Charlene!" a girl's voice yelled. "He found her!"

I was only vaguely aware of the firemen who appeared at my side, relieving me of my heavy burden. I dropped helplessly to my knees, totally oblivious to the sharp rocks that embedded themselves into my flesh. I barely registered being picked up under each arm and carried toward the waiting ambulance. My vision blurred from a fresh rush of tears, and I lost all contact with reality.

I faintly remembered being lifted high in the air before my eyes closed, then I willingly surrendered myself to whatever fate had in store.

I slept for a long time. When I awoke and opened my eyes, the memories of the fire rushed back, and I expected to see doctors and nurses all around. I was surprised to find myself lying on my own bed, staring at the ceiling. *I'm home already?* I puzzled. *I don't remember anything about going to the hospital. Boy, I must have really been out of it.*

I tried to sit up in bed and was immediately seized by a splitting headache. After the room stopped spinning, I carefully lowered my feet to the soft, carpeted floor. I stood slowly and stumbled toward the door, surprised at how weak I was.

Mom and Dad must be having a tizzy fit after having to get me out of the hospital again, I thought. *They're starting to think I live there.* Then it dawned on me. *Wait a minute! The house burned down! What's the deal? And Charlene! What happened to Charlene? Is she alive?*

In my anxiety, I tripped going down the stairs and hit my head on the railing, doubling the effects of my headache. Dad was sitting in his recliner in the family room comfortably watching the news, and didn't even blink as I stumbled in. I stopped and looked at him for a second. Then I held out my hands and studied them. *Am I Inviz?* I wondered. *Can't he see me?*

"Hi, Bart," he said with a quick glance in my direction. "How was your day?"

How was my day?! How was my day?! I just about died in a fire, and he asks me how was my day?! I was speechless.

I shuffled past him into the kitchen and found Mom at the counter cooking something. "Mom?" I said hesitantly.

I expected her to turn and swallow me up in one of her big, smothering bear hugs, but she just glanced at me quickly over her shoulder and returned to her work. "Are you ready for dinner, hon?" she asked. "You can set the table, if you like."

"Dinner?" I asked stupidly. *That's all she's worried about is dinner?*

"Oh, I know it's early, but your dad has a meeting tonight, so we're trying to hurry."

"A meeting?" I echoed. *What's going on here?*

"His weekly Thursday night presentation," she explained. "You know that."

"Thursday?" I said, dumbfounded. *It can't be Thursday. Yesterday was Thursday. The fire was Thursday.*

"Is there an echo in here?" Mom asked as she turned and put her hands on her hips, "or are you just hard of hearing all of a sudden?" She smiled and opened the fridge as I sat cautiously on the edge of the nearest chair. *Did I just dream this whole fire thing?*

"Mom?" I asked tentatively. "Where's Charlene?"

"She's at a friend's birthday party. They went roller-skating. Why?"

Just then the phone rang, and Mom went to answer it. At the same time, my ears caught the words of the TV newscaster from the family room, and I swung around to watch.

". . . have just about contained the blaze that erupted suddenly here at the skating rink less than an hour ago. Authorities speculate that the fire was caused by a faulty gas line that exploded in a back room. The building was totally engulfed in a matter of minutes."

Now this is strange, I thought.

"Yes?" I heard Mom say behind me. "I'm Mrs. Elderberry."

". . . miraculously, no one was killed, although there was one close call. As the occupants flooded into the parking lot, it was discovered that one young girl was still in the building, apparently in the rest room at the time of the explosion. Firemen had to physically restrain several friends to keep them from rushing back in to find her."

"Could it be?" I asked quietly, my interest piqued.

The scene changed from the live broadcast to a pre-recorded segment showing the skating rink building with black smoke billowing out the front door and into the sky.

" . . . then, from nowhere, this young man came stumbling out the front door, carrying the missing girl in his arms . . ."

I watched in utter amazement as a dark figure emerged through the smoke, carrying the limp body of a girl in his arms. As the camera zoomed in on the dramatic scene, I immediately recognized the blackened face and tattered clothing of the rescued girl.

"Charlene!" Dad yelled, bolting from his chair.

"Charlene!" I yelled, jumping to my feet.

"Charlene?" Mom squeaked into the phone, her face suddenly white.

As the firemen rushed forward to retrieve the limp body, the rescuer fell to his knees and was prevented from toppling headfirst to the pavement by a nearby police officer. The camera zoomed in on his face and his bare, sweaty, black chest as he was hoisted back to his feet. My mouth dropped open in utter disbelief.

"What?!" I gasped. *THAT'S NOT ME! That's not—! But how—? Who—?*

The scene switched back to the anchorwoman speaking to the camera. "We have just received word that the girl and her unidentified rescuer are both in serious condition at the Utah Valley Regional Medical Center, and are being treated for burns and smoke inhalation. We'll have more on this and other news at ten, when, hopefully, we'll have discovered the identities of the young girl and her brave hero. Back to you, Mike."

"We're on our way right now!" Mom yelled, slamming the phone down. "Phillip! Charlene—!"

"Charlene's in trouble!" Dad yelled, running into the kitchen. "I just saw her on TV!"

"They just called from the hospital!" Mom cried, grabbing Dad by the arms.

"Let's go!" he ordered, pulling Mom toward the garage.

"I'm going with you!" I yelled, running right behind them.

We had to wait a while before we were able to see her. She was under constant supervision in the intensive care unit and hooked up to dozens of wires and things. Her face had been cleaned up some, but her wavy blonde hair was still streaked with black. When she was able to talk, the nurse invited us in to see her for a few minutes.

I could tell Mom wanted to pick her up and hug her to pieces, but she was afraid to touch her anywhere. Finally she rubbed her cheek gently with the back of her finger. "Oh, baby," she said through her tears. "Don't worry. Mommy's here. Daddy's here. You're going to be all right, honey." Dad bent down and gave her a tender kiss on the cheek, but was too choked up to say anything.

Charlene smiled and closed her eyes. After several minutes, when we thought sure she was sound asleep, she suddenly opened her eyes wide and looked at me. In a soft, raspy voice, she said, "Thanks, Bart . . . for saving me."

Mom smiled condescendingly. "Char, it wasn't Bart. It was someone else. We don't even know his name yet."

She looked at Mom with a puzzled expression, then back at me. "It WAS you, wasn't it, Bart?" She looked back at Mom and Dad. "I saw him pick me up . . . and he talked to me . . ." She looked back at me questioningly, and her eyes started drooping again. "I was sure it was . . ." She closed her eyes and drifted off to sleep again.

Later, as we left the hospital, I was taken aback when I saw my reflection in the glass of the outside door. I was still wearing my favorite Lakers T-shirt.

Chapter 4

- Speeding -

Friday afternoon we visited Charlene again in the hospital. We also met her rescuer, who turned out to be an employee of the skating rink named Andy Riggins. Apparently, he had been in a storage room when the water heater had exploded from a gas leak, and he'd been knocked out by the blast. He didn't remember a thing about saving Charlene. In fact, he didn't remember anything at all between the explosion and waking up in the hospital. He was totally surprised—probably even more than I was—by all the reporters and visitors, and especially by the video clip of the rescue.

I still couldn't explain my involvement. I had started and ended lying on my bed, and the whole thing had only lasted a few minutes. The only explanation I could come up with was that maybe the Lord had shown it to me in a vision or something. If that was the case, it was the most realistic vision on record, because I distinctly felt the smoke in my eyes and the heat on my face, as though I had been there.

Of course, the hair on my arms was not burnt, and my lungs were as clear as a bell.

And the real clincher—why did Charlene think I had saved her? She said she had seen me pick her up, yet my recollection was that she had been unconscious the whole time.

I was still working it over in my mind later that evening while sort of watching a movie on TV. I don't even remember the movie ending, but suddenly I was jerked out of my reverie by the sound of the names that had haunted me for the past several months. It was the ten o'clock news.

". . . the escapees have been identified as Samuel Clawson, Derek Monroe, and an Indian who goes by the name of Silver Hawk . . ."

I gasped as their mug shots were projected on the screen.

". . . all three were serving life sentences for the murder of Clawson's stepdaughter, Tiffany Short of Payson, along with various other crimes including—"

"Mom!" I yelled as Tiffany's picture popped up. "Come here, quick!" The phone rang, and she was detoured to answer it.

". . . details about Wednesday's escape are being kept hush-hush by prison officials, but it appears that they may have had some help from the inside, possibly a prison guard or—"

Mom interrupted by handing me the phone. "It's for you."

"Bart? This is Paul," blared the familiar voice from Payson. "Turn on your TV to channel four! Hurry!"

"I'm already watching."

". . . police are warning all residents in the area to use extreme caution, as the three are believed to be armed and extremely dangerous. If you observe anything or anyone of a suspicious nature, please notify the police immediately."

"Bart, they're out," Paul whispered hoarsely.

I was too stunned to answer.

"Bart? You there?"

"Yeah," I responded.

"What are we going to do?"

"What CAN we do?" I answered.

"Do you think they'll come after us?"

"I don't know, Paul. I don't know."

"Jeez Louise, this wasn't supposed to happen! They weren't supposed to EVER get out."

"I'm sure they'll get caught. How far can they get?"

"I don't know, but be careful."

After I hung up, I realized that Mom had been standing by, watching the TV and listening to my conversation. I detected a trace of fear in her eyes. Instinctively we embraced and hugged each other hard.

"They're probably halfway to Mexico by now," I said, trying to sound reassuring. She just hugged me harder.

Before bed, Dad double-checked all the windows and doors to make sure everything was locked tight, and Mom insisted on leaving all the lights on in the house and yard. Needless to say, I didn't sleep well that night. Every time I dozed off, I was assaulted by nightmares of Mr. Clawson staring down the three-foot-long barrel of a gun pointed at my face, or Derek ripping me apart like a rag doll, or Hawk yanking me out of my body and setting fire to my lifeless form with a torch. Every little noise in the house made me jump.

Finally sleep came. And morning came, and with the brightness of the sun our fears subsided. We all spent the morning commenting optimistically either about how close they would be to Mexico or how close they would be to getting caught and thrown back in jail. I attacked my chores in a daze, trying to keep myself occupied.

Until Curtis called at around two o'clock, I had completely forgotten about the Buzz game.

"I don't think you should go, Bart," Mom said anxiously. "What if—"

"Mom, we're going to a crowded ballpark on a crowded freeway in the middle of the day. What could happen? Besides, I'm probably better off away from home right now, anyway."

A few minutes later I backed out of the driveway, leaving Mom clutching her chest and Dad with his hands in his pockets. I picked up Curtis first, then George. We hit the freeway right at two-thirty, as planned.

Curtis and George were both oblivious to my silence and apprehension, and were busy talking about baseball and how all the major league teams were doing. I tried to listen, but couldn't get myself into the conversation.

We were just rounding the point of the mountain when Curtis turned around to say something to George and stopped in mid-sentence. "There's a cop behind us," he announced.

"Shoot!" I cussed, glancing quickly at the speedometer. We were going about fifteen miles over the limit.

"He's right behind us with his lights on," George said, turning around and pointing over his shoulder out the back window.

I looked in the mirror and saw the police car swerve suddenly, like he was dodging something.

"Better hurry and pull over, Bart," Curtis advised.

I pulled off the side into the emergency lane and coasted to a stop, rolling down my window as I went. With the brake set, I began fishing around in the glove box for the registration. Sitting back up, I turned to face the officer standing by the side of the car.

"I guess we were—"

The words died abruptly in my throat as I found myself staring cross-eyed at the end of a gun. Everybody froze.

They've found me, was my first thought. *My nightmare has come true. I'm dead.*

Then I looked past the gun. It wasn't Clawson or Hawk or Derek, like I had feared. It was just a cop, standing in the ready-to-fire position. I was really spooked, and the look I saw on his face scared me a lot more than his gun did. He was dripping with sweat, and his eyes were bugged out in sheer terror. His hands were shaking badly, and I started to worry about him accidentally pulling the trigger. If I was scared, HE was petrified.

I felt the car jerk, like someone had jumped on the bumper. I looked in the mirror and saw another cop lying on the trunk, pointing a shotgun through the back window at George.

For several seconds, nobody moved.

"Don't . . . don't move!" the first cop finally squeaked. His voice was high-pitched and extremely nervous.

"We're not moving," I answered softly.

"Get your hands up where I can see them! Slowly!"

We all raised our hands over our heads.

"What's going on?" Curtis asked.

"Out of the car!" he yelled at us. "Spread-eagle on the hood!"

This guy is out of control, I realized. *He wants to shoot us!*

I carefully and slowly opened my door as he backed away from the car. I was afraid he was going to get hit by traffic if he wasn't careful. Curtis got out next, followed by George. When we were all safely spread out on the hood, he finally pried his left hand away from his gun and fingered the microphone clipped to his collar.

"Dispatch? Jones here. We got them!"

"What's your twenty, Jones?"

"I-15. Point of the mountain. Northbound."

"Backup units are on their way."

His partner—name tag said Peterson—handed his shotgun to Jones while he frisked us. He pocketed my knife and threw all three wallets on the hood.

"Nothing," he said, disappointed. Jones never took his eyes or his gun off of us.

Peterson cuffed me, and then Curtis. Jones clumsily fished out another pair of handcuffs for George with the same hand holding the shotgun. Watching him, I got nervous again. *He's going to blow his own head off.*

Satisfied that we were secure and no longer a threat, Peterson read us our rights from a card he pulled from his pocket. Then, while Jones stood guard, he popped the trunk and searched it thoroughly, pulling out the spare tire and toolbox and everything else. Next, he crawled through the whole inside of the car, looking under the seats, in the glove box, everywhere. Finally, he lay down on the asphalt, studied the underside of the car with his flashlight, then popped the hubcaps off the tires.

"Nothing," he said again. "What gives?"

Jones keyed his mike. "Dispatch? Jones. Repeat suspect description."

"White four-door sedan, late model, Honda or Toyota," the radio squawked. "Three assailants. White, males. Late teens or early twenties."

A highway patrol car pulled up alongside us, diverting traffic into the two left lanes, and the patrolman stepped out. He relieved Jones of the shotgun.

"What do you have?" he asked.

"So far, nothing," Peterson answered.

Dispatch continued, "One dark hair, dark complexion, wearing a white T-shirt . . ." I glanced down at my shirt. "One sandy blond hair, wearing a red T-shirt . . ." Everyone looked at Curtis. "And one wearing a ball cap and dark blue shirt. All wearing blue jeans." I looked at the Buzz cap George was wearing. His shirt was white, though, not dark.

What in the heck's going on here?

Two more cop cars pulled up.

"I have two white T-shirts and a redhead," Jones said, looking confused. "No dark shirt. Did they get a plate number?"

"The witness reported that he chased the car, but the rear plate was too dirty to read."

Peterson went around to the rear of the car. "This plate is clean as a whistle," he said, rattling off the numbers.

"No guns? No money?" asked another newly arrived cop.

"Zip," answered Peterson.

"Looks like you might have the wrong guys here," spoke up a veteran trooper who immediately took charge. We were all herded to separate patrol cars and questioned. After being relieved of command, Jones dropped heavily into the seat of his car and stared blankly into space for several minutes, his gun still in hand.

Several calls were made, all our parents notified, and our stories verified. The car was searched again. Finally, they uncuffed us and gathered us around Jones' car.

"We're really sorry about this," Peterson apologized. "There was a convenience store holdup in Orem just a while ago, and you and your car matched the description almost to a tee."

"That's okay," I managed.

I expected an apology from Jones, too, but he had his head back against the headrest with his eyes closed. Judging by his age, I guessed he had probably just pulled his gun for the first time in his short career. *When he walked up to our car, he thought he was facing three armed and dangerous men, ready to kill him,* I realized. *Poor guy.*

Peterson told us that when George had turned and pointed at them through the window, they thought they were being shot at, and they had swerved to dodge bullets.

Amazing. No wonder Peterson was on the trunk with shotgun ready.

As we pulled back out on the freeway into traffic, the thought "three armed and dangerous men" came to mind again. *What a coincidence,* I thought.

The Buzz were losing five to three at the bottom of the fifth inning by the time we got to the game. None of us did much cheering. We didn't even buy hot dogs. Poor little George was a nervous wreck. I guessed it would be days before he got over it.

On the way home, when we passed the Bluffdale exit and the state penitentiary, I told them about the prison escape.

"You mean to tell me the same guys you put in jail are out running around free right now?" Curtis asked incredulously.

I nodded.

"Including that lunatic devil Indian?"

I shot him a quick glance to remind him that George was listening.

"Jeez. No wonder all the cops were so nervous," he breathed. "What a coincidence."

I had an uneasy feeling that there was a lot more to this so called coincidence than met the eye, but I couldn't put a finger on it.

The rest of the evening was spent working in the garden with my family, followed by a late outing to the theater, so I didn't have much chance to think about the incident on the freeway or to worry about the fugitives.

Our meeting schedule for Sunday was from eleven to two, so we all slept in. Later on, after our Sunday dinner, I decided I'd better call Paul and tell him what had happened. He listened intently without interruption until I finished.

"Bart," he said breathlessly, "you're not going to believe this. I had the same thing happen to me yesterday morning."

"What?"

I sat in stunned silence as Paul related to me his own experience. He and his sister had gone out early in the morning to go to BYU. They'd only been on the road for ten minutes when they were pulled over and given more or less the same rough treatment we had just endured—guns pulled, cuffed, frisked, searched, the works. It had turned out to be another case of mistaken identity—a guy and a girl in a red pickup truck who had just robbed a grocery store at gunpoint.

"This is getting way past the coincidence stage," I said when he had finished. "Something awful funny is going on here."

"You think all this has something to do with Clawson?" he asked. "That doesn't make much sense."

"Maybe not, but I think we need to do some serious talking. Let's get together as soon as possible."

"Okay. You want to drive down here, or you want me to drive up there?"

I thought for a second. "How about I meet you halfway. Let's say Spanish Fork. In thirty minutes."

"That's not halfway. That's only ten minutes from here."

"I know. I thought maybe the cemetery would be a good place."

"What?"

"Tiffany's grave. Thirty minutes."

"Bart, that's morbid."

"Just trust me on this," I said. "I have my reasons."

"Okay," he sighed. "Thirty minutes."

Dad had the car at some meeting or other, so I had to use the family station wagon. On the freeway, about halfway to Spanish Fork . . . he came.

"So, it IS you," I said, glancing in the mirror at the empty backseat. "What do you want? What are you trying to prove?"

There was no answer, of course, but the car was heavy with his stifling, evil presence.

I got off the Spanish Fork exit and worked my way through town. When I neared the cemetery entrance, I thought to myself, *Now we'll see if I'm right.*

No sooner did I drive through the gate than the evil feeling left. It was like coming up for air after being under water forever.

YES! I breathed in deeply several times and smiled.

Paul was already there, pacing a circle in the grass around Tiffany's headstone.

"So, what's happening?" he asked as I rolled down my window. He looked upset. "What are they doing?"

"They're trying to scare us," I answered.

"Well, it's working," he said bluntly.

"Get in."

As Paul climbed in, I rolled my window back up, turned the radio on, and cranked the air conditioner up to high.

"Tell me something," I asked. "Was this trip to BYU a spur-of-the-moment thing, or was it planned in advance?"

Paul looked at me, puzzled. "We planned it several days ago. Diane was going to perform in a dance competition in the Marriott Center, and I was going to tape her with our video camera. Why?"

"Because I think we were set up."

Paul's mind raced. "You think Clawson called the cops on us? But why? How would he know we were—?" Understanding flooded his face.

"Hawk," we said in unison.

"I've been feeling his presence all week," I explained. "He's been watching me. He knew I was going to the ball game yesterday, and he knew exactly what time and with who."

"And you think he sent the cops after you? What about the convenience store robbery?"

"All planned," I answered. "Clawson and Derek probably paid big-time for some cheap thugs to pull it off as if they were us. They knew what kind of car to have, what descriptions to match, and at the last minute, even what clothes to wear—right down to the ball cap."

"Yeah, the two that the Payson cops were after were described as wearing the exact same things Diane and I had on."

"All Hawk had to do was report to Clawson every few minutes," I said.

"And all Clawson had to do was make a phone call and say 'Go'," Paul concluded. "Jeez Louise. You mean he's been hanging around my house all week, too?"

"Probably."

"But why is he going to so much trouble?"

"We're a threat to them. At least I am."

Paul looked lost.

"Don't you get it?" I asked impatiently. "They just escaped from prison. They're wanted by the FBI, and they're on the run. I'm sure they're going to try to leave the country. But they're afraid of me, because I can identify them."

"So can I," he challenged, almost proudly.

"Yeah, but the difference is you probably couldn't find them. I can. No matter where they go in the whole world, I could find them in a heartbeat—right now, if I wanted to. Even if they changed their identities, went to Antarctica, and had plastic surgery done, I could still find them. I'm the only person on earth who can do that."

"Then why don't you?" he asked in desperation.

"If I start looking for them, Hawk will know for sure. You saw how fast they were able to set us up. How hard do you think it would be for them to hire an assassin?"

"Oh my gosh, Bart," he exclaimed. "They're going to kill you anyway. Sure as heck."

Suddenly, Paul looked around suspiciously in the air. "Hawk could be here right now," he whispered.

"He was, but he's not now," I answered confidently. "My guess it that he's right over there by the front gate."

"Huh?"

"I took a gamble that he might be superstitious, what with all his talk about magic and being a medicine man and all. I read somewhere that Indians are afraid to enter sacred burial grounds. I felt him real strong in my car, right up until I drove through that gate."

"No kidding? He stayed out? That's why we're here?"

"I figured meeting on the headstone of his own murder victim would give him the heebie-jeebies."

"Cool."

"But I'm sure he could still hear us from there. When I go Inviz, I can pick out sounds a lot farther away than that."

"That's why you've got the radio and air conditioner going," he concluded. "To cover our conversation."

"Exactly."

"You know, there are two other people who can identify them."

I looked at him questioningly.

"Roshayne and Cindy," he said.

I closed my eyes in agony. "Oh, great," I whispered. "We'd better call them right away."

It was just getting dark as I drove out the gate, and I was immediately met by Hawk's presence again—reminding me that he was not going to leave me alone. After a couple of minutes, though, he left again, presumably to report back to Clawson—wherever he was.

Chapter 5

- Setup -

After leaving the cemetery and feeling Hawk leave, I pulled over to the nearest phone booth. Paul stopped behind me. I thumbed through the directory, then dialed Cindy's number. Four rings later, the answering machine picked up with a message about them being on a cruise for the next two weeks. I tried Roshayne next. Her mom answered on the second ring.

"Is Roshayne there?" I asked.

"No, she's not. Can I take a message?"

"This is Bart. Bart Elderberry. I don't know if you still remember me—"

"Of course I do, Bart." She had always been keen on me liking Roshayne, I remembered. "She's staying with a friend for a few days up in Ogden," she continued. "She drove up on Wednesday and should be back next Thursday. Would you like the number?"

"Yes, please," I answered with relief.

She gave me the number. "Her name's Maureen."

"Thanks."

Ogden was long distance, so we had to change a couple of dollars at the service station first. After several rings, I was about to hang up when a kid's voice finally answered.

"Hello?"

"Hi. I'm looking for Roshayne Pennini. Is she there?"

"You have the wrong number," he answered.

"Wait!" I yelled before he could hang up. "Maureen! Is Maureen there?"

"Sure. Just a sec."

A moment later, a girl's voice came on. "This is Maureen."

"Hi. I'm looking for Roshayne Pennini. I understand she's staying with you."

"Who's calling?" she asked politely.

"My name's Bart Elderberry. We're good friends. Just tell her Bart's calling."

"Roshayne isn't here."

"Will she be back soon? I can leave a number."

"I mean she's not here at all."

"But I thought—"

"She was going to come, but she left a message on my answering machine saying she had something come up at the last minute. A funeral or something . . . in Arizona, I think."

My heartbeat started picking up, and Paul looked at me anxiously, mouthing the word "what."

"When was that?" I asked breathlessly.

"Wednesday afternoon. Why? Is something wrong?"

"No! I . . . uh . . . I guess I didn't hear about her change of plans, that's all. Sorry to bother you."

After hanging up, I turned to Paul. "She's not there. Her friend said she called and canceled the whole thing because of a funeral or something."

"A funeral? Whose funeral?"

"I don't know. Something's fishy."

I dropped another quarter in the phone and dialed again.

"Mrs. Pennini? This is Bart again. Hey, I called Maureen's house and they said Roshayne isn't there."

"Oh! I forgot," she blurted out. "I'm sorry. She called Thursday morning and left us a message on the answering machine. She said that she and Maureen were driving up to Logan to see some friends at USU. I guess they haven't made it back yet."

"Logan?"

"That's right."

"But they . . ." I started.

"Yes?"

"Nothing. It's nothing," I said quickly. "Just ask her to call me when she gets home."

I hung up the phone heavily, and Paul saw the panic in my eyes.

"Now what?"

"Her mom says Roshayne called and left a message about her and Maureen going to Logan."

"Well, maybe she—"

"Paul, Roshayne's been missing for four days, and nobody even knows! Her mom thinks she's in Logan, and her friend thinks she's in Arizona. Why do you think that is?"

"No way!" he said, shaking his head. "You don't think—"

"I don't know, but Hawk or no Hawk, I'm going to get to the bottom of this, if it's the last thing I do," I said, running to my car. "I've got to get home."

"I'm going with you," Paul said as he ran to lock up his truck.

We drove to Orem in silence, each of us wrapped up in our own thoughts and fears, and both of us too afraid to validate them by voicing them out loud.

As we rounded the last corner in my neighborhood, we were met by yet another surprise. At the end of the street, there were three police cars parked in front of my house, lights flashing. I pulled over to the curb and turned off the lights.

"Oh, no," I said in exasperation. "Now what?"

"After everything else that's happened, I'm not sure I want to find out," answered Paul.

I put the car in reverse and slowly backed around the corner, the same way we had come. Once the house was out of sight, I turned around and headed in the opposite direction.

"Bart, I'm really getting scared about this. Maybe we better go back and see what they want."

"I'm not going back until I know what's going on. We were both framed yesterday, did you forget? And Roshayne is missing. Do you think those cops are at my house for punch and cookies? They're there because Hawk and Clawson sent them there, that's why. I need to make a phone call."

I was about to turn and head for Curtis' house, then changed my mind at the last minute. *Cops might be there, too. Everybody knows we're friends.* I turned around again and, five blocks later, parked in front of George's house.

"Who lives here?" Paul asked.

"A friend," I said, not believing my own ears. *Well, a friend in need is a friend indeed,* I thought.

I ran to the front door like a CIA agent on the chase, looking around in all directions at once. George was excited to see me and invited me right in.

"George," I said, before he could offer me anything, "I need to use your phone. It's an emergency."

"Okay," he said, puzzled. "What's happening?"

I grabbed the phone and dialed.

"Hello?" Mom said. I didn't say anything. "Hello?" she said again.

"Mom?" I asked hesitantly. "What's going on?"

There was a long silence on the other end. "Why, of course, Mary. Come on over," she said loud and sweet.

I breathed a sigh of relief. Mom was still on my side. "Mom, why are they looking for me? What do they want?"

"It's no trouble for me if it's no trouble for you, dear," she answered. "What's the problem?"

"I don't know!" I yelled into the phone. I spun around to see George staring at me.

"Well, come on over, and I'll see what I can find."

"Mom, I'm not going anywhere until you tell me what in the heck's going on!"

"I'm afraid that's the strongest DRUG I've got," she answered. "Especially for little PAULY."

"Drug? Pauly?" I repeated. Then it dawned on me. "Drugs?! They think we're involved with drugs?" My voice squeaked. I was practically hyperventilating.

"Yes, among other things," was all she could come up with. I could tell the charade was wearing thin.

"Holy cow, Mom! It's Clawson! They're trying to set us up! They're trying to frame—"

"Well, maybe I could bring it over—"

"No, no, no! If you leave, they'll wonder for sure. Is Darin home?"

"Yes."

"Give him a bottle of Tylenol and send him . . ." I stopped. *The cops still might be listening in.* "Send him to Tommy's house as fast as possible. Understand? As fast as possible."

"Okay. I hope he gets better soon. Goodbye."

I slammed the phone down and ran out the front door. "George!" I yelled back over my shoulder, "if anybody asks, you haven't seen me since the ball game!"

I jumped in the car and peeled out. Paul was beside himself. "Where we going?"

"To find Darin," I answered, flooring the gas pedal. "We've got to cut him off before he gets to Tommy's house."

"Darin? Your brother?"

"Yeah. If he does what I said, he'll be cutting through the block through the empty lot, then jumping the fence behind Cordners' and cutting through the next block at Andersons'. If the cops are trying to follow him, they'll be having fits. We've got to get there first."

I rounded a corner with tires squealing and raced the length of two blocks. Just as I turned the next corner, I caught sight of Darin coming out from behind Cordners' house on the run. I floored it and managed to get a couple of houses away, just before he disappeared again behind Andersons'.

Paul rolled down his window. "Darin!" he yelled as loud as he dared.

Darin stopped and spun around.

"Get in! Quick!"

Darin raced for the car and dove into the back seat. I peeled out again before he could even close the door.

"Is that Rangers hat still back there?" I yelled over the seat.

"Yeah," came Darin's shaky reply.

"Hand it to me. You two duck down."

Darin and Paul hit the floor. I put on the hat and pulled it down over my eyes just as we reached the corner. As we were turning right, a patrol car came from our left and turned down the street we were leaving. He looked at me briefly, but didn't stop. He was obviously looking for Darin on foot. As soon as he was out of sight in the mirror, I sped up and turned left at the next block. Then another right and another left and straight on down for several blocks until I was comfortable that we were far enough away from the neighborhood. I spotted an elementary school and pulled around to the back of the parking lot and stopped.

"Okay," I announced. "It's safe."

Darin sat up slowly with the look of death on his face. He was scared silly.

"Darin, what's going on?" I demanded, turning around to face him.

"They found a whole bunch of money under the seats in Dad's car," he answered nervously. "Thousands!"

"What?!"

"And a whole bunch of drugs in the trunk . . . under the spare tire."

"Impossible!"

"And a real gun in the glove box, Bart. It was loaded and everything!"

"I don't believe it!"

"I didn't hear the whole thing," he continued, "but they came knocking on the door about an hour after you left. They had search warrants and everything. They said something about confirming the license plate number with the convenience store and wanting another look. They searched Dad's car and found it all pretty fast."

"I thought they searched your car on the freeway yesterday," Paul cut in, "when you got pulled over."

"They did," I answered. "Twice. They must have planted that stuff while we were at the game, or maybe this morning during church."

"The police?"

"No. Clawson's hoods."

"They think you're in on it, too," Darin said to Paul. "Something about you and your sister?"

"Oh, that's just great," he said disgustedly.

"What about Mom and Dad?" I asked Darin. "What did they say?"

"They told the cops you were being set up by those guys who broke out of jail, but they just laughed at them. Mom and Dad know you didn't do anything."

"We're in big trouble, Bart," Paul said. "They'll lock us up forever."

"Well, we can't go home. That's for sure."

"We can't?" Darin asked, his voice squeaking.

"Not you. I mean Paul and I."

Darin heaved a sigh of relief as I started the car and headed back toward home.

"What are you doing?" Paul asked.

"Dropping off Darin at Tommy's. I don't want him involved in this."

We drove slowly and carefully back into the neighborhood. I decided a couple of blocks from Tommy's wouldn't hurt. Darin jumped out at the corner. After two steps, he stopped and turned around.

"Oh, Mom said to give this to you," he said, tossing a Tylenol bottle through the window. He turned and raced off at full speed.

"Let's get out of here," Paul urged.

I stepped on the gas and raced south. We were just about to Center Street when a cop car came around the corner and passed us going in the opposite direction. I tried to slow down, but it was too late. I watched him closely in the mirror for a whole block and thought for a minute that he would keep going.

Then, all of a sudden, his lights and siren went on. He popped a U-turn, tires squealing, and came chasing after us. Without even thinking about it, I punched the gas and took off.

"Bart, what are you doing?" Paul yelled. "You're going to get us killed!"

I made a quick left, raced to the next corner, and hung another left. I could see the lights from the cop car reflecting off of everything behind us. Another right and another left.

"Get ready!" I yelled to Paul as we raced down a long block.

"What?"

"On the count of three!" I yelled back. I grabbed the door handle with my left hand.

"You're crazy!" he yelled as his right hand went to the door. He stared at me in abject horror.

"One!" I yelled. I let go of the handle briefly and spun right around another corner.

"Two!" Another glance in the mirror confirmed that the cop was closing in. Grabbing the handle again, I slammed on the brakes and skidded through the intersection and into a driveway. We stopped mere inches from the garage door.

"Three!" I yelled.

We bailed out in unison. Paul clambered over the hood, and we sprinted around the corner of the house and through the open gate into the backyard. There was a four-foot-high block fence at the back of the house, which we vaulted easily.

Instead of hitting the ground where we should have on the other side, we kept falling and falling, at least twelve or fifteen feet. Then we crashed into bushes and tumbled head over heels down a steep hill for another fifty feet, finally coming to rest in a heap at the bottom.

For a couple of seconds neither of us moved, too stunned by the assault on our bodies. Then I remembered what we were doing. I jumped up, ignoring the pain in my left leg, and hauled Paul to his feet.

"Ouch!" he screamed.

"Come on!" I yelled.

We took off running to the right. I caught a quick glimpse of a man climbing over the fence at the top of the hill. He stopped just short of jumping, waving his arms and struggling to keep his balance when he realized what a long drop it was.

After running about fifty yards, I pulled Paul into the bushes, and we stopped to catch our breath. "Why didn't you tell me we were jumping off a cliff?" he demanded between gasps.

"Because you wouldn't have jumped."

"Darn right!" he snapped. We both gulped air for a few more seconds. "Now what, Einstein?"

"Back the way we came," I said.

"Are you crazy?"

"I hope not."

Reluctantly, Paul followed me back to where we had tumbled down the hill. It was dark enough that we were almost impossible to see, if we moved slowly. I gazed back up at the block fence for several seconds. There didn't appear to be anyone there.

"They'll expect us to hightail it south along the river bottoms," I explained in a whisper. "That's where they saw us heading. They'll have all the roads blocked off within seconds."

"So you want to go north instead?"

"No. I want to go back up the hill."

"I should have known."

We followed the hillside another hundred yards north, then turned and laboriously pulled ourselves back up the hill. Every other plant I grabbed came out by the roots, and it was difficult to keep from falling back down again. Finally we came to a tall, wood retaining wall approximately twenty feet high. "So, Batman," Paul asked sarcastically, "you going to use the grappling hooks or the rope ladder?"

I crawled a few yards along the bottom of the wall. "Right here," I announced.

"Piece of cake," Paul answered, seeing what I had in mind.

The wall was made of several rows of square timbers, like long railroad ties, about twelve inches thick, stacked on top of each other. Right above where we were standing, there was an end of a timber protruding out about three inches from every other row, the long end of which went back deep into the dirt to help hold the wall in place. Paul kept watch as I slowly and carefully scaled the side. The timbers weren't as flat as they looked, and I almost slipped off twice, both times barely catching myself by my fingertips. Paul held his breath. At the top, I poked my head carefully over the wall. Seeing nothing out of the ordinary, I slipped over and fell several feet onto the grass. Two minutes later, Paul dropped over beside me.

"I suppose you're going to break in and hide out in this house," Paul said, following my gaze.

"Hide, yes. Break in, no."

I led Paul across the yard to the north end of the house and up the steps to the top of the redwood deck. It was a huge deck that ran the entire length of the house. It was also non-stop windows, most of which were lit up inside. It wasn't so much a problem of being seen from inside as it was being silhouetted perfectly to an outside observer. Spaced evenly between the windows were three sets of sliding doors.

"We want the one on the other end," I whispered in Paul's ear.

"Figures."

We crouched down and crept quietly along the railing, pausing briefly as someone went in and out of the family room. By the side of the last door, I stopped. The lights were on, and I could hear soft music playing inside. I tapped quietly on the glass.

"Obviously, you know these people," Paul whispered.

"Obviously." I tapped again a little louder. Suddenly the curtains flew open, and a girl looked out at us. She smiled and slid the door open.

"Bart?" she said, "What—?"

"Shhh!" I said quickly, grabbing the back of her neck with one hand and covering her mouth with the other. Her eyes went wide open as I guided her back into her bedroom. Paul followed quickly and closed the door and curtains.

"Are you going to be quiet?" I asked in a whisper. She nodded. I took my hand off her mouth and let her go. "Angela, Paul. Paul, Angela," I said, making quick introductions. I turned to Paul. "Angie and I have a few classes together at Orem High."

"Pleased to meet you," Angela said to Paul. Turning to me, she asked, "What on earth are you doing sneaking into my room, you sly devil?" She had a sudden mischievous look in her eye.

"Not what you think," I answered.

After making sure her door was locked, we sat on the bed and finally relaxed.

"We need to hide here for a bit," I explained.

"Hide?"

"Can I use your phone?" Paul interrupted.

"Sure. Go ahead," she said, motioning toward her nightstand.

While Paul was making his call, I told Angela what was happening, starting with the search on the freeway and ending with our climb up the hill into her backyard. Her eyes grew gradually wider and wider as I went.

When I finished, she squealed with delight. "My gosh! You're fugitives!" she exclaimed. "How exciting!"

"Keep your voice down," I cautioned.

She bombarded us with questions, most of which we were able to answer. It wasn't long before we heard the doorbell ring, and Angela went out to see who it was. When she came back, she was more excited than ever.

"It's the police!" she said in a conspiratorial whisper. "They asked Daddy if he had seen any suspicious men around. He told them no, and they asked if they could search the backyard. This is SO cool!"

My blood ran cold.

"They're back there right now snooping around," she added.

Paul and I both stood up. "Can we borrow your closet?" I asked, opening the bi-fold doors.

"What—?"

We didn't wait for permission. Once we had crammed ourselves in, I racked my brain trying to think what the police might find in the yard. *Grass flattened down near the fence? Footprints leading to the deck?* I decided both were unlikely, it being such a hot, dry summer evening. *Maybe a piece of torn clothing hanging somewhere?* I felt my shirt and pants for damage.

"So, who's the babe?" Paul asked in a whisper.

"Just a girl," I answered.

"And you just happen to know where she lives? And where her bedroom is?" I could see in the dim light that he was smiling suspiciously.

"We did a group biology project here a few weeks ago," I explained. "She insisted on taking us on the grand tour."

"Sure." Paul glared at me with furrowed eyebrows.

"Honest," I said firmly. "We're not dating, if that's what you're thinking. She's . . . not my type." I dropped my voice to a bare whisper. "A little too anxious, if you know what I mean."

"Apparently."

We listened intently as Angela moved around the room, opening and closing the door to the hallway a couple of times. After ten minutes or so, she whispered through the closet door, "They're gone. You can come out now."

"I think we'll just stay in here a while longer, if you don't mind," I answered.

She was quiet for a few seconds. "Okay," she said finally. "Whatever."

It was another fifteen minuets and three leg cramps later when we heard the doorbell again. Angela went out and came back immediately.

She yanked open the closet doors, exposing us like a couple of trapped rats, blinking in the sudden light. "You have a friend waiting for you in the driveway," she said with a hurt look. "A girl."

I looked at Paul in surprise.

"I called for reinforcements," he explained.

We bailed out of the closet and carefully exited through the sliding doors to the deck.

"The gate's open," she whispered as we scurried off into the darkness. "Be careful. Nice seeing you." As we reached the stairs, she whispered loudly. "Come again when you can stay longer."

After double- and triple-checking the neighborhood from the safety of the fence, Paul and I made a beeline for the waiting pickup truck and vaulted over the side into the open bed. I recognized the truck immediately as Paul's. We scrunched up under the oversized white toolbox that sat right behind the cab.

"Go!" Paul whispered as loud as he dared.

"Where?" came a girl's voice.

"Anywhere!" he answered desperately. "The freeway!"

The engine started, and the driver ground the gears getting started. We didn't move a muscle and hardly breathed until we were sure we'd been on the freeway for several minutes. Finally, Paul climbed out from under the toolbox, tapped on the back window, and signaled the driver to pull off at the next exit. We turned west into the shelter of the Camelot campground and stopped under some big, dark trees. I climbed out to meet my rescuer.

"Hi, Bart," she said cheerfully, stepping out of the truck. "Long time no see." It was Tamara Edmonds, one of the old gang from Payson High.

I wrapped my arms around her and gave her a big hug.

"Hi, Tammy."

Chapter 6

- Fugitives -

"You're in a real pickle, all right," Tamara said ten minutes later, after we had briefed her on our situation. We were back on the freeway, heading south toward Payson. "What are you going to do?"

"I'm not sure," I answered. "I was hoping you two might have some suggestions."

Paul spoke up. "Well, our biggest problem right now is that the police are looking for us—not only for supposedly dealing drugs and whatever else they think we did, but because we just ran away from them. That's called 'resisting arrest,' in case you didn't know," he said, glancing accusingly at me, "and it makes us look awful guilty."

"I know," I answered meekly.

"If you turned yourselves in right now," Tamara suggested, "I'm sure you could prove you're innocent soon enough."

"Maybe," I answered.

"Especially if we explained our connection to those three recently escaped convicts everybody's looking for," Paul added.

"Possibly."

"You've both got lots of alibis," Tamara added, "and plenty of people who can testify that you're not involved with drugs or stuff like that."

I didn't answer.

"Well?"

"I've been thinking," I said at last. "Why is Clawson doing this? I mean, besides just to scare us. What does he have to gain if we get in trouble and get thrown in jail for a few days?"

Paul and Tamara stared at me blankly.

"It can't possibly make any difference to their own escape. They've got FBI all over the country looking for them, but I'm sure they're well on their way. What difference do WE make? And if I'm such a big threat to them in the long term, like we talked about before, why go to all this trouble? Why not just kill me?"

"Bart!" Tamara exclaimed. "How can you say that?"

"Well?" I persisted. "Why not?"

"Well—?"

"And, more importantly, why did they kidnap Roshayne?"

"That part's easy," Paul answered. "To get you to do what they want. That is, if they even HAVE her in the first place."

"That's the question," I agreed. "The first thing I need to do is find Roshayne." I turned and faced them both. "What we need to do now is keep moving. If we stop anywhere, even for an hour, Hawk will find us, and Clawson will report us."

"How can he do that?" asked Tamara.

"He just picks up a phone, makes an anonymous call to the sheriff, and says, 'I just saw those two guys you were looking for. They're in a red pickup with a girl at such-and-such a place,' and the cops close right in and catch us. If we keep moving, and keep changing directions, maybe Clawson won't know far enough in advance where we'd be at any given time to report our location."

"So where do you want to go?" asked Paul. "Las Vegas? Montana? Or just around in circles?"

I paused for a moment, trying hard to sense whether Hawk was anywhere nearby at that moment, listening or watching. Satisfied that he wasn't, I answered in a whisper, "I want to go wherever it is they are."

"Oh, sure, Bart," Paul said. "That's just asking for trouble."

"It's the only way. We've got to find them. Somehow we've got to outsmart them and get THEM on the run. Why do WE have to be playing defense all the time? Let's turn the tables on them. THEY'RE the real criminals, not us."

"They're also the real killers—not us."

"How much money do you have on you?" I asked.

"I've got about eighty bucks," Paul answered. "Why?"

"I've got about fifty," I said, "and a gas card with a two-hundred-dollar limit. That ought to take us a ways, if we budget carefully."

"I've got a VISA card," Tamara added, pulling her wallet out of her purse, "with a thousand-dollar limit, and . . . ninety-three dollars cash."

We both looked at her and shook our heads. "No, Tammy—"

"What?" she demanded. "You're going to dump me? I bum a ride to Spanish Fork in the middle of the night to find your truck, and crawl around all over the ground trying to find your stupid spare key—look how dirty my hands are!—and drive all the way to some girl's house in Orem that I don't even know, and then smuggle you right out from under the noses of half the Orem police force, and all you have to say is 'Thanks for the ride. See you later'?"

"Tammy, it's—"

"Forget it! I'm going with you, and that's final."

"But—"

"And don't give me any of your macho sexist garbage about how dangerous it is for a girl," she said heatedly, wagging her finger in my face. "I'm as smart and as tough as either of you. Besides, I'm a fugitive now, too, for 'aiding and abetting,' and . . . and 'harboring a fugitive,' and—"

"Okay, already," I said. "Chill. You can go."

She stared at me speechless for a second. "Really?" she asked, suddenly all smiles.

"Really."

She faced quickly to the front and bounced quietly up and down in her seat like a five-year-old. "Oh, cool!" she said under her breath.

Paul spoke up. "We need to get some things, Bart. Like sleeping bags, maybe a tent. Some clothes. What are we going to eat?"

"Convenience store junk food, of course," I answered.

We had arrived at the Payson off-ramp, and Paul pulled off the freeway.

"Wait a minute," I said, suddenly alarmed. "We can't go to YOUR house. You're already on the suspect list. There could be cops waiting for you. Your truck's a sitting duck."

"See?" Tamara spoke up brightly, "you DO need me. We can go to my house. We've got camping stuff all over the garage."

"What are you going to tell your parents?"

"Nothing," she said simply.

"Her dad doesn't live with them anymore," Paul explained, "and her mom doesn't tell her what to do these days."

"She thinks I'm pretty much old enough to decide for myself," Tamara added.

"How would it be?" I asked.

Tamara instructed Paul to park in the neighbors' driveway, who, she informed us, were out of town. She produced a key from under a rock in the bushes and let herself in the dark garage. Then, like the criminals we were, we quietly smuggled out three sleeping bags and pillows, two foam pads, a water jug, a small pup tent, and a box full of odds and ends like cooking utensils, flashlights, and paper towels.

On the last trip out, Paul spotted a small toolbox and grabbed it, too. Tamara wrote a note on a flap she ripped off a cardboard box, explaining how she had gone with some friends on a camping trip, and left it propped against the steering wheel of her mom's car.

It was two o'clock in the morning when we finally pulled out and hit the freeway again.

"Where to now?" Paul asked.

"South, I think," I answered. "Last time we saw Clawson, he talked about going to Mexico or Brazil."

"Wait a minute," he responded, letting his foot up off the gas. "You telling me we're going to leave the country?"

"I don't know yet, but it's possible. Just start driving, and keep your eyes peeled for cops."

None of us broached the subject of what to do if we found any.

Leaving Tamara in the front with Paul, I crawled through the rear sliding window and set about making myself at home in the open bed of the truck. I lined up the two foam pads side by side, and stacked most of the gear on one of them. Then I unrolled one of the sleeping bags on the other side, arranged a pillow so my head was under the truck's big toolbox, removed my shoes, and climbed in. Even though it was the middle of June, the evening was brisk, and the wind rushing over the truck made it rather cold. By the time I got in, I was pretty chilled, and it took nearly half an hour to warm up and get comfortable again. I had to fight the whole time not to fall asleep.

Finally, I felt ready. I concentrated hard and allowed the rush of the wind and the gentle rocking of the truck to help me bring on the vibrations.

Roshayne, I thought over and over. *I've got to find Roshayne.*

I visualized her in my mind, the way I'd seen her last. It had been at a basketball game between Orem and Payson, just a few months earlier. As usual, she was breathtaking. It didn't seem to matter what she wore—formal dress or blue jeans—she always sparkled. There was something about that combination of dark, shoulder-length hair, with the bangs hanging precisely down to her eyebrows, the smooth, unblemished, dark complexion of her face, and the deep, dark mystery of her brown—almost black—Latin eyes that just set my blood on fire every time I saw her. I smiled to myself and started reminiscing about the first kiss she had given me.

Careful, Bart, I thought suddenly. *You're drifting off. Keep cool.* I pulled my mind back into focus.

I need to get out, I thought. The tingling vibrations were almost lost in the gentle movement of the truck, but I felt myself pull loose, just the same. The most obvious and immediate sensation was the sudden lack of motion. It was as though everything had been stopped in a freeze-frame. I opened my eyes and found myself still looking at the underside of the white toolbox. I commanded myself to rise in the air, and wondered briefly if I might be blown away by the wind. It didn't happen, though. I went straight up and rolled over at about five feet above the truck. It was an exhilarating experience, floating along at seventy miles an hour so close to the ground.

My body looked funny lying there in the back of the truck with my head hidden from view. Since I was already in the prone, facedown position, I stretched out my arms and pretended I was Superman.

I could see Paul and Tamara through the rear window, and was concerned about seeing Tamara asleep against Paul's shoulder. I knew Paul had to be just as tired. I was also a little jealous at the way she was snuggled up so close to him. I hadn't been that close to a girl for a while. Somehow, I just couldn't get interested in any of the girls I'd met and dated in Orem. Roshayne seemed to always be in the forefront of my thoughts, and I meticulously compared everyone to her.

Roshayne, I thought, remembering the purpose of my mission. *Find Roshayne.* There was a quick sense of movement, a second or two of blurred semidarkness rushing by, and then I came to an abrupt stop again.

It was like déjà vu city. There I was, hovering over the most beautiful girl in the world. She was lying peacefully asleep in bed, her long hair fanned out on each side, just the way I had seen it the first time I projected to her. She even had her arms on her stomach, her hands clasped loosely together, just like before. She was striking, and I couldn't help just staring at her and admiring her for several seconds.

Something is wrong here, my subconscious finally butted in. I looked around to take inventory. I was surprised to find that we were in an elegant suite, like the penthouse of a ritzy hotel. The bed she was sleeping in was covered with an expensive-looking bedspread, and the pillows were blue satin. There was a nightstand on either side, with fancy lamps and a digital clock radio. All the walls were finished in a rich, medium brown wood paneling, like oak or cedar, with nice paintings, and the floor was covered with thick, plush carpet. Opposite the foot of the bed there was a large overstuffed couch and a small table, and in the corner, a TV equipped with a VCR and a whole rack of tapes. Off to one side was a doorway, through which I could see a shower and a sink—also expensive-looking, with black marble and gold fixtures. On the other side of the room was a door that led to the hallway.

This is not what I expected. She's supposed to be kidnapped. My mind immediately brought back images of the basement room in Provo where Cindy had been kept—fastened to a steel cable, curled up in a ball on an old, musty mattress, eating oatmeal on a paper plate. It made my skin crawl just thinking about it.

I was momentarily torn between moving outside, to see where in the world we were, and making myself visible so I could talk to her and find out what was going on.

I didn't have a chance to do either, for at that moment I felt a powerful jerk backward, and the next instant I was banging my forehead sharply against the bottom of the toolbox. My body was flying around all over the place, up and down like a trampoline, along with all the camping equipment in the truck. I fought desperately to grab something, and finally managed to get a grip on the side of the truck bed. I hauled myself up to a kneeling position and looked through the windows just in time to see Paul jerking the truck back onto the freeway. After being sure he was on solid ground again on the paved shoulder, he let the truck coast to a stop.

"What happened?" I yelled.

Paul turned and opened the sliding window. "I . . . I dozed off, I guess."

Tamara was sitting up as straight as a board, clutching the dashboard and looking like she had just faced the grim reaper.

"We all need to get some sleep," I said, "before we kill ourselves." I climbed out of the back and got in the right side of the cab. "I'll keep you awake until we find a place."

Paul started out onto the freeway again, but didn't exceed fifty-five miles an hour. "So, where are we going to sleep?" he asked.

"I think we need to just find a deserted little side road and sack out in the back of the truck."

"Won't Hawk find us?"

"Yeah, probably, but I think Clawson might have a bit of a credibility problem trying to drop an anonymous tip about 'just happening' to see us and our truck out in the middle of nowhere. What cop is going to believe that? Besides, Hawk would have a hard time pinpointing our exact location when every sagebrush looks like the next one. We'll just have to take our chances."

"One thing's for sure," Tamara spoke up. "We're better off hiding somewhere than driving off the road."

"Sorry," Paul said meekly.

"It's not your fault," I consoled. "We've been on a wild goose chase all day long. I'm just as exhausted as you are. Let's just hope Hawk is, too, and is sleeping somewhere."

After driving in silence for a few minutes, I asked, "Where are we, anyway?"

"We're about ten or twenty miles south of Nephi."

"Do you have a map?"

"No, but I've been down this way plenty. We can get off the freeway at Scipio, and drive out into the farms someplace."

Ten minutes later, we found the exit and drove out into the dark farmland. The whole area was laced with roads, but they were all paved and appeared more or less traveled. Paul finally found a dirt road that looked promising. It dropped down into a gorge along a creek that was lined with big trees on the creek side and big weeds and bushes on the other. We followed the road for half a mile, then pulled off and parked between a couple of particularly tall trees.

The sudden silence and darkness that engulfed us after turning off the truck was eerie, and nobody moved for several seconds. Finally we gathered up our courage and climbed out.

Even though we were miles away from the nearest house, we went out of our way to be quiet. Paul stored most of the gear in the cab while I arranged the bedding. The two foam pads fit just about perfectly in the bed of the truck. We arranged the sleeping bags and pillows as best we could, although they overlapped each other by several inches.

As soon as they were ready, Tammy slipped off her shoes and climbed in the middle one. Paul and I each chose a bag and followed suit.

After a few minutes of listening to the brook and the crickets, Paul whispered softly, "Bart? You still awake?"

"Yeah," I answered quietly.

"You sure you want to go through with this?"

"No, but . . ." I paused a moment, trying to formulate the right answer. "I don't really want to, but I don't see any other choice. Clawson has us hamstrung. First thing in the morning, I've got to find them. Then maybe we'll have a better idea what we're up against."

"Did you find Roshayne?" Tamara asked.

"Well, yes and no."

"What do you mean?"

"I found her, but I don't know where she is. I was about to go exploring when I was jarred back by our side trip off the shoulder of the freeway."

"Sorry," Paul apologized again.

"Is she all right?" Tamara asked.

"She seemed to be. Maybe TOO all right." I told them what I had seen and how plush and unexpected her surroundings and circumstances were.

"Sounds pretty fishy," Paul said. "Why would she be in an expensive hotel? Doesn't sound like the place for fugitives on the run to be hiding out."

"No, it doesn't," I agreed.

With that, we all slipped into our own thoughts, each trying to make some sense out of all the madness that had cascaded down on us during the day. Even as nervous and scared as we were, fatigue won out quickly, and we were all sawing logs in a matter of only minutes.

Chapter 7

- A Prayer? -

I couldn't remember the last time I'd slept so soundly. It seemed like only minutes later that the sunlight was working its way through my eyelids. Not wanting to wake the others, I opened one eye and pushed myself up slowly on one elbow. I half expected the truck to be surrounded by the entire National Guard, waiting and pointing M-16s at us. I was relieved to find they weren't. There were a couple of stray cows standing by the side of the truck, though, chewing their cuds and staring off into space. *What a boring existence,* I thought briefly, wondering what it must be like being a cow.

By the looks of the sun, we had slept in quite a bit. A quick look at my watch confirmed that it was already past nine. *We've got to get a move on,* I realized, suddenly remembering our plight.

I climbed out of the bag quickly and put my shoes on. Paul rolled over and squinted at me. "Where? . . . What? . . ." he asked, surveying our strange surroundings. "Oh, yeah."

"Where are the keys?" I asked. "We need to get moving before Clawson catches up with us."

"I'm surprised he's not here already," Paul answered, fishing under the foam pad and handing me his key ring.

"Me, too."

I unlocked the door and moved some of the gear from the cab into the back. "Take your time," I said. "You and Tammy can get up as we go." Without further ado I started the truck, backed out, and headed for the freeway.

A few minutes later, Tammy poked her head through the window. "Where's breakfast?" she asked. "I'm starving."

She reached in, grabbed an armload of stuff off the seats, and pulled it out through the window. Next thing I knew, her feet came shooting past my ear, and she adeptly maneuvered herself into the cab. It was a great performance of feminine dexterity. Her next priority was to take over the rearview mirror and examine her face.

I chuckled.

"Keep your eyes on the road, buster," she said, punching me playfully in the ribs. "Nobody in the world is allowed to see me like this." Soon she had the dashboard converted into a beauty salon. I didn't think it was possible to put so many things in one little purse. She brushed and painted and dabbed, then re-brushed and re-painted and dabbed some more. Finally she was satisfied, and, I had to admit, she looked gorgeous.

"Is Paul up?" I asked.

"He's rolling up the sleeping bags and trying to keep the pads and pillows from blowing all over the road."

Paul came through headfirst a few minutes later, and pretty much just tumbled in on top of us.

"Glad you could join us," I said, closing the window. "Where can we get some breakfast?"

"I think we're only a few miles from Fillmore," he answered. "We need some gas, too."

We spent a good half hour at the gas station, taking turns using the facilities, buying gas and maps, and stocking up on food and drinks, including plenty of Hostess brand goodies. Tammy bought a new backpack to put it all in. We decided we'd better use cash, since credit card purchases could be easily traced. Since I was responsible for the whole mess, I spent my money first, nearly exhausting the entire fifty dollars.

We were just entering the freeway on-ramp when I suddenly remembered about my family. "My folks are probably having a heart attack by now," I said. "I should have called them."

"Too late now," Paul answered, as we pulled onto the freeway. "Unless you want to get off at the next exit."

"No. Keep going. I'll call later."

Tamara spoke up. "I was wondering . . ." She looked in her lap, kind of bashful-like.

"Yeah?" I prompted.

"Well . . . it's probably . . . I mean, I was thinking maybe we should start out . . ."

"Start out what?" Paul asked.

"Well, my mom and I always have a little . . . prayer. First thing in the morning." She glanced up at the two of us in turn, looking for approval. "We made a mess out of Sunday yesterday," she said. "You know . . . camping out, running away . . . all that."

I felt a twinge of guilt. "Couldn't be helped," I responded. "We'll just have to repent hard later, I guess."

"I guess so," she agreed. After a short, silent pause, she asked, "So . . . is it okay if we have a prayer?"

"Right now?" I asked. "We're on the freeway." I looked at Paul, and he nodded ever so slightly. "Okay. I guess we could use some extra help right now. Pull off to the side, Paul."

"Right here on the freeway?"

"Under that next overpass," I said, pointing.

Once we were stopped, Tamara instructed us to fold their arms. I felt pretty strange doing that out in the middle of nowhere on a freeway, but I did as she asked.

She prayed for a good fifteen minutes—probably the longest prayer I've ever heard in my whole life. After giving thanks for still being alive and free, she explained to the Lord how Paul and I had been set up and that we were innocent of any serious wrongdoing. She told Him we were afraid and desperately in need of his help and protection. She asked Him to bless our families and help them understand what was happening, and to not be too scared for us. Then she asked a special blessing on Roshayne, wherever she was, that she would be safe from harm and abuse, and to be comforted.

I got goosebumps all over my arms. It was like she was talking face-to-face with God.

"Father," she concluded. "I know you've given Bart a special gift, and I know it's supposed to be used only for righteous purposes. Our big desire is to find Roshayne and help her escape from the trouble she's in. And if we can, in the meantime, to bring Mr. Clawson and Derek and Silver Hawk back to justice. Please, please help us."

She added a few other requests, thanked Him again for everything, and closed.

"Tammy," I said softly, placing a hand on her arm. "That was beautiful. Thanks."

Tears were running like rivers down her face, and she gave me a quick hug and a kiss on the cheek.

Paul wiped at his eyes with the back of his hand when he thought I wasn't looking, but couldn't trust his emotions to say anything. The whole truck was filled with an incredible feeling of peace and warmth. It was a wonderful feeling that none of us wanted to see end.

"How do you feel about all this now?" I asked Paul.

"Like I could conquer the world," he said.

"Then let's do it!" I shouted, making Tamara jump.

"Okay!" Paul yelled back, giving me a high-five in front of Tamara's nose.

"All right!" she piped in, high-fiving us each in turn.

Paul put the truck in gear and was just about to go when we heard a knock on the window.

My heart stopped. There was a highway patrolman signaling Paul to roll down his window. Tamara gasped audibly and covered her mouth with her hand. Paul's hands were shaking as he rolled down the window.

"You kids in some kind of trouble?" he asked.

We're in ALL kinds of trouble, I thought. *What a stupid question.*

"No," Paul answered hesitantly.

"It's against the law to stop on the freeway unless you have an emergency, you know."

"We know," I answered.

He was staring at Tamara and studying her up and down. "So why are you parked under this overpass?" he asked. His eyes came to rest on Tamara's WWJD ring that she was twisting nervously around her finger.

"We're just heading out on a trip to Arizona, and Tammy remembered that . . ." I looked down at the floor, embarrassed. "that we hadn't said a prayer first," I answered.

He laughed. "A prayer? Ha! That's a new one."

None of us said anything, and he grew serious again. "A prayer," he repeated, mostly to himself.

We all continued to stare at the floor.

"Well, in all my days, this is the first time I've ever pulled over a bunch of teenagers for praying," he said.

"Sorry," Paul said meekly.

"On your way," he ordered, with a wave of his hand. He turned and headed back to his car. "A prayer," he muttered again, shaking his head.

Paul put the truck in gear again.

"Wait," I said. "Let him leave first."

"Why?"

"I don't want him following us for the next who-knows-how-many miles. That'll give him too much time to look at us and the truck . . . and the license plate. Obviously he didn't call us in, or he would have arrested us on the spot."

Paul waited for the patrolman to get several hundred yards down the road before pulling back into traffic.

"That was awfully close," Tamara said, breathing heavily. She rested her head back against the seat and closed her eyes.

"You can say that again," I answered. "We should say another prayer and thank God for getting us out of that one."

"Say it in your head," Paul said. "I'm not pulling over again."

Chapter 8

- Fishing -

Not wanting to waste any more time waiting, I decided it was time to find Clawson and figure out what was going on. I traded places with Tamara and slid out through the rear window. "Try not to fall asleep this time," I cautioned Paul.

I arranged the bedding the same as before, which got my face and head out of the sun, and lay down on top of the sleeping bag. It only took a couple of minutes, and I was set.

Ready or not, here I come, I thought.

Without further hesitation, I closed my eyes and lifted out of my body effortlessly. My destination was so well ingrained in my subconscious that I didn't even have time to think about it before I was streaking along the surface of the earth at breathtaking speed. I was surprised that the trip was not instantaneous, like it so often was. Instead, I was able to glimpse clouds and mountains as they flashed by, and the entire trip lasted almost ten whole seconds. At last, all the blur of varied colors changed to a steady streak of dark blue, and I stopped.

There he was, mere feet in front of me: Samuel Taylor Clawson, the master of blackmail and extortion, skillful liar, professional thief, kidnapper, and cold-blooded murderer. Just seeing his face brought back a whole avalanche of feelings and emotions—fear, disgust, anger, contempt, revulsion. I had a sudden, powerful urge to punch him in the face and stomp him into the ground; and, had I been in my phyzbod and capable, I would surely have tried. As it was, I was powerless to do anything other than observe and simmer.

I backed away several feet, more to distance myself from him than for any other reason, and began to examine the area.

To my surprise, I found myself hovering over water, overlooking the fore deck of an extremely big and very expensive yacht.

Clawson was seated atop a chair, which was elevated several feet from the deck. I immediately recognized it as a deep-sea fishing seat. In front of him stood a thick, sturdy fishing pole in its holder, the heavy line trailing out into the water behind me. He was strapped into the chair, with his feet firmly planted against the footrests. I knew this was not a restraint, but a protection to keep him from being yanked suddenly off the boat, should he snag a big enough fish.

As he alternately pulled and relaxed the line, he laughed and joked with his companions, waiting for his prize-winning catch to bite. He was dressed in tan Bermuda shorts, thongs, a sleeveless T-shirt, and a fishing hat. His arms were showing the beginnings of a healthy tan, as though he had been out in the sun for several days already.

How did he get out here so fast? I wondered. *It's only been four days since his escape.*

To the right a few feet, in a similar chair, sat the ominous Herculean bodyguard Derek Monroe, also manipulating a fishing pole, but with considerably less enthusiasm than Clawson. In his tank top and shorts, the finely tuned muscles of his chest, arms, and legs rippled and flexed, reminding me of his sheer brute strength.

To the side of each of them stood a deeply tanned, bikini-clad girl—Clawson's fingering his hair, and Derek's caressing his bulging biceps. Behind them was Silver Hawk, lying comfortably on a padded lounge chair, dressed in frayed Levi's and a button-up flannel shirt, and wearing the usual assortment of turquoise and silver jewelry. His eyes were covered with sunglasses, so I couldn't tell if he was asleep or not, and his hands were crossed over his chest.

The last time I saw him like that, I remembered, *he was jumping out and coming after me.*

A chill of terror ran through my entire being as I hurriedly scanned the air around me. There was nothing in the world I feared more than being attacked by the evil spirit of Silver Hawk. Once before, I had come dangerously close to spiritual destruction at his hands.

Seconds later, he sat up abruptly in his chair and began looking around in the air.

Well, he knows I'm here, one way or the other, I realized.

It occurred to me that he might be just as adept at sensing my presence as I was getting to be at sensing his. I attributed that to the vast differences between the goodness and badness of our conflicting spirits.

He calmly rose to his feet and walked to Clawson's side. After tapping him on the shoulder to get his attention, Hawk leaned over and whispered something in his ear.

"Are you sure?" Clawson exclaimed, abandoning his fishing. "Where?"

Silver Hawk pointed so directly at me that I wondered if he might actually be able to see me.

Clawson looked in my general direction with a wry smile on his face. "So, Mr. Elderberry," he said, crossing his legs and leaning back, "you've come at last. Welcome to our party. Do you like the accommodations?" He gestured widely to the yacht and its occupants.

Looking around, I saw that there were a few others on board, presumably crew members, since it was unlikely Clawson and company could manage a boat that size by themselves. It was at least a hundred feet long.

"We've been expecting you," he continued. "I'm surprised it took you so long. Then again, you HAVE been busy, haven't you?" He laughed, and Derek joined him.

"Where to begin," he said, stroking his chin. He turned to the girl behind him. "Why don't you and Cherica go on up to the sundeck and work on those tans." He gave her a pat on the rump as she and her companion grabbed their towels and things and retired to the other end of the ship. "Carlos!" he yelled to one of the crew. "We are in conference. See that we are not disturbed."

"Sí, señor," he answered.

Since he couldn't look me in the eye while he spoke, Clawson resumed his fishing and watched the pole and line. Derek reeled his in and sat back to listen.

When the deck was cleared, he continued. "You're probably wondering how we managed all this instant comfort. Well, maybe I should thank you for that. You see, you set us up with a wonderfully efficient office environment for the last year and a half. Prison is an interesting place, Bart. You should visit sometime." He and Derek laughed again.

What a creep, I thought.

"See, we never quit. Going to jail didn't put us out of business. We just changed locations. Hawk has been very busy these past months finding worthy candidates from which to extract generous contributions to our cause. I think you call it 'blackmailing.' We call it 'placing penalties on the white-collar criminals.' We have become very good at it. You could say I'm a modern-day Robin Hood. I collect from the rich and rotten, and give to the poor and deserving—like Derek and Hawk here, and those gorgeous beauties who just left." He motioned toward the sundeck and chuckled.

This guy's got an ego the size of Mount Everest.

"You know, we've managed to amass a small fortune from behind bars. We have numbered accounts at several offshore banks where deposits are made regularly. Derek's friends on the outside have been most helpful in enforcing our prompt payment plan.

"They were also very accommodating in arranging our rapid departure. We were provided with transportation, disguises, false ID's, and the works. We were across the border inside of twelve hours. Does that surprise you? We thought about altering our appearance—you know, mustaches, wigs, maybe some surgery—but there's no need. Where we're going, it's highly unlikely anyone will ever find us. And we have learned that we can carry on our business from just about anywhere. Like from this yacht, for instance. Distance is no obstacle. Hawk makes visits, I make phone calls with my neat little satellite cellphone, and Derek pays his vast army of minions to do the legwork. Life is good."

He sat quietly for several minutes, and I started to wonder if he had finished his speech.

"There's just one little problem," he said finally, growing serious, "and I'm sure by now you've figured out what—or should I say WHO that is. What are we going to do about Bart Elderberry?"

I figured he'd get to this sooner or later.

"I can't be wondering and worrying every day of my life if you're going to come along and ruin my day. And Hawk can't spend his whole life watching you. He's got more important things to do.

So, here's my plan—there's no use hiding it from you, since you can drop in and eavesdrop on us anytime you want, anyway. We're just going to have to get rid of you."

He said it so casually, you would have thought he was talking about fumigating a house for bugs.

"During my first few months in prison, I devised half a dozen different ways to kill you when I got out. Fast and quick ways. Slow and painful ways. But I realized that the reason I was in jail in the first place was for not sticking to the rich and rotten. I messed around with innocent people when I kidnapped that stupid girl, and my stepdaughter's death just screwed everything all up. No, I can't just kill poor, innocent, respectable, fine, upstanding Bartholomew Elderberry. Everybody would know I did it. Just one more thing for me to worry about later.

"So I worked out a couple of things to make you look not-so-innocent. And now, all of a sudden, you're a local thief and a two-bit drug dealer. Naughty, naughty. How does it feel to have cops breathing down your neck? How does it feel to be wanted, Bart?"

Well, at least I know I was right about the setups.

"But, knowing the goodie-goodie you are, I figured you'd get out of trouble eventually. So I had to convince the cops you were real guilty before you got a chance to prove otherwise. I had to make you run. And that's where your girlfriend comes in. I knew if she disappeared, you'd come looking."

Roshayne! He DID take her!

"And I was right. Here you are. She was very obliging, by the way. She packed a suitcase and said goodbye to Mommy and everything. All we had to do was pick her up. No one has the slightest idea that she's even been kidnapped—except you, of course. She left her car in long-term parking at the airport, with a note on the dash explaining why she ran away from home. Pretty creative, don't you agree?"

You dirty rotten scum! You're going to pay for this!

"So, now she's safely stashed away, and everybody with a badge is out looking for you and your friends. It's actually been quite entertaining. I just wish I could see it all personally instead of getting it secondhand from Hawk."

Roshayne must be here on this yacht! I realized. *I've got to see her!*

"So now things start to get interesting—"

I didn't wait around to hear any more. *Roshayne!* I screamed.

Instantly, I was transported to her side—but, surprisingly, she was still in the same room where I had seen her before. *What gives? Why would Clawson leave her here?*

She was lying on her side on top of the bed, fully clothed, staring off into space. Nothing else had changed. I was on the verge of materializing and showing myself to her when the door flew open with a loud bang, causing both Roshayne and me to jump.

In walked Mr. Clawson, followed by Derek and Hawk. Roshayne shrank back against the wall.

"How rude!" Clawson yelled at the ceiling. "Walking out on me like that and leaving me talking to the air!"

Roshayne was totally perplexed. "But I—" she started to say.

"Not you!" he yelled, cutting her down with his stare. "Your ghost boyfriend."

"My—?" She glanced quickly at the ceiling and flashed a tiny smile, then grew serious again. "What makes you think—?"

"Oh, he's here all right," Clawson assured her. He turned to Hawk, who nodded slightly in the affirmative.

"So, here she is, Bart," he said without taking his eyes off of Roshayne. "Now what are you going to do? Play the knight in shining armor and come rescue her? I hope you do. In fact, I'm counting on it. And, in case you have some preconceived notion that you can lead the cops to me, let me remind you that you're not exactly in good with the authorities right now. They aren't likely to believe a word you say. You're a wanted criminal. How does THAT feel? And besides, where are we? Take a look around, Bart. Nothing but miles and miles of ocean. No landmarks. No road signs.

"Oh, sure, you can just shoot up into the air and figure it out, but by the time you get high enough to see land, we'll be too small to see. Hawk already tried it. And we have lots of fuel on board. We can wander around out here for days."

"You creeps!" Roshayne yelled. "You can't get away with this! Bart will find a way!"

"Shut up!" Clawson screamed, his eyes burning with fury. Without warning, he reached over and slapped her face, sending her reeling off the bed and crashing to the floor.

I was so mad, I wanted to strangle him.

"I'm done playing around, you little jerk. No more Mr. Nice-Guy. Within forty-eight hours you'll be dead of your own doing, and your little sweetheart here will be shark bait!"

With that, he stormed out of the room. Derek followed, but Hawk remained behind. "Yes, boy," he hissed like a snake. "You are dead. You are no match for me. You cannot win. Soon, I will watch your spirit leave your miserable body for the last time. Then you will be taken away where you can never escape. The Great Spirit awaits!"

Hawk stared hard at Roshayne, who was still sitting on the floor. Then he spat on the carpet beside her and left. Derek reached in from the hallway and pulled the door shut, and I heard a heavy padlock being snapped shut.

"Bart?" Roshayne whispered softly, looking at the ceiling. "If you're really here, remember the mirror."

Yes, I'm here! I yelled silently. *What mirror?* I looked around the room, but didn't find a mirror. Roshayne sat cross-legged on the bed with her arms folded and stared blankly at a picture on the wall. I followed her gaze and pushed my head through the picture and into the wood paneling. Behind the glass frame, I found one of Derek's toys—a miniature video camera. *So, she's being watched. Good thing she warned me before I showed myself.*

I spent the next few minutes checking out the room. I found two more cameras: one in the ceiling, disguised as a sprinkler head, and one behind the mirror in the bathroom. *Dirt bags! Perverts! Filthy rotten—!*

Looking around a little more, I found a couple of microphones also embedded in the walls, and I was sure there were plenty more elsewhere. *It figures. They're worried about her talking to me and giving me information. This is going to be harder than I thought.* Roshayne said nothing. I hovered in the middle of the room, feeling totally helpless and defeated. *Don't worry, Rosh. I'll think of something. I'll be back. I'm not going to leave you out here.*

Reluctantly, I rose up through the ceiling and found myself over the aft deck dining room of the yacht. Rising higher, I scanned the horizon again and was discouraged to find that Clawson was right. There was nothing in sight for me to relate to except miles and miles of endless water. I rose higher until the yacht looked like a toy in a bathtub. Nothing. I went up again until the yacht was just a tiny white speck on the ocean. Still nothing. Higher and higher I rose until I finally detected some brown and green on the west horizon. When I looked back down, the yacht was gone from view. I rose again until I was high enough to make out a string of islands. To the northwest I finally recognized the tail end of Florida. I was so high by then that I could see the curvature of the earth, and looking down was like looking at a map in a history book.

I've got to get back to the truck, I decided. *Back to body!*

In a heartbeat, I was yanked back. I quickly climbed out from under the toolbox and knocked on the window. Tamara slid it open.

"Where are we?" I asked urgently.

"We just passed Beaver," she answered. "Why?"

I crawled halfway through the window. "Give me the map. Hurry."

Tamara unfolded the Utah map and handed it to me. After studying it a minute, I asked, "Is this I-70 right here?"

"Yeah," replied Tamara. "We passed it just a while ago."

"Turn around as soon as you get a chance, Paul. We've got to get on I-70."

"Why?" Paul asked. "Where we going?"

"To Florida."

Chapter 9

- The Freeway -

Within a few minutes, we were eastbound on Interstate 70 and heading toward the Colorado border. I spent the next hour or so relating to Paul and Tamara everything I had just seen and heard. Both listened quietly, asking only an occasional question until I was finished.

"So, this is it," Paul said finally, breaking the long silence that followed. "You were right all along. Clawson and Hawk are going to kill us all."

"If he can catch up with us," I answered.

"What do you mean?"

"The faster we move, the harder it's going to be for him to nail us down using the police."

"Maybe. Maybe not," Paul said. "For all we know, there could be a roadblock waiting for us just over the next hill. I don't like this at all."

"Well, what choice do we have?" I asked. "We can't go home, or we'll be thrown in jail in five minutes. By the time we get out, Roshayne could be dead. We've got to try."

Tamara spoke up. "What do you think he meant when he said you were going to get yourself killed 'by your own doing'? Does he think you're going to kill yourself?"

"Of course not," Paul answered. "He means we're going to run into so much trouble that sooner or later we're going to get ourselves shot by somebody."

"That's comforting," Tamara said sarcastically. "Really, Bart. What do you plan on doing? You know darn well that Silver Hawk will be watching us the whole way. What can we do?"

"I'm not sure," I said, staring off into space. "There's got to be a way we can get by Hawk undetected. We've got to figure out some way to hide from him."

"How are you going to do that?" Tamara asked.

"I don't know. He finds us by homing in on our brain waves," I said, stroking my chin thoughtfully. "Maybe we could figure out a way to scramble or block the signals, or divert him somehow."

"You mean like flying low, below radar," Paul volunteered.

"Something like that."

"Well, we could sleep in cemeteries on the way," he joked. "We know he doesn't like them."

"Cemeteries?" Tamara asked, looking back and forth from Paul to me.

"Cemeteries," I repeated thoughtfully.

"Hey, I'm just kidding," Paul said. "I know we can't—"

"Yes!" I said, slapping my leg. "Why didn't I think of that!"

"What?" they both asked.

I turned to them and grinned wickedly. "I have a plan."

"Then let's have it," Paul demanded.

"We could use a—" I stopped abruptly, looking around in the air. "I can't tell you right now."

"Why not?" he asked, a little annoyed.

I mouthed the words *Silver Hawk,* and he nodded in understanding, looking around nervously.

The very idea that Silver Hawk could be hanging around watching and listening threw us into another prolonged silence, and we traveled for the next several hours without saying much of anything. We spotted two highway patrol cars going in the opposite direction on the freeway, but neither of them even gave us a sideways glance. Then we passed one on our side sitting in the shade of an overpass checking for speeders. We all stared holes in the mirrors and held our breath, expecting him to chase after us at any moment. But he didn't.

Gradually our nerves settled down, and we relaxed a little. Tamara fell asleep again on Paul's shoulder, and I watched the sagebrush and telephone poles fly by.

Under different circumstances, this could be a pretty exciting vacation, I thought. *If only Roshayne was here with us.*

That thought brought back to the forefront the reason for the trip, and I felt the hair stand up on the back of my neck when I remembered the way Clawson had knocked her off the bed. *You'll get yours,* I promised, clenching my teeth so hard my jaw popped.

We crossed the Colorado border at around four o'clock. Half an hour later, we stopped in Grand Junction for gas and food. We made it a point to hurry, and got back on the road as quickly as we could. I took over the wheel so Paul could rest for a while. He propped a pillow against the window and was out like a light.

"Can you tell every time Hawk is around?" Tamara asked quietly a few minutes later.

"I've felt him around a lot of times," I answered. "Sometimes it's very strong, and sometimes it's just an uncomfortable, uneasy feeling. But I have no way of knowing if I can always tell. It's the same with him, I think. The first time I saw him in Clawson's office, I was out-of-body and only a few feet away from him, but he didn't give any indication that he knew I was there. Ever since then, he's sensed my being there sooner or later. Maybe he got to know my smell," I joked.

"It sure is weird, all this out-of-body, jumping out, going Inviz stuff you do. What does it feel like? I mean, what do you see? Where do you go?"

"It doesn't really feel like anything at first," I answered. "Sometimes I don't even realize I'm out. But once I do, it's a great feeling. There's no weight or gravity at all. It's kind of like floating in outer space, I guess."

"Can you hear and touch and smell and all that?"

"It's funny you would mention that. I was just thinking the other day about how the five so-called physical senses aren't really all that physical at all. I mean, I can see and hear just fine when I'm out . . . better, in fact. I can focus right next to my eyes and see in the dark, and I can hear things miles away."

"What about touching things?"

"Touching is a different story. My spirit body, and all spirit matter, I guess, is so fine that it just melts through physical stuff like it wasn't there. But if I concentrate and touch slowly and carefully, I can feel things. I can even feel if things are hot or cold, even though I don't ever actually feel hot or cold myself. You know what I mean?"

"No. Not really."

"Well, it's like I always feel perfectly comfortable. There's never any pain or pressure or heat or anything like that. But if I put my hand in a fire, I can tell—sense somehow—that it's hot. It's weird."

"How about tasting and smelling?"

I laughed. "Well, I've never eaten anything as a spirit, so I don't really know if I can taste or not. Come to think of it, I don't think I've ever seen anything spiritual to eat."

"You mean spirit people don't eat?" she asked, surprised.

"I guess not. It's not like they're going to starve to death."

"That's terrible," she said seriously. "I don't think I could survive without chocolate."

I looked at her funny. *Give me a break. That's all she worries about?*

"You did solve one big mystery for me, though, Bart."

"What's that?"

"I always used to worry about . . ." She stopped and glanced at me, then looked at the floor, embarrassed. "About whether or not I would have clothes on when I died."

"Huh?"

"Well, think about it. When you die, your physical clothes stay with your physical body. So, do you go out naked or what? Is there going to be some spirit lady—or guy, in your case—standing there with a robe or a towel or something to cover you up right away?"

"I never thought about it," I admitted.

"Well, I have. It's bothered me a lot. But when you appeared to me at Mervyn's that one time, you were dressed . . . just like you always are. Not even in white robes or anything like that. Just regular, everyday clothes."

"Really?" Thinking about it, I realized that in all the times I had projected, I had never even once bothered to look and see what I was wearing, or IF I was wearing. *I'll have to make it a point to look next time,* I decided. "Well, the scriptures say that everything physical has a spiritual equivalent," I reasoned. "So maybe whatever clothes you put on physically are also being put on spiritually."

"Cool."

"Or maybe when we were born, we came already spiritually dressed. Maybe we've had on the same old spirit clothes ever since."

"That makes more sense. So, after you get out, how do you get back in? Aren't you afraid someday you won't be able to get back?"

"Someday I won't," I replied. "That's called dying."

"You know what I mean."

"Getting in is a hundred times easier than staying out, believe me. When my body wants me back, it yanks me back. And if I want to go back, all I have to do is think 'back to body,' and I'm back. It's usually instantaneous. Although . . ." I stopped, remembering what had happened just a couple of days before, during the fire.

"Although what?"

"Sometimes weird things happen."

I proceeded to tell her about how Charlene had almost burned in the fire, and how I had supposedly saved her. How I had felt the smoke and heat, and carried her out of the building.

"I heard about that, Bart," she said. "I thought it was some guy who worked there."

"I know. I met him. But I was just as much there as he was. I know I was. I just can't—"

I let the thought die, not knowing what else to say or how to explain the incident.

"Weird," Tamara responded.

She reached up and twisted the mirror around where she could check up on her face and her makeup. After fussing with her eyelashes for a few seconds, she paused and squinted into the mirror. She turned around and looked over her shoulder for a second, then jerked back around.

"Bart, I think we're being followed."

I was about to look over my shoulder. "Don't turn around!" she said quickly.

I straightened up the mirror and surveyed the road. About fifty yards behind us was an old gray sedan, following at our same speed.

"He's just taking advantage of our cruise control," I said, "so he doesn't have to worry about speeding."

"Are you sure?" She pulled the mirror back where she could use it, and I watched from the side mirror for a while.

"Well, there's one way to find out," I said. I turned off the cruise and gradually increased our speed another ten miles an hour. At first he dropped behind, but then he caught up again and matched our speed. I passed a station wagon pulling a U-Haul trailer and then moved back in the right lane. He did the same. I sped up another five. He did also. I slowed down and reset the cruise. He fell in at the same speed, but farther back than before.

"Paul," I said. "Paul, wake up."

Tamara shook him and roused him. "What's up?" he asked groggily.

"I think we have company." I glanced again in the mirror.

Paul started to turn around to look. "Don't look!" yelled Tamara, grabbing his arm.

Paul studied the car for a while from the other side mirror. "They don't look like cops," he said.

"I was thinking the same thing," I answered nervously.

"This could be serious. Do you think Clawson's sending his own guys after us?"

"That would explain why the police aren't interested in us around here," I answered.

"How long have they been following us?"

"I'm not sure. They could have been there for hours, for all I know."

"Do you think they want to catch us?" Tamara asked fearfully. "Or kill us?"

"They've had plenty of time to do that already," I answered. "All they'd have to do is pull up alongside and blast away. We're sitting ducks."

"Maybe," Paul answered. "Or maybe they're just waiting for us to get off the freeway and go somewhere less traveled."

"You think we should try to lose them?" Tamara asked.

"How?" I asked. "We're on a freeway with nothing but mountains on either side. How do you lose somebody on a freeway?"

"And Denver's still a hundred miles from here," Paul added. He stared thoughtfully at the mirror for a few seconds, then turned and smiled at us. "I guess we'll just have to scare them off, won't we?" he said casually.

"How you planning on doing that?" Tamara asked. "You going to pull faces at them or something?"

"No. We're going to use my secret weapon."

Chapter 10

- Jet Fighter -

While I wound my way up the mountains, Paul and Tamara climbed out the rear window into the back of the truck. I noticed that the car following us immediately backed off a little more. *Paranoid guys,* I thought.

Using a key that he had extracted from the key ring in the ignition, Paul proceeded to unlock and open one of the lift-up lids of the big white toolbox. He rummaged around in the box and pulled out what looked like a big radio set and a cardboard box full of stuff. Those he handed to Tamara. Then he opened the other lid. Slowly and carefully, he began pulling out something big and silver. I watched intently in the mirror, almost missing a curve in the road that came up in a hurry. I overcorrected and knocked Paul off his feet. He dropped to his knees, protecting his cargo with his arms and chest. "Be careful!" he yelled at me angrily.

After making sure I was on a long straightaway, he stood back up, proudly cradling his surprise in his arms and bracing himself against the headwind.

"Holy cow!" I yelled back at him, gawking in the mirror. "It's a jet! Holy cow!"

It was a perfect scale model of an F-16 fighter jet, measuring almost four feet long. Paul had always been a big fan of remote control aircraft. He had two or three little planes that he flew around regularly.

"How do you like the newest member of my fleet?" he asked, tipping it forward so I could get a better look.

"Awesome!" I replied. "How does it fly? Does it have a real jet engine or what?"

"The whole fuselage of the jet is filled with a mini-turbo," he yelled back. "It flies a simulated mach-two—about two hundred actual miles an hour."

"You're kidding."

"What are you going to do with it?" Tamara asked as Paul squatted down in the truck and laid the jet in the bed.

"I'm going to buzz those guys in the car back there and see if I can't scare them off."

"You're what?" I asked in surprise. "Don't you need a runway or something? We're not stopping."

"Don't need to," he yelled back. "We've already got a sixty-mile headwind blowing right over the top of the truck."

Paul fiddled with his equipment, presumably filling the fuel tank or something. I watched anxiously as the gray car started getting closer and closer. They were just as curious about what was going on as I was. When he was finally ready, Paul held the plane up in the air so it was pointing forward.

"Okay, get under it," he told Tamara. "Hold it real tight right here on the wings where I'm holding it."

Tamara scooted under the model plane, sat back on her haunches, and grabbed the wings firmly. Paul picked up the radio transmitter that he used to control the plane and made some adjustments. I saw the flaps and things move when he wiggled the knobs.

"Hold on real tight. I'm going to start the engine."

"Is it going to take off?" Tamara asked nervously.

"Not yet."

"This is crazy, Paul," I yelled back. "You're going to wreck that thing. It must have cost you a fortune."

"Yeah, pretty much," he answered.

I expected the high-pitched, squealing noise that goes with most remote-controlled planes and was genuinely surprised at the loud, deep roar that soon filled the air. It sounded every bit like a real jet engine. Tamara's face stretched tight as she fought to hold the plane still and overcome her urge to cover her ears.

"I'm going to increase the throttle," he yelled right into Tamara's ear. I read his lips more than heard. "When you feel it pushing forward, lift it up just a little bit so it can catch some wind—but don't let go!"

Tamara nodded quickly and nervously. Her hands and knuckles were turning white from the grip she held on the jet. Paul tweaked one of the knobs, and the noise gradually increased. After a couple of seconds, I saw Tamara slowly rise up onto her knees. Her face was totally distorted from the agony of the exercise. The noise increased more and more in pitch and volume.

"Get ready to stand up . . . real slow and careful," Paul instructed.

Tamara brought one knee up and proceeded to stand. She stumbled from the effect of the headwind, and my heart skipped a beat. Paul grabbed her arm with his free hand and steadied her. Finally she was standing up, legs spread with one back and one forward for support, the jet just inches over her head.

"Lift it higher!" Paul yelled.

Tamara straightened her arms to full length as Paul continued to gun the engine.

"I can't hold it anymore!" she yelled. "It's pulling loose!"

"Backward or forward?"

"Forward!" she answered.

"When I count to three, let it go . . . slowly and carefully!"

I felt the sweat forming on my forehead as I strained to negotiate the curves and keep the truck steady, and still watch the action in the back. My arms ached from the effort. Tamara closed her eyes and bit her lip.

"One!"

A tighter than usual curve came up that I tried to take wide and easy, forcing us out into the opposite lane. Fortunately, the only traffic within a mile was the bad guys' car behind us.

"Two!"

I held my breath as the truck came straight again.

"Three!!"

Letting go was anything but slow and careful. Tamara basically abandoned the plane and collapsed. I saw Paul's eyes following the jet—up and back—and to my horror, saw the plane disappear down behind the tailgate.

It's going to crash! I thought. *It's ruined!*

I waited breathlessly, expecting Paul to throw down the controls in disgust any second. But he just stood there like a statue, right behind the window, gently massaging the controls. Suddenly, I heard Tamara let out a war cry and caught a glimpse of the jet rising into the air about fifty feet behind the truck, its speed matching ours perfectly.

"YES!!!" I yelled. "All right, Paul!!"

Paul settled back against the toolbox for support.

"Move over so I can see!" I yelled back.

He shifted to the right a couple of feet, and I saw immediately that the pursuing car had dropped back dramatically. Paul experimented a little, trying to get the feel of the plane. Ascending and descending were easy maneuvers, but when he tried some bank and turns, the jet went the opposite direction from where he intended. "It's like flying in a mirror!" he complained. "I have to think backwards!"

"Turn around so the controls face forward," I suggested, "and watch over your shoulder."

He got the hang of it pretty quickly once his front and the plane's front got in sync with each other. I had a hard time following everything, seeing how I was still in charge of keeping us on the freeway, but from what I saw, Paul conducted a spectacular air show. He moved the jet back and forth slowly in front of the car and allowed the jet to slow down. The car dropped back to avoid a collision. Paul managed to get the jet within three or four feet of the hood, then he moved it out and along the right side and let it drop back even with the car. The guy riding shotgun tried to reach out and knock it down, but Paul kept it out of reach.

It was obvious they were not enjoying Paul's experiment, and several times they were so busy watching the jet that they nearly ran off the freeway.

"Another curve to the right!" I yelled back, warning him of our changes of course.

Paul tried a couple of quick ins and outs, coming within inches of the driver's mirror and forcing them to swerve from one lane to the other. After a couple of attempts to hit it with his left hand, the driver found something longer to swing with.

"That looks like a gun!" Tamara yelled.

I looked closer in the mirror. Sure enough, the driver was swinging what looked like a sawed-off shotgun.

Paul saw the danger and maneuvered the jet out of the way, then flew it directly over the car. I watched in dismay as the guy riding shotgun started climbing out his window WITH the shotgun.

"He's going to shoot it!" Tamara yelled frantically. "He's going to shoot the jet!"

Paul pulled back on his remote control stick and gunned the throttle. Instantly the jet shot a hundred feet into the air. The guy finally got himself out of the window far enough to sit on the door and proceeded to pump off three shots in quick succession straight up into the air. From his point of view, the jet was a stationary target exactly over his head, but fortunately he failed to take into account the effect the wind would have on the buckshot, which was swept clear of the jet by a couple of yards.

Paul decided his fighter was in mortal danger and flew the jet way out to the right and up along the mountainside where we could barely see it. I was afraid he would crash it into the pine trees. He increased its speed to the max for a couple of seconds and brought it way out in front of us.

When I looked in the mirror again, I saw that the shooter had re-entered the car, and the driver was maintaining a cautious distance, wondering what Paul intended to do next.

"I'm going to bring it back into the truck!" Paul yelled. "Get ready to grab it when it comes overhead!"

"What if they shoot at us?!" Tamara yelled back.

"Throw something at them," he yelled back.

Tamara found the small toolbox Paul had picked up in her garage and pulled out a handful of wrenches and pliers, which she stuffed in her back pockets.

Almost immediately, the bad guys started moving in. I couldn't see the shotgun, but I was plenty worried.

Tamara saw them closing in and promptly launched a crescent wrench at their car. It bounced wildly on the road in front of them and banged noisily several times under their car as they drove over it. I was hoping it would hit the oil pan or something, but they kept right on coming. Tamara displayed the hammer in her hand, and the car backed off again.

As Paul was bringing the jet back toward us from the front and

Tamara was bracing for the catch, I came up behind a diesel truck pulling an empty flatbed and moving just slightly slower than we were. Paul saw the problem and flew the jet up higher where he could see it. "Go around and get in front!" he yelled.

I passed on the left. Our pursuers came right behind us. As soon as I had barely a car-length on the diesel, I cut back in front of him. He laid on his air horn, nearly scaring me out of my wits. I glanced in the mirror, expecting to see the driver flipping the bird at me or something, but instead he was grinning from ear to ear. Then, without warning, he swerved into the left lane, practically forcing the gray sedan off into the median. They fishtailed back onto the road and attempted to pass the truck on the right, but as soon as they made the attempt, the truck driver pulled his rig back into the right lane, cutting them off again.

"All right!" I yelled. "He's running interference for us!"

Paul had been too busy to notice as he coaxed his jet down directly over his head. Tamara dropped the hammer, stretched out her hands and wiggled her fingers, as if coaxing the plane down to her. Finally she was able to grab it by the wings, and they reversed the takeoff procedure, cutting the engine and slowly squatting down with the plane to get it out of the direct blast of the wind.

"Hold still right there!" Paul yelled to Tamara. "I'm going to try something else."

"What?" she asked in desperation.

By that time our trucker friend had cut off our hunters three more times, and they finally decided to keep their distance behind the truck for the time being.

Confident that Tamara had the plane under control, Paul set aside the radio and started scavenging frantically in the bottom of the big toolbox. He came up with three red road flares.

"What are you going to do with those?" I asked through the window.

"We're going to dive-bomb them," he answered.

"What?"

After some rummaging around in Tamara's small toolbox, he came up with a roll of electricians' tape, which he used to strap the flares together. Then he stuck some loose wires haphazardly in and out and around, and taped them to a big voltmeter.

Finally, he strapped the meter to the side of the package with the display facing out, and turned it on.

"It's dynamite," he said triumphantly, holding it up for my inspection, "with a timer. We're going to do some dive-bombing."

"You've got to be kidding," I said. "How are you going to drop it?"

"From here," he said, pointing to the underside of the jet. Looking closer, I detected a small device that resembled a claw protruding from the center of the fuselage. "I use it to do bombing raids with water balloons," he explained. "I added a remote switch to my controls for it."

With the makeshift bomb in his left hand, Paul retrieved the radio with his right and flipped a switch. The four curved arms of the tiny hook swung open. Then he carefully held the "bomb" under the plane and flipped the switch again. Just like they had been designed especially for that purpose, the hooks closed perfectly around the top flare and hung on tight.

"Hurry up!" Tamara yelled. She was sweating profusely and nearing the point of no return.

Paul looked around to make sure we were running steady on the freeway, then began the takeoff routine. It went much faster and smoother than before, and the jet lifted cleanly into the air overhead. Our trucker friend had been right behind us the whole time and honked his horn repeatedly when the jet took off. He looked like a kid with a new toy on Christmas morning, bouncing up and down on his air-cushioned seat and making all kinds of wild faces.

"Speed up!" Paul shouted. He swung the jet out several yards to the right as I accelerated to around sixty-five or so. "Faster!" he yelled.

I gunned it to seventy. A glance in the mirror let me know that the diesel had dropped a considerable distance behind, and while the driver was busy watching us, our self-appointed executioners had passed him and were closing in again.

"Faster!" Paul yelled again.

I nudged the needle to seventy-three. "It's too steep to go any faster!" I yelled. "And the curves are too sharp!"

Paul didn't waste any time. In seconds, he had his jet coasting comfortably only a few feet in front of the gray car. I took great pleasure in seeing the expressions on their faces when they spotted

Paul's care-package hanging underneath.

They slowed down immediately, and the jet raced ahead. As expected, the shotgun shooter started to get out of his window again with his weapon. The driver grabbed him by the belt and yanked him back inside with a jerk. I couldn't hear their conversation, but it was obvious the driver was explaining to his not-too-bright partner about the stupidity of shooting at high explosives at close range.

I didn't have to be much of a lip reader to recognize the dozen or so swearwords, either.

"They fell for it," I shouted over the noise of the wind.

Paul steered the fighter out to the side, then behind and over the top of the car. They tried in vain to see it from their windows, but Paul had found the perfect blind spot and kept the plane right down low—almost resting on the top of the car—just above their rear window.

"Here goes nothing!" he yelled.

With a slight bump of the throttle, the jet floated out over the front windshield, and before the bad guys could react, Paul hit the switch and dropped his bomb. Then he yanked back on the stick and raced away as though fully expecting a nuclear explosion to occur.

The driver slammed on the brakes, causing the tires to smoke and the car to careen wildly all over the road as it squealed to a stop. I expected the bomb to tumble off the car, but Paul's profusion of wires had entangled themselves in the windshield wipers, and the bomb held fast.

The last thing I saw, as we rounded the next curve, was the two of them bailing out both sides and running at top speed in opposite directions off the sides of the freeway. The driver narrowly missed getting plastered by our trucker friend.

"Yahoooo!" Tamara yelled, swinging her arms in the air.

"We did it!" Paul yelled.

"Paul! We've got a big problem!" I yelled back frantically. "There's a tunnel!"

Paul whipped around just long enough to catch sight of the Eisenhower Tunnel coming up, barely a quarter mile away, then frantically began maneuvering his jet. Fifteen seconds later I raced through the opening of the mile-and-a-half-long tunnel, sure that Paul's jet was going to slam into the mountain overhead. I was surprised and shocked to look in the mirror and see it closing in on us at barely six feet above the pavement.

The speed limit in the tunnel said fifty, but I didn't dare slow down for fear the jet would stall. There were a couple of tense moments as Paul expertly maneuvered the jet up from the rear. Tamara faced backward and caught the jet in her hands when it came overhead, then sank quickly to her knees. The roar of the engine was amplified a hundred times in the tunnel, and we all just about lost our hearing before Paul cut the engine.

"That was awesome! Totally awesome!" Tamara said a few minutes later as she climbed through the window into the cab. I threw her a high-five.

Paul poked his head through the sliding window. "It's only a matter of time before they realize they've been had, you know. We've got to get off the freeway . . . and fast!"

A quarter mile after leaving the long tunnel, we saw an exit marked LOVELAND PASS, and I pulled off. I was disappointed to find that our only options were to go under the freeway and climb the mountain on our left, or continue along the frontage road, which merged with the freeway again a mile ahead. I pulled off to the side and stopped.

"I don't think they'll see us here," I said, pointing at the hillside to our left. We were down much lower than the freeway, and all we could see of the traffic were the tops of the diesel trucks that went by. Quickly, we bailed out and climbed the hill, then crouched down behind the guardrail where we could spy on the traffic. There were suddenly a lot of cars on the road, and I was amazed that we had managed to avoid them all during our run-in with the bad guys.

"Maybe we missed them already," Tamara said after watching for almost five minutes.

"We better wait some more, just to be sure," I said. After another few minutes, I was ready to give up. "We must have—"

"There they are!" Paul yelled. We instinctively ducked down and watched through the openings between the posts. The gray sedan came racing around the bend, then shot past us at close to a hundred miles an hour.

"They look awful mad," Paul said slowly.

"Sure do," I replied.

We watched them speed down the canyon until they were out of sight, then we returned to the truck. Paul took the wheel.

Moments later we were silently coasting down the canyon, conscious of our speed and the surrounding traffic. Another forty minutes later, we came over the Buffalo Lookout and were awed by the sight of the Mile-High City and the endless Great Plains stretching out in front of us.

Chapter 11

- Busted -

The Monday afternoon traffic in Denver was relatively light, and we sailed through the center of the city on I-70 with no problems at all. Being in the middle of a big city was suddenly comforting after our episode with Clawson's thugs, and we were grateful for the surrounding civilization. We didn't even give the police a second thought. We had "bad guys" on the brain.

"Surely they wouldn't dare do anything to us here . . . would they?" Tamara asked.

Paul said nothing.

"I wouldn't think so," I answered.

"I mean . . . not with all these people around. Right?" she added, trying her best to be optimistic.

I just shook my head.

But our comfort zone soon faded away as the businesses and houses got thinner and farther apart, and we again found ourselves studying the oncoming traffic and looking nervously in the mirrors.

"Where do you think they went?" Tamara asked.

"Hopefully they gave up and went home," Paul said gruffly.

"What would YOU do if you were them?" I asked Tamara. "Assuming you were working for Clawson."

"Probably find a phone and tell him the bad news," Tamara answered.

"And then what would Clawson do?"

"I don't know," Tamara said. "What COULD he do?"

Paul turned and stared at me. "He'll send Hawk again, won't he?"

"More than likely."

"Have you felt him here?" he asked, somewhat accusingly.

"I think so. About five minutes ago, but I'm not one hundred percent sure."

"Oh, great. That's just great," Paul said loudly. "Bart, this is totally out of hand. We've got to re-think this whole thing." He drummed the steering wheel nervously with his fingers. "We should never . . ." He stopped short, muttered something under his breath that I didn't catch, and fell silent, staring hard at the road ahead. The look on his face told me he was not a happy camper, so I didn't say anything.

Tamara shot me a quick glance that basically said "I'm scared" and "What are we going to do?" at the same time.

For several minutes nobody said anything. Paul gripped the wheel so hard his knuckles turned white, and his face got deeper and darker red by the minute. Tamara stared intently at her lap, wanting only to stay neutral. I watched out the side window and tried to think of something appropriate to say.

It was obvious that I was becoming the bad guy. Paul was mad at me, and he had every right. Here we were, trying to outrun every law enforcement agency in the country, with paid killers hot on our tail at the same time.

Who wouldn't be mad?

Maybe I should have just gone straight home the first time, I thought. *I should have just turned myself in last night and let the cops and the lawyers do their thing. I should never have dragged Paul and Tamara out here like this. What ever possessed me to do such a crazy, stupid, irresponsible, idiotic thing like this?*

The answer was obvious, of course. *Roshayne.*

The image of her being struck to the floor by Clawson came blazing back into my mind's eye, and I felt myself getting angry again. I clenched my fist and tightened my jaw, and burned holes in the passing sagebrush with my eyes. Clawson's words rang in my ears. "Within forty-eight hours, your little sweetheart here will be shark bait!"

I remembered the look in Silver Hawk's eyes as he breathed his threats against me. "The Great Spirit awaits." I started absent-mindedly thumping my leg angrily with my fist.

I recalled the silent promise I had made to Roshayne, and vowed again to do everything possible to get her back safely.

I'm going to have to do this on my own, I decided, *without Paul and Tamara. There's no reason to keep putting them in danger. I'm the only one Clawson really wants, anyway.*

I spent the next few minutes tossing around some ideas and formulating a new plan. When I was fairly sure what I needed to do, I turned around to break the news.

"Paul—" I started.

Without warning, Paul slammed on the brakes, throwing Tamara and me against the dash, and yanked the truck roughly across the shoulder and into the dirt. We came to an abrupt stop in a thick cloud of dust. Before I could recover from the jolt, Paul was out the door, storming around the truck and off into the weeds. I got out and followed.

"What was THAT all about?" I asked testily.

He stopped with his back to me and looked at the ground, one hand on his waist.

I decided to try a softer approach. "Paul, I'm sorry, okay? What—?"

"Sorry?!" He yelled, spinning around and glaring at me. "Sorry? We're out here being hunted like rabbits, and all you can say is 'Sorry'?"

"Well, I—"

"We're going to get killed, Bart. KILLED! As in DEAD!" He walked off another couple of feet and spun around again. "Those guys have real guns, Bart, with real bullets!" He marched off again.

"Okay, all right," I said quickly, trying to keep up with him. "So we'll turn ourselves in. We'll take our chances with the cops. At least maybe they won't shoot us first."

"No. They'll just throw us in jail for ninety years and throw away the key!"

"My dad will get a lawyer. We can explain—"

"How are you going to explain running from the police for the last two days? How are you going to explain that gun and all that stuff they found in your dad's car?" He took a couple of steps menacingly toward me and pointed angrily at his truck. "And how are you going to explain all that stuff in MY TRUCK?!"

"Huh? What stuff?"

"In the toolbox!"

I turned and looked at the truck. Tamara was standing right outside the door, watching our heated exchange and chewing on her fingernails.

"Go ahead!" Paul yelled. "Look for yourselves!"

Tamara raised the lid slowly with her right hand while she looked Paul steadily in the eye. Then she turned and looked inside. "Omagosh!" she yelled, jumping back, her eyes wide. "Omagosh!" She covered her mouth with both hands.

I ran to the truck. There in the bottom of the box, underneath where the jet had been stored, lay several big ziplock bags stuffed chock full of hundred-dollar bills. Nestled comfortably right in the middle of them was . . . a gun!

"Holy smokes!" I exclaimed. I couldn't believe my eyes. My mind went into hyperdrive. "They must have planted all this stuff while you and your sister were at BYU—same as they did with us at the ball game."

I started to reach inside.

"Don't touch it!" Paul yelled, running over and grabbing my arm. "The last thing we need is your fingerprints all over it!"

"We're in big trouble," I conceded, looking back into the box.

"We better get moving!" Tamara said. "And fast!" She grabbed her new backpack from the front seat and dumped the contents out on the floor. Then she fished a handkerchief out of her purse, and before Paul or I could say or do anything, reached in and grabbed the gun by the barrel. After depositing it carefully in the bottom of the bag, she pulled out each of the ziplock moneybags by the corners, using the handkerchief to avoid fingerprints, and dumped them in on top of the gun.

"Let's go," she said. She grabbed the backpack by the shoulder straps and climbed into the truck. "We'll figure this out on the way."

I slammed the lid closed. Paul started to head around the back of the truck, but came to an abrupt stop in the gravel after only two steps, staring at the road behind us. "Oh, no!" he muttered under his breath.

I stepped to the side to see around him—just in time to watch a highway patrol car pull to a stop twenty feet behind the truck, its red and blue lights flashing away.

"We're dead," Paul said. "We're dead."

We were both too stunned to move, so we just stood there glued to the ground while the patrolman climbed cautiously out of his car.

"What's the problem here?" he asked, looking back and forth at Paul and me.

"Uh . . . nothing," Paul stammered. "No problem at all." He glanced back at me over his shoulder and rubbed his sweaty palms on his pants. He had "guilty" written all over his face and looked suspicious as heck.

After a few seconds of uncomfortable silence, the patrolman came to the same conclusion. "Okay, step slowly away from the truck. Keep your hands where I can see them."

With our hands at our sides, we both backed away a few feet as the officer came around between the two automobiles. Tamara started to get out of the truck.

"Hold it right there!" he yelled, pointing at her with his left hand. His right hand rested lightly on his holster.

Tamara panicked and instantly shot both hands high in the air, sending the backpack tumbling out on the ground. It rolled and rolled, over and over, for what seemed an eternity in slow motion before finally coming to a stop, leaving a trail of ziplock bags scattered all along the ground.

The cop's gun came out in a flash, and he pointed it stiff-armed at Tamara. Then he spun around to me, then to Paul, then back to Tamara.

"Don't shoot," I said feebly. "We can explain—"

"Shut up!" he yelled, spinning back around on me. I could see beads of sweat popping out on his forehead. It was I-15, point-of-the-mountain all over again, with one big difference—we weren't going to come up clean like we did the first time.

I started to get really scared.

"On your knees! And put your hands behind your head!" he yelled at me. I did what I was told. "Now you!" he said, pointing his gun at Paul. "And you!" he said to Tamara. Once we were all down, he backed slowly to the side of his car and reached in the window for his microphone to call for backup, never once taking his eyes off us.

Before long, the place was swarming with cops. Patrol cars were parked at odd angles everywhere. So many, in fact, that they blocked the right lane, causing a congestion of rubber-neckers, anxious to see blood and guts or whatever was available. I felt like a first-class criminal and wondered what people would be thinking as they drove by. After all, it's not every day you see a full-scale felony arrest going down.

We were grabbed and thrown around pretty roughly as we were frisked and handcuffed. The moneybags were retrieved, along with the backpack. The cop picking them up whistled softly when he looked inside. "Well, lookie here," he said, pulling out the gun with his own handkerchief and displaying it proudly to the other officers. The cop holding me tightened his grip.

Several other officers were searching the truck. They were particularly interested in Paul's jet, which was still lying in the back. One cop lifted the lid on the toolbox where the money and the gun had been. Another did the same on the other side.

"Sergeant!" the second one yelled, holding the lid open. "Take a look at this!"

I glanced at Paul, and he gave me a look that said, "I was going to tell you." When I looked back, the officer was pulling out what appeared to be more ziplock bags . . . full of white powder. My heart sank and my stomach tightened up as he extracted a second, then a third.

"Three kees," the sergeant said. He opened the top of one of the packages and poked his little finger in, then touched it lightly to his tongue. "Pure," he announced. If looks could kill, I'd have been shriveled up and dead under his stare.

After several more long minutes of exhaustive searching and questioning—to which we answered nothing—we were finally led to separate cars, where officers were holding the back doors open for us.

Just as I was about to be pushed inside, Tamara gasped, "Bart!" She caught my eye, then looked quickly at the road.

I followed her gaze and found myself locked eye-to-eye with the shooter in the gray sedan as they slowly drove past with the rest of the traffic. He had a wicked grin on his face that made my skin crawl.

"Get in!" the cop beside me said, pushing my head roughly down into the car. When he had me bent over, he bumped me hard in the rear with his knee, sending me flying crazily into the backseat. By the time I got straightened up, the door had been slammed shut and the gray sedan was long gone.

The last thing I remembered seeing, as we were taken away, was a big yellow tow truck backing up to get a grab on Paul's brand-new, shiny red truck. After that, I closed my eyes in agony and kept them that way all the way to the county jail.

What have I done?! I moaned over and over. *What have I done?*

I went through the whole booking process in a daze.

We were fingerprinted, pushed in front of a camera for mug shots, and relieved of all our personal possessions. The backpack full of money, the three sacks of drugs, and the gun, which had been put in its own ziplock bag, were all put in a small safe behind the desk. Our things were put in manila envelopes in a drawer.

In the midst of the confusion, I vaguely remembered hearing someone mention that they had pulled up the APB on us, and that there would be some Utah County sheriffs coming to get us the next day sometime.

Then we were paraded down the hall through two separate, heavy metal doors, and Paul and I were shoved roughly into a cell. The door banged shut, echoing loudly through the jailhouse. Tamara was taken around the other side where the women were kept.

I looked around at the cell, taking inventory and trying hard to avoid making eye contact with Paul. He hadn't said a single word to me since we were arrested, but had glared accusingly at me several times.

The cell was about ten feet square and pretty typical-looking, at least compared to what I had seen on TV. The outside wall was made of brick or block and had a long, narrow window with bars. The two side walls, floor, and ceiling were made of thick, heavy hardwood timbers.

And, of course, there were the expected bars along the front. A beat-up looking set of bunk beds hung suspended from one side, and a stainless steel toilet and sink were mounted on the opposite wall. Nothing surprising, except that the place stank to high heaven and was as hot as an oven. There were two ceiling fans in the hallway, but they didn't do much good.

"Well," I said, trying to make conversation, "it could be worse. We could be in a swampy dungeon, chained to the walls."

"Oh, give it up, Bart," Paul shot back angrily as he threw himself on the bottom bunk. "I'm not in the mood for your stupid jokes, okay?" He crossed his arms over his chest and stared at the rusty springs of the top bunk.

There was nowhere to sit, and nothing else to do, so I climbed up on the top bunk and lay down. After several minutes of staring at the ceiling, I said softly, "I'm sorry, Paul. I'm really sorry." I heard the squeak of the springs as he rolled over, but he didn't answer.

I kept still for nearly an hour after that, hands behind my head, waiting and thinking. Eventually, Paul's breathing became regular and heavy, and I concluded that he was sleeping. As the tension gave way to fatigue, I found it harder and harder to stay awake myself. I wondered if the deputies might bring us supper, but eventually gave up on the idea. Apparently, we had checked in too late.

At last, satisfied that I would not be interrupted, I placed my arms straight along my side, closed my eyes, and summoned the vibrations.

Had anyone been watching, they would surely have wondered if I had just up and died. For over two hours, my body lay perfectly still, without so much as a muscle twitch. My breathing was so slow that even if they had licked the back of their finger and held it directly under my nose, they wouldn't have felt anything. To the casual observer, my chest would have appeared motionless; and even with a stethoscope, one would have had to listen intently to hear my barely detectable heartbeat once every five or six seconds.

But finally, they would have seen my chest heave suddenly as I drew a deep breath, and my eyes opened and closed briefly. After that, they would have been serenaded by my usual, obnoxious snoring until morning.

Chapter 12

- Spooks -

After what seemed like only a few brief minutes of sleep, I was jarred abruptly awake and sat straight up on the bunk. I looked all around and listened carefully, trying to identify whatever had awakened me. The whole building was quiet and nearly pitch-black. I realized I must have been asleep for several hours, although I had no idea what time it was. I lay back down very slowly. Listening more intently, I detected Paul's steady, heavy breathing below, and someone else's quiet snoring coming from down the hall. Neither was anywhere near loud enough to wake me.

All of a sudden, I was overcome by a nauseous feeling and wondered if I might have gotten food poisoning from something I ate. I made a sour face and instinctively moved my hand to my stomach. Then I realized the nausea wasn't physical. I didn't have a stomachache, or any other kind of bodily ache. It was an ugly, sickening, evil presence.

SILVER HAWK!

His unseen spirit had entered the cell and seemed to fill the whole room like a dark, smoky mist. I felt my heart start to race, and began breathing rapidly. I felt a terrible squeezing pressure bearing down on my chest and arms. Beads of sweat popped out on my forehead, and I thought my whole body was going to explode. I clenched my fists and tensed every muscle in my body. With my eyes shut tight, I tried desperately to endure. But the more I strained, the more the horrible feelings grew and intensified, until I was sure I would be crushed to death.

When I couldn't stand it anymore, I bolted upright, pressed my hands against the sides of my head, and screamed.

"HAAAAAAAAAAAAAWWWWWWKKK!!!"

Paul sprang from his bunk like a jack-in-the-box and flattened himself against the far wall. He stood frozen in place, watching me sitting there with my eyes bulging out, my bloodcurdling scream reverberating off the walls and echoing through the whole jail. For several seconds nobody moved, and the silence was profound and absolute.

Then the jail erupted in shouts and foul language as all the other inmates in the place hurled angry threats at me. The big iron doors at the end of the hall slammed opened, and the deputy on duty came charging down the hall.

"What in the heck's going on here?" he demanded, stopping in front of our cell.

"It . . . it was a devil," I said, still shaken from the experience.

"Say what?" He looked at Paul, still scared out of his wits and cowering against the wall.

My mind raced. "A devil!" I said with more conviction. "There was a devil . . . a ghost! Right here in front of me! I thought he was going to kill us both! He—"

"Oh, shuddup!" he yelled. "You think I'm fool enough to believe a cockamamie story like that? I wasn't born yesterday!" He started walking away.

"But it's—"

"Next time you holler like that, I'll bring my gun in here, rules or no rules, and plug ya 'tween the eyes!"

Both doors slammed loudly as he left.

The other inmates let loose with a series of catcalls, taunting us and making fun for several minutes. I ignored them, and Paul just stood there looking at me like I'd lost my mind.

Finally, after the noise died down, he whispered, "Bart, what in the heck happened? You scared me to death!"

"Silver Hawk was here. It felt like he was going to crush the life out of me."

Paul looked nervously around the cell. "Is he still here?"

I looked at the ceiling, then closed my eyes and concentrated for a few seconds. "I don't think so," I answered. "Paul, we've got to get out of here—fast!"

"What?"

I jumped down from the bunk and started pacing the floor. "Clawson's got something planned, and if we don't get out real quick, it's all going to end right here."

"You think he's going to come charging right into the county jail? With cops all over the place?"

"That guy who just went storming down the hall is the only cop in the building. It wouldn't take much—"

"So what? We can't exactly leave when we want to."

I paced faster and faster, my mind in high gear. "If we could get him to open the door somehow, we could jump him and take his keys."

"Bart, get real. You can't—"

"We could scream about devils and ghosts again, and convince him we're crazy."

"No way, Bart. He'd shoot us first."

"He's not allowed to bring a gun—" I stopped pacing. "Wait a minute! I can BE a ghost. I can go out there!"

"How's that going to get us out? You can't bring the keys back."

"If Mohammed can't go to the mountain, bring the mountain to Mohammed," I said. "Or something like that."

"What the—"

"I'm going to get Tammy to do the screaming," I said, climbing back up on the bunk. "Who can resist a damsel in distress?"

Paul just stood there with his mouth open.

"Be quiet . . . but be ready. This won't take long."

I closed my eyes, stretched out, and, for the second time in the same night, projected from my body and went airborne.

I'd already been around the jail during my earlier episode and knew the layout by heart. I went straight into the outer room and found the deputy sitting back in his chair with his feet on the desk, reading a magazine of ill repute. I noticed that his gun was on the desk, and his keys were hanging from his belt.

From there, I went directly to Tamara's cell in the women's section. She was sharing a cell with someone else and was on the top bunk. My screaming had awakened the women as well as the men, and they were just starting to get settled down again.

Tamara was curled up in a tight ball, facing the wall with her eyes shut. I maneuvered myself right into the wall, brought myself up slightly above her eye level, stuck my head and chest out through the wall, and materialized.

"Tammy," I whispered.

At first she didn't move. Then it dawned on her that someone had spoken her name, and she opened her eyes.

"Tammy—"

That was as far as I got. She let loose with a scream that was easily twice as loud as mine, and lasted a full three seconds before she recognized me and cut it off. Her cellmate came out from under just about as fast as Paul had, and stood staring right at me, wide-eyed and open-mouthed, before I had the presence of mind to disappear. No sooner was I invisible again than the iron doors in the hallway were thrown open, and the deputy came charging up to the bars.

"What in tarnation?" he yelled. I moved to the middle of the cell where I could see everyone.

"There was a ghost!!" yelled Tamara's cellmate. "Right there! In the wall!" She pointed steadfastly at the spot where I had appeared.

Tamara nodded vigorously in agreement. "A ghost," she echoed in a hoarse whisper.

"It this some kind of joke? What do you take me for?" He grabbed the bars and pushed his face in close. "I ain't got time for this, ya hear? You and your boyfriends over there can holler all night for all I care. It ain't gonna do ya no good." He shook the bars. "NOW GO TO SLEEP!"

Boots stomped, and doors slammed again. Tamara's cellmate was about to say something, but Tamara waved her off quickly and lay back down on the bed where she had been before. The other girl shrugged her shoulders and climbed back into her bunk.

After I was sure the place had settled, I moved back over to my spot in the wall. Tamara was expecting me and was staring right at me before I even appeared, but it still made her gasp and jerk when I did.

"What are you doing?" she demanded in a barely audible whisper.

"I'm trying to scare you," I whispered back.

"Well, you did," she said flatly. "Now go back where you came from before I have a heart attack."

"We need to get out of here, Tammy. I need your help."

"Are you crazy? We're in jail . . . in case you haven't noticed."

"All we need to do is get his keys. I'm going to scare you and your friend again—maybe even appear to the cop for a second or two and try to get him to open your door and come in. Once he does that, you can just take the keys, throw him on the floor, and lock him in. Piece of cake."

"Bart, this is totally random. Totally."

"We can—"

"Who you talking to?" came a loud whisper from the lower bunk.

"Nobody," Tamara answered. "Myself. Chill." Turning back to me, she asked quietly, "How are you going to scare me now? I already know you're here."

"I can make a mean face, and you can scream and pretend you've just seen the devil," I answered. "Like this." I held up my hands like claws, furrowed my eyebrows, and made the meanest face I could, complete with growling. In my mind's eye, I pictured a gruesome monster with fangs, and blood dripping from the corners of his mouth, razor-sharp claws, hairy arms, horns, and fiery red blazing eyes.

To my surprise, Tamara's eyes flew wide open, and she screamed like there was no tomorrow. She acted so terrified that she actually backed right off the bunk and crashed to the floor. Then she stood up, screamed some more, and collapsed on top of the toilet, shaking like a leaf. The cellmate came shooting out again, took one look at me, and split the air with ultra-frequency screams like I'd never heard before, jumping up and down and waving her arms like a crazy woman.

I made myself invisible as the heavy doors crashed open yet again. The screams died down to a whimper as they scanned the empty air, but they both looked positively spooked.

"Dad blast it all to heck!" the deputy yelled. "If you don't shuddup, I'm gonna hog-tie and gag the both of ya!" He hit his baton against the bars several times for effect and finally got them quiet. He paced back and forth a couple of times. "Shuddup!" he yelled again. "Just SHUT UP!" Then he stormed back down the hall, leaving the doors open and cussing a steady stream. "Why me?

This wasn't even supposed to be my night, gall darn it!"

A few seconds later, I materialized again in the center of the room in full view.

"Ahh!" yelled the cellmate, jumping back. Then she clamped both hands over her mouth and shrank as far into the corner as she could. I decided it was way too late to hide from her anymore.

"That was great, Tammy. You were wonder—"

"Bart! How did you do that?" she demanded. "I swear, you nearly killed me, scaring me like that."

"What do you mean?" I asked, puzzled. "All I did was—"

"You turned into a MONSTER, Bart! You had horns and fur, and . . . and blood all over, and . . . claws, and fire coming out your eyes! You freaked me out, Bart!"

"I did?" *How is this possible? She described my mental image exactly.* "I turned into a monster?" I asked innocently. "For real?"

"Yes, you did!"

"With fangs and blood and everything?" I smiled.

"Yes, yes!"

I floated around the cell a couple of times, absorbing what Tamara had just told me. Then I stopped right in front of her again.

"Tammy?" I said, all soft and sweet.

"What?"

"DIE!!!!" I screamed as loud as I could. I immediately formed the mental image again, and yelled and screamed like a wild banshee, flying around the cell in all directions. Tamara and the other girl both came unglued. I added pitchforks and swords, and breathed fire out of my mouth, and they screamed and screamed.

I shot through the wall into the neighboring cell, where two other girls were pressed against the bars, trying to see what was happening. I let out another ferocious growl. They spun around and saw me and screamed at the tops of their lungs. I crossed the hallway into the other two cells, where I got the same results. The noise was absolutely deafening. Hair-raising.

The deputy sheriff came racing down the hall with his baton raised high. "That's it!" he yelled. But that was as far as he got. I zoomed in on him face to face, and raised swords and spears over his head in a death stance. At first he just stood there, frozen. I growled at him, and he turned and ran for his life back down the hall.

I can't let him get away! I thought desperately. I rushed right through him and stopped him at the doors. He slowly backed up, swinging his baton at me and finding nothing but air. Slowly I maneuvered him back down the hall, growling and baring my fangs, until I had him right up against the bars of Tamara's cell. Her cellmate was still hysterical, but Tamara finally got herself under control and realized what I was doing. As the deputy shrank down onto the floor, Tamara rushed up and snatched the key ring from his belt. Then she reached around and worked a half dozen keys in the lock before the door snapped open. The deputy never even noticed, until he fell backward through the open door.

By that time, Tamara's cellmate had recognized the golden opportunity and overcame her fear immediately. Before Tamara could even think about it, her cellmate had grabbed the deputy by the collar, dragged him into the cell, dumped him unceremoniously on the floor, grabbed Tamara by the elbow, and yanked her out into the hall, pulling the metal door shut behind her.

I made myself invisible in the middle of that maneuver, and the noise in the cellblock slowly died down again.

It was several seconds before the deputy came to his senses. Then he rushed to the front of the cell and grabbed the bars. "Crazy witches!" he yelled. "I don't know how you done it, but you ain't never gonna get away with this! Ya hear? You ain't never gonna get away with this!"

His outburst brought Tamara to her senses, and she rushed down the hall.

Back to body! I yelled to myself.

Chapter 13

- Escape -

I opened my eyes and leapt off the bed. Paul was pacing like a caged animal and nearly clobbered me when I hit the ground.

"What's going on over there?" he demanded. "You kill somebody or something?"

I ignored him and rushed to the bars. "Tammy! Down here!" I heard her footsteps running through the outer office. "Quick. Get us out of here!"

The doors were closed to our hallway, and it took her several attempts before she found the right keys. Finally, with hands shaking like a tambourine, she worked the lock on our door and let us out.

"Hey!" someone yelled from down the hall. "Let us out! Open the doors!" Several others joined the chant and started pounding on their doors.

"Forget it!" Paul yelled back, and we took off on the run.

We fairly flew off the front porch and across the parking lot, and didn't even slow down until we were deep into the weeds in the empty lot on the other side of the road.

Suddenly, I was overcome with a terrible, foreboding feeling that something really bad was about to happen.

"Hold it!" I cried, grabbing their arms. "Stop!" I grabbed the deputy's keys from Tamara.

"What now?" Paul asked between breaths.

"We've got to go back," I said, turning around and heading for the jail.

"Are you nuts?"

"We've got to let the rest of them out."

"Why?!"

Tamara followed me back in, but Paul hung back in the weeds. We raced down the men's side and opened all the doors, turning loose a flood of derelicts and drunks and two-bit thieves. A couple of them thanked us, but most just beat a path for the front door.

On the women's side, we opened the remaining cells, except Tamara's, and let loose a whole collection of call girls in miniskirts. The deputy just glared at us through the bars.

In the foyer, as we were about to crash through the exit doors again, Tamara stopped abruptly, causing me to practically plow her over. "Wait!" she yelled. "The money!" She ran back to the front office and around the desk, grabbing the keys from me as she went. "Dang!" she said, squatting down in front of the safe and staring at the combination lock.

"Don't worry," I said. I pushed her gently aside and started spinning the lock. After three easy turns, the latch clicked and the door swung open.

"How—?"

"I saw them open it late last night," I said, smiling, "while I was casing the joint."

Tamara looked at me and smiled. "So, you've been busy." She grabbed her backpack and the moneybags from the safe. I salvaged our personal things from the drawer and stuffed them in the bag on top of the money, then we made a hasty exit.

Tamara was several yards ahead of me and was just disappearing into the weeds when I was hit with the same powerful feeling as before. I came to a stop in the middle of the road.

"Come on!" Paul coaxed from the darkness. "Let's get out of here!"

I stood there like a statue for a couple of seconds, debating what to do next.

"Come on, Bart. What's the matter?"

"I forgot something," I called back, then turned and ran back into the jail alone.

Instead of running through, like before, I walked in quietly and slowly. When I came to the front desk, I spotted the deputy's gun and carefully picked it up with both hands. Then I tiptoed down the women's cellblock.

At Tamara's cell, I stopped. Pointing the gun through the bars, I announced quietly, "I can't leave you here."

"Well, it's about dag-on time!" he shouted, coming toward the front of the cell.

"Back up!" I ordered.

Seeing the gun, he stopped and backed up. When he was against the wall, I opened the door and swung it inward.

"Put your handcuffs on . . . with your hands behind you."

He looked at me funny for a second, then cuffed himself.

"Turn around, so I can see them."

He did.

"Okay, let's go. But don't try anything funny," I said, trying to sound mad and mean. "I'm already wanted for everything under the sun, so one more won't matter."

He decided I was serious and went peacefully through the jail and out the front door.

"Into the weeds," I ordered. I was relieved to see that it was still dark out. *Not any too soon,* I decided.

Paul and Tamara were shocked to see me come back with the deputy.

"Jeez Louise, Bart," Paul said. "Why'd you bring HIM here?"

"Because," I said simply.

I squatted down in the weeds, and the others followed suit.

"Why are we staying here?" Tamara asked nervously. "We're going to get caught again."

"Shhh," I answered, my finger to my lips. "Just watch."

While we were waiting, Tamara handed us our personal envelopes and we retrieved our wallets and watches. As soon as Paul got his keys in his hands, he whispered to the deputy, "Where's my truck?"

The deputy just smiled and stared at him.

I prodded him in the back with the gun. "Answer the question."

He relented. "Half a block down that way. Big fenced-in area."

Paul grabbed the deputy's keys from me. "I'll be back in a sec."

Not two minutes after Paul left, a car with its headlights turned off pulled up in front of the building next to the jail and stopped.

"It's them!" Tamara whispered hoarsely, recognizing the gray sedan.

"I know," I whispered back. "I was expecting them any minute."

She glanced at me funny. "You have been busy tonight, haven't you?"

I poked the deputy in the side with his gun and whispered, "Don't get any crazy ideas. Those are not nice guys over there. Just sit here and be real quiet."

After a couple of agonizing minutes of waiting, the front doors of the sedan finally opened quietly, and our two pursuers got out. The shooter was carrying a couple of big, heavy-looking gunnysacks, and the driver was wearing a long trench coat, obviously hiding the infamous sawed-off shotgun. The shooter disappeared down the side of the jail building, and the driver walked carefully up the porch and inside the jail. After only a couple of seconds, he came running back out, shotgun plainly in hand, and called softly to his buddy. The other guy came around the far corner.

"It's empty!" the driver called out in a loud whisper. "There's nobody in there!"

"Nobody? What about the cops?" asked the shooter.

"Gone," he said softly as they approached each other.

"And the kids?"

"Gone."

"Now what?"

The driver looked around in all directions. "Torch it anyway!"

He grabbed one of the gunnysacks and began tossing what looked like water balloons through each of the outside cell windows. The shooter disappeared around the back with the other sack. When the driver reached the end, he pulled out a lighter and lit a cigarette. After taking a couple of long drags, he tossed it through one of the windows, grabbed the half-full sack, and ran back around to the front. After making sure the street was empty, he pitched the sack through the front doors and ran for his car. The shooter met him at the curb, and they jumped in the open doors and sped away.

Seconds later, it became clear to us that the balloons had not been filled with water. Smoke started billowing out of the windows from a couple of the cells.

"They're burning down the jail!" exclaimed the deputy, standing up. I quickly pulled him back down.

"They intended to burn it down with us in there," I said.

He turned and looked at me quizzically. "Who the heck ARE you guys?"

"Just some innocent teenagers being chased by some very bad dudes," I answered. "We haven't done anything wrong. We're being framed, and they want us dead."

"But they would have killed twenty other people with you."

"You included," I added. "That shotgun had your name written all over it."

His face went sober. "Now what are you going to do?"

At that moment, Paul's truck pulled up to the curb, and the door opened. Tamara took one look and ran for the truck. The smoke from the jailhouse was becoming thicker, and we could hear the crackling of growing flames.

"Time to go!" Paul called out.

"I'm going to give you back your keys and your gun," I said to the deputy, "and I'm going to leave you right here. We don't want to hurt you or anyone else. Do you understand?" He nodded. "Paul, throw me his keys," I said over my shoulder. He tossed them, and I snatched them out of the air. "We just saved your life," I said to the deputy. "Think about that while we're driving off down the road."

With that, I set the keys and the gun on the ground and backed out of the weeds toward the truck, maintaining eye contact the whole way. The look on his face was one of total bewilderment. When I made contact with the door I stopped, and for several seconds we just stared at each other. Gradually, a look of understanding and maybe even compassion came over him, and he smiled.

We were jolted abruptly by an explosion from somewhere in the jail. The deputy looked panic-stricken at his burning jailhouse. "Get going!" he yelled. "Get out of here!"

"What are you going to tell them?" I asked.

"Don't worry. I'll think of something."

Tamara tugged on my sleeve, and I got in. Before I could close the door, Paul was burning rubber. Seven blocks and two corners later, a fire engine passed us going in the opposite direction. We could see the thick, black smoke billowing into the sky behind us.

Just before we got to the freeway, I directed Paul to pull off the road, and we took cover behind a billboard.

"Now we wait some more," I said in answer to their unspoken question.

Chapter 14

- Reinforcements -

"What are we waiting for?" Paul asked impatiently.

"For the second-string team to arrive," I answered. "But I've got something I need to do first, before they get here." I climbed out of the truck and checked the back. "Good. The foam pads and stuff are still here."

"Go ahead," Paul said, folding his arms in disgust. "We'll just sit here like good little boys and girls while you have your fun."

Tamara rolled her eyes.

I made myself comfortable as quickly as I could, then jumped out.

Silver Hawk! I commanded to myself.

In seconds, I was hovering over the yacht again. Being three time zones ahead of Colorado, it was already mid-morning there, and the sun was shining brightly. As soon as I spotted Silver Hawk and Clawson at the sundeck table, I shot up into the air as high as I could go and still see them. I watched intently to see if Hawk reacted to my being there, but he didn't seem to notice. If he did, he didn't say anything.

Maybe a little distance is all I need to avoid detection, I thought.

They were both sipping at their coffee mugs when Derek walked onto the deck to join them.

"Any word?" Clawson asked.

"Not yet," Derek answered, checking his watch. "If everything goes as planned, they should be hitting the jail just about now. I expect they'll have to run for a while before they can stop to call us."

"Good," Clawson said.

Just then, one of the crewmembers came on deck and took their orders for breakfast. After he left, Clawson turned to Silver Hawk.

"When we get done eating, I want you to go see how things are going."

"Yes, sir," Hawk answered.

"As soon as I know the kid's dead, we can dump the girl and get on with business."

I was afraid for Roshayne and really wanted to check on her to see how she was doing, but I was afraid of getting too close for too long. I didn't want to give Hawk a reason to come looking for me any sooner than absolutely necessary.

Back to body!

"That didn't take long," Tamara said, leaning over the side of the truck where she'd been watching me. "Where did you go?"

"To check on Clawson and Silver Hawk," I answered. "I didn't want to talk about anything with you guys until I was sure Hawk wasn't around listening. He's busy eating breakfast right now, but he'll be coming soon enough."

"How's Roshayne?"

"Alive," I said. "Other than that, I don't know. I didn't dare stick around to find out."

Paul climbed out of the truck. "Bart, I've been thinking, and I've decided—"

"I know," I said, cutting him off. "You don't want to go any farther with me." He looked at the ground, embarrassed. "It's okay, Paul. I want you and Tammy to go back home now, anyway."

"What do you mean, go back home?" Tammy asked, alarmed. "I don't want to go back home. I want to—"

Just then, I spotted an old black funeral car cruising by and ran out into the road and whistled. The hearse stopped abruptly and backed up. "You found us," I said.

"It wasn't hard," answered the driver.

"Pull over here in front of Paul's truck," I told him. "We're just about ready." He spun around and parked. "Paul and Tammy, this is Curtis," I said as he got out of the car, "a good friend of mine from Orem."

"Hi, guys," he said, extending his hand and smiling. The passenger door opened and a tall, blonde girl stepped out.

"And this is Curtis' older sister, Candy," I continued.

"Hi," Candy said shyly.

"You're trading us for them?" Tamara asked, the hurt apparent in her eyes. "I don't understand."

"You drive a hearse?" Paul asked, admiring Curtis' car. "Where'd you get it?"

"My dad's a mortician," Curtis answered as he admired Paul's truck. "He doesn't use this one anymore since he bought his new one, so I claimed it."

"Cool," Paul answered, running his hand along the side.

"Bart?" Tamara persisted. "Explain."

"Okay," I answered. "We need to hurry, anyway." Paul and Curtis leaned against their respective vehicles and folded their arms. The girls sized each other up. "I think I've figured out a way for me to get to Hawk and Clawson without Hawk knowing where we are."

"How?" Tamara asked.

"Well, we know Hawk can jump out and zoom in on me anytime he wants, right?"

"Yeah."

"So, I'm thinking that if I'm out first, it's my spirit he'll find, not my body. So, what I plan to do is go Inviz and stay out as long as I possibly can while my body is being transported to Florida. That way, Hawk won't know where my body is, and Clawson and Derek won't be able to set traps."

"That's no good, Bart," Paul objected. "You can't possibly stay out that long. It'll take two or three days to get to Florida. You've got to eat and stuff."

"Not if I fly," I answered. Paul and Tamara responded with blank looks. "Curtis has a cousin who owns a plane, and he's agreed to fly us there. If I can stay out long enough to get my body on the plane, we'll be in the air and on our way in no time. Once we're airborne, it'll be just as hard for them to pinpoint our position as it is for us to pinpoint theirs. Kind of evens the score a little bit."

"Might work," Tamara conceded. "So let's get to the airport and get going."

"The plane's not here," Curtis said. "It's in Laramie, in Wyoming. That's where my cousin lives."

"You've got to be kidding," Tamara said. "So . . . Bart can lie in the back of the truck. How far is it? A couple of hours?"

"More like three," Curtis answered.

"You still can't go, Tammy," I said softly.

"Why not?" she asked, pouting.

"Because if Hawk can't find me, he'll look for you and Paul. He already knows you both. He'll assume that wherever you are, I am."

"That makes sense," Paul said agreeably.

"So, I want you and Paul to head home. Then when he finds you, it'll be obvious that I'm not with you, and since you're going in the wrong direction, he'll know I've gone on by myself. I don't think he'll cause you any more trouble after that." Tamara looked defeated. "I'm sorry, Tammy. Really, I am."

"So," Paul concluded, "Curtis and the 'Candy Cane' are taking you to Wyoming in this fancy body-mobile because Hawk doesn't know them?"

"Exactly," I answered.

Paul looked in the front seat of the hearse. "You can't very well be sitting up while you're doing your spirit thing. You want to take the foam pads and sleeping bags and put them in the back?"

"That won't be necessary," Curtis said, swinging open the back door of the hearse. "We've got a pretty comfortable place all ready for him."

"You've got to be kidding!" Tamara said in shock, looking in the hearse, then at me. "You're going to ride in a coffin?"

Curtis pulled the dark, walnut-colored coffin partway out the back. "Oh, it's okay. It's not a real one. Well, it was, but it got damaged during shipping, so no one will buy it. I use it for parties and things." He opened the lid to reveal the plush interior silks and satins. "I put a thick foam pad in the bottom to make it more comfortable."

"What if the lid falls shut?" Tamara objected. "He'll suffocate."

"Nope," he answered. "Already thought of that. See this gold-colored metal grillwork on the end here? That's a cleverly disguised air vent, and I installed a neat little electric fan on the other end that moves air through the whole coffin. Plus I extended the air conditioning into the back of the car, so it stays nice and cool."

"I'll have to borrow this sometime," Paul spoke up. "I can think of a hundred things I could do with a car like this."

"Be my guest," Curtis said, "as long as you leave me your truck in the meantime."

"Deal."

"Okay," I interrupted. "Let's get going before Hawk gets here. Did you bring the clothes?"

"Right here," Candy answered. She reached in the front behind the seat and pulled out a black tuxedo, complete with bow tie, frilly white shirt, and the works.

"Why do you need those?" Tamara asked. "Can't you ride in a coffin in regular clothes?"

"Well, let's just say this is insurance, in case Hawk CAN find my body." I took the clothes and walked around the other side of the truck to change. "I'm banking on the hope that he won't like snooping around in coffins any more than he does cemeteries. But in case he does, I want to look real dead."

"I've got some makeup for your face," Candy added. "I've had a lot of practice painting dead faces."

"That's SO morbid!" Tamara exclaimed.

"So, we're set. You two take off for home," I said to Paul and Tamara, "and try to stay away from cops."

"I think I'll unbolt the toolbox and drop it down in the back," Paul suggested. "That way the cops won't see it from their cars. It'll change our appearance a little."

"Good one," I said. "And be real careful what you talk about, in case Hawk does find you." Looking at Curtis, I said, "You two hit the freeway and head straight for Laramie. I'll stay out-of-body as long as I can—hopefully until you get to the airport."

"We need to stop somewhere for gas and food," Curtis said, "but that won't take long."

"Yeah, I need to eat something, too." Straightening my tie, I came around for inspection. "Well? How do I look?"

"Handsome," Candy said, smiling.

"Stuffy," Paul said with a sour face.

"Tammy, I need the backpack with the money."

"Why?"

"I'm thinking we might have a few expenses before we get done. I'd just as soon let Clawson pay for them as us, don't you agree?"

"I guess so," she said reluctantly, handing over the backpack. I stashed it away behind the seat of the hearse along with my clothes, then sat on the end of the car by the coffin.

Candy produced her bags of tricks and started dabbing makeup on my face.

"So, what are you going to do when you get to Florida?" Tamara asked.

"I'm going to rent a fast boat and go find that yacht," I answered.

"How are you going to do that?" she asked. "You said yourself that they're out in the ocean in the middle of nowhere. You could be days and weeks looking out there."

"I'm hoping Roshayne can tell me where they are . . . or at least find out."

"If you show up in her room, their cameras and mikes will pick you right up."

"I know. I'm still working on that part."

Candy finished her job, and I crawled into the back of the car.

"Then what? You going to just pull up alongside the yacht and ask Clawson to hand Roshayne over to you?"

"I'm still working on that part, too," I admitted lamely.

"Bart?" Paul said, when I was ready to get in the coffin. "Hey, I'm . . . sorry about getting mad at you yesterday. It was stupid."

"Don't worry about it," I said. "I understand. I'd have done the same thing, probably."

"Be careful, okay?"

"Count on it." We bumped fists.

"Bart, aren't you forgetting something?" Tamara spoke up, making a last-ditch effort at changing my plans.

"What?"

"What are you going to do when Hawk finds you?—your spirit you? He nearly killed you the last time, remember?"

"Yeah, I remember," I responded solemnly. "It was the scariest thing I've ever done in my whole life."

"So, what's your plan?"

"I'm going to hide out spiritually where hopefully he won't be able to go."

"In a cemetery?" Paul asked.

I climbed in the coffin and stretched out. "No," I said, lowering the lid. "In a church."

Chapter 15

- In Church -

A few minutes later, we were pulling into a gas station by the freeway on-ramp. By that time, any anxieties I might have had about suffocating had been put to rest. Curtis had done an excellent job of ventilating the coffin, and it was cool and comfortable. I could see how he could have so much fun with it. The only thing that really bothered me was that he had to latch down the lid. "Anybody who wants to look inside will naturally expect it to be sealed," he said.

"Anybody who?" I asked.

"I don't know. Just . . . anybody."

While Curtis filled the tank, Candy brought me some donuts and milk. It must have looked pretty funny to the people in the car next to us when she disappeared into the back of the hearse with food and came right back out empty-handed. Unfortunately, the windows were too dark to allow anyone to see in. I would have loved to pull a face or two at them when I sat up.

Finally, we were on our way. After making sure I was in the official coffin position, I floated up through the coffin lid and the roof of the car, and tailed Curtis for a few minutes just to see how he was doing. It hadn't occurred to me until that moment that he and Candy had already been driving all night to get to us. I was relieved to see that Candy was taking a turn driving, and Curtis was tipped back and sleeping.

I directed myself back to Paul and Tamara, and found them still at the same place I had left them. Paul was just about finished unbolting his toolbox, and Tamara was straightening up the gear in the back.

Okay, I thought. *Everything's in order. Let's go back to Utah.*

I knew there must have been hundreds of churches close by, but the only one I could picture solidly in my mind was the one in our neighborhood in Orem, so that's where I went. After the brief blur of motion, I came to a stop hovering over the street in front of our church. It was still pretty early, and the sun hadn't quite made its way over the mountains yet.

As I stood gazing out over the neighborhood, my attention was drawn to an unusual aura of light coming from the church area. It looked like a huge biodome-shaped force field that rested on all the outside fences and arched right over the whole property. It was strange—like a covering of glass all lit up from the inside. I couldn't resist the temptation to go in.

As I crossed through the "force field" into the church grounds, I felt a rush go through my spirit body, sort of like walking through one of those air doors at Smith's where the air shoots down from the ceiling and into the floor. It was a cleansing feeling, though, and it was immediately apparent that I was on holy ground—or holy air, in my case. The feeling was overwhelming and gave me a real spiritual high.

As I hovered there enjoying the sensation, I was taken aback by another brilliant white dome of light covering the church building—much brighter than the one covering the whole property. It arched way up and over the tall, pointed steeple. The whole thing was shimmering and pulsing and sparkling like it was alive. I moved cautiously above the sidewalk.

As I got closer, I realized that it WAS alive. It wasn't just a light, but a whole army of spirit beings—angels—completely surrounding the whole building and guarding it. There were thousands of them, all facing out, shoulder to shoulder, and stacked on top of each other. They were clothed in battle attire, like ancient Egyptians or something, with swords and spears and everything.

Needless to say, I stopped in a hurry. I had not considered being confronted by the hosts of heaven. For several minutes I just floated in place and watched.

Eventually, after I had properly recovered, I worked up a little courage and approached the guards to talk to them. I didn't have to move far before two of them broke ranks and came out to meet me. They were plenty fierce-looking with their swords in hand, but for some reason I wasn't afraid of them. They were putting out too much love and peace for me to fear them. The feeling was so strong, it was almost touchable.

"What is it you seek in the chapel of God?" one of them asked sternly.

"Well . . . I . . . uh." My mind went blank.

"Only those who believe and have accepted the Lord in their lives are permitted to enter here in spirit," said the other one.

"Oh, I believe," I said. "I'm a member already."

The first one studied me curiously up and down, and said, "You are not deceased. You are one of the gifted mortals."

"Yeah, I guess so," I answered uncertainly.

"Why do you want to meet with the immortals?"

"I don't," I answered. "I'm . . . uh . . . hiding from a bad guy who follows me around spiritually. It's very important, for my friends' safety and my own body, that I hide from him for a while."

At that moment, a third angel-person approached from the wall of guards and summoned the first angel to withdraw and talk to him. After a brief conversation, he returned.

"You have been granted permission to enter," he said with a friendly smile.

"Come with me," commanded the third angel, motioning with his hand.

He was taller and older-looking than the other two, and was not dressed in battle gear. Instead, he had on the expected Bible-style, long, white robes. As I got closer to him, I had a nagging feeling that I knew him from somewhere.

"You must stay by my side," he cautioned as we moved toward the army of guards. When we were only a few feet away, the wall of angels-guards parted and allowed us through.

This guy must really carry some clout, I thought.

"It is not position that allows us to enter," he said, apparently perceiving my thoughts, "but righteousness. I am known to be worthy, and I have vouched for your worthiness."

"How do you know I'm worthy?" I asked without thinking.

He smiled and looked lovingly at me. "I know," he answered.

As we entered the building, the rushing, cleansing feeling happened again, only a hundred times more powerful. I felt wonderful and extremely privileged to be allowed in—even though I'd been there physically a hundred times. It was all familiar, but . . . different somehow.

After we passed through the foyer, he directed me to the left and into the chapel meeting area. We came to a stop in the air near the back, and the angel turned to face me.

"I know of your plight and your need to remain hidden. Your enemy will not know your whereabouts. Even should he know, he would not be allowed to enter here in spirit. You are safe here. I have been authorized to allow you to observe the services for a short while. This is a rare and sacred privilege, Bartholomew, as you surely know."

Hearing my full name, I suddenly remembered the meeting I'd had with an angel during my near-death experience just over a year earlier. He had called me by my full name and had drawn me up into heaven to meet him. I was never quite able to focus on his face, since some sort of mist or fog separated us the whole time.

Could it be? I questioned silently.

"I will return when it is time," he said.

Before I could respond, he disappeared—not by leaving, though. He just . . . disappeared—the same way I did when I was materializing to Tamara in the jail or to Becky on the mountain.

But how can he just disappear, when we're both spirits already? I wondered.

My attention was drawn to the chapel area, as I became aware that I was not alone. There were dozens of other people—spirit people dressed in white—standing around and talking quietly in small clusters. They didn't seem to notice me at all. If they did, they didn't care. Occasionally, one of them would leave one group and join another, and the second group would all stop and listen while he spoke to them. Then a different one would leave and go to another group, where they would all stop and listen. I watched and listened intently, trying to understand what it was they were doing. But I couldn't quite make out their words.

Then gradually I became aware of one person in the room that didn't seem to belong. At first, I wasn't sure why. Then it dawned on me that he was the only one not in a group. He was sitting all alone on the front bench, staring blankly into space. The others didn't seem to even notice that there WERE benches. They walked through them without giving them a thought.

Gathering courage, I moved slowly along the wall until I was near the front and could see the man better. Then I saw that he wasn't really staring. His eyes were closed. And his mouth was moving a little bit.

He's praying, I realized. Then I looked closer. *And he's mortal!* He was wearing Dockers and a blue pinstriped shirt. *Just a regular guy praying in church.*

At that moment, three of the spirit people—two women and a man—stepped up beside the mortal guy and watched him for a few seconds. Then one of the women bent over and whispered something in his ear.

This is weird, I thought. *Surely this guy doesn't hear her.*

He didn't move or react, but just kept on praying. The spirit woman leaned over and whispered again. Still no change. Then she whispered a third time, much longer than before. As she straightened up, a big smile filled the man's face from ear to ear, and he opened his eyes, staring straight ahead at nothing. The three spirit people all smiled at each other and moved away to join one of the groups. After several minutes, the man stood, walked down the aisle wiping the tears from his checks, and left the chapel.

Whatever he was praying about, I guess he got his answer, I reasoned. *That was pretty cool. I wonder if that woman was his wife or his mother or someone like that.*

I became lost in thought and wondered what it must be like, being really dead and really a spirit. I wondered if any of my relatives had ever tried to whisper to my mind. *Like Grandpa Elderberry,* I thought. *Good ol' Gramps. He would like doing that.*

After a good, long while, the angel suddenly appeared in front of me again. "It is time, Bartholomew. The services have ended." I looked around and realized that the chapel was empty. All the spirit people had left. "You can exit the chapel the same way we came in," he informed me.

"Wait," I said. "Before I leave, I want . . . that is, I'd very much like to know who you are. I mean . . . well . . . what's your name?"

He paused a moment and smiled at me. "Very well. You may refer to me as David."

"David," I repeated. "Are you the same one I talked to in heaven?"

"Yes, Bartholomew," he explained. "I am your guardian angel. It is my assignment to watch over you throughout your sojourn on earth. I am always by your side."

"Then why haven't I ever seen you before? When I go Inviz, I mean."

"I am not permitted to show myself to you, except at special times and in special places. At the entrance to paradise was one such place. Here in this chapel is another. But I am always near."

I smiled. "I'm glad. It makes me feel really good knowing you're around."

"Come now," he said, "you must go."

I followed him through the foyer and out through the closed glass doors. The guards parted for me to leave, and the angel David stopped me again just outside the chapel grounds.

"You can defeat your enemies, Bartholomew," he said, "if you do so righteously. Do not seek for vengeance, for vengeance is the Lord's. Do not seek to satisfy your carnal wants and desires. Control them. Keep your heart pure, and seek only to do right." He reached out and took my hand, and the feeling that shot through me was almost electric. "As you saved your sister from the fire, so shall you conquer those who seek to destroy you."

With that he disappeared again, leaving me alone in the middle of the street where I'd started.

"Wait," I said. "What—?"

But he was gone. His last comments left me puzzled, but I didn't dare spend any time thinking about them until I could establish where I stood with Silver Hawk. Since I was no longer in the safety of the chapel, I was vulnerable again.

I'd better see what's going on, I thought. *Silver Hawk!*

Chapter 16

- Airborne -

"I don't believe it! He's got to be somewhere!" It was Clawson, pacing the foredeck and cussing a steady stream.

"I tried everywhere," answered Silver Hawk, standing calmly off to the side. "I cannot find him."

I was hovering almost directly overhead. Worried that I might be detected, I quickly rose up into the air a few hundred feet.

"How about his friends? The ones in the truck?" Clawson barked at Hawk.

"I found them easy. They are driving back to Utah."

"Back to Utah? Are you sure?"

"Very sure."

"Maybe he's hiding in that toolbox or somewhere."

"I looked there. Also underneath truck and in engine. I followed them for many minutes. He is not with them."

"And they didn't say anything?"

"Nothing important. The girl seemed very angry . . . or sad."

Clawson paced in silence while Hawk and Derek looked on.

"Maybe his family knows something. Have you checked?"

"I spent many minutes with his brother and two sisters. Also with parents. None say anything of Bart, but his mother has worried look on face. I don't think they know where he is."

"How about Tiffany's friend . . . what was her name? Cindy? She was involved with them in Payson, remember?"

"I have found her on large cruise ship near Mexico with her parents. She knows nothing."

Derek spoke up, "How about those two punks he was with when the cops stopped Bart's car on the freeway?"

"Young one is called George. He is home and knows nothing. Other one is called Curtis. There is strangeness about him. I found him and a girl driving a funeral car on the freeway."

Clawson's eyes perked up. "A funeral car? Where?"

"I do not know the area well, but it looked like they were going north . . . to Wyoming. His father owns a . . . what do you call it? A house of the dead?"

"A mortuary," Derek answered.

"Yes." He paused, appearing nervous. "There was a casket in the back."

"And did you look in the casket?"

"I do not enter the place of the dead bodies, and Bart's body would not be in a casket unless he was dead."

"Maybe he IS dead," Clawson said, standing only inches away from Hawk's face. "Did you think of that?"

"He is not dead," Hawk answered simply.

"How do you know? Maybe he died in the jail."

Derek spoke up. "My men were clear about that. They insisted all the cells were open and empty. The building was vacated before they torched it."

"If he WAS dead," Clawson said, facing Hawk again, "would you still be able to find him?"

"It would be almost impossible to find his outer body—it would have no life. But I would find his inner body. I have seen the spirit dead many times. They spend a short time in a waiting area before they are taken. If he was dead, I would have found him there."

"So, maybe he's alive and hiding in outer space somewhere . . . billions of miles away."

"I would have found him in a heartbeat," Hawk answered confidently.

Clawson smacked his fist into his open hand and swore loudly. "Then where is he?!"

"I do not know," answered Hawk, looking at the deck.

Clawson paced silently for several seconds, then sat heavily in one of the lounge chairs on deck. "Leave me now," he said, waving Derek and Silver Hawk away. "I need to think."

I was curious to see what Hawk and Derek were going to do next, but at that moment I was alerted by the pull of my physical body calling me back.

Hawk can wait, I decided. *Back to body.*

I opened my eyes and was suddenly blinded by brilliant sunlight.

"What?" I said, sitting up. "Why—?"

A girl's hand mysteriously appeared over my forehead and pushed me back down into the coffin.

"Don't move!" she whispered. Then her hand disappeared.

I obeyed and held my breath. I could hear traffic zooming by and figured we must still be near the freeway, but I couldn't imagine why we were stopped. And why was the coffin opened? After a minute or two, Curtis and Candy appeared, leaning over the coffin. They both looked like they'd seen a ghost.

"What's going on?" I asked nervously, looking from one to the other.

"That was TOO close," Candy answered. "You started to sit up just seconds after that cop got done looking at you."

"A cop?" I asked.

"We just got a ticket," Curtis explained. "For speeding. He's gone now."

"Oh, for cripes sake," I answered. "What happened?"

"I don't have a cruise control in this thing, and we got a little carried away," he defended. "You know how it is."

"Then he wanted to know why we were driving around in a hearse," Candy continued. "He kept looking through the windows at the coffin."

"So," Curtis said, "I told him we worked for my dad's morgue and were delivering a body to Laramie, which was actually the truth. I even showed him the paperwork." He held up a sheaf of papers for me to see. "Candy typed them up last night before we left."

"But he HAD to see for himself," Candy said with disgust. "There's no trust in this world, you know?"

"And?" I prompted, sitting up.

"He looked," Curtis answered with a grin. "And he really, really wanted to feel you and see if you were cold. He stuck his hand halfway in about four times before he finally got up the nerve."

"He touched me?" I gasped, climbing out of the coffin and straightening my tux.

"On the forehead," Candy answered. "Very fast."

"Lucky for us the air conditioner had been blowing full-blast on your head right up until I pulled out the casket, or we'd have been goners for sure."

"Holy schmoly!"

Curtis closed the lid and pushed the coffin back into the car, and I climbed in the front seat with Candy. It wasn't until I was closing the door that I even thought about the traffic going past—much slower than they should have been. We really had to laugh at the looks we were getting. I'm sure they could hardly wait to get home and tell everybody about the resurrection they saw on the freeway.

Ten minutes later, we were pulling into the Laramie airport where Curtis' cousin was leaning against his plane, waiting. We parked the hearse near the fence, locked the car, and made our way across the tarmac.

"Bart, this is my cousin, Alan. Alan, Bart."

I shook hands with Curtis' cousin, a short, pudgy-looking guy that appeared to be around his mid-twenties. "Pleased to meet you," I said.

"My pleasure," he replied, studying my attire.

"So, let's get this show on the road, shall we?" Curtis said. "I'm ready to let somebody else do the driving for a while."

"That's your luggage?" asked Alan, seeing my backpack. Candy and Curtis were carrying similar ones.

"We left in a hurry," I answered.

I was expecting a little Cessna or something, but Alan's plane was a model I'd never seen before. It was a real beauty—painted bright yellow with a single, DeLorean-type door opened up over the left wing.

"Who wants to ride co-pilot?" Alan asked.

"I think I'll ride in the back," I said, "where I can relax and sleep."

"Me, too," answered Curtis.

"I guess that leaves you and me, cousin," Alan said to Candy. "You guys get in first and climb back between the seats."

Stepping gingerly on the wing, I ducked through the door, but stopped halfway in when I read the word EXPERIMENTAL stenciled vertically along the doorjamb.

"What's this 'experimental' stuff?" I asked suspiciously, looking at Curtis and Alan.

"It's nothing," Alan said. "The FAA requires all kit-built planes to have that written on them somewhere."

"Whoa," I said, backing out the door. "Kit-built? Are you telling me you built this thing?"

"Yeah, I did," he said proudly.

"Is it safe?" I asked nervously. "I mean, isn't it risky flying around in something you made yourself?"

He laughed. "Of course not. I've flown over two hundred hours in it already. It's a quality kit."

I ducked back through the door and into the backseat. After we all got buckled in, I took a closer look at the interior. "Hey, what gives?" I asked. "There's no steering wheel! How do you fly this thing?"

Alan laughed again. "It's not a steering wheel, it's a yoke, and this plane doesn't have one. I fly it with this joystick here on the armrest."

"Okay," I said uncertainly, eyeing the stick and the modern dashboard full of state-of-the-art gauges and avionics.

Moments later, Alan had the plane's engine running, and we headed down the taxiway. Alan had already filed a flight plan for Miami, per my instructions to Curtis the night before, and all the paperwork had been done before we got there. After getting the necessary clearance from the tower, he gunned the engine and hurtled the plane down the runway. I was surprised at how fast we picked up speed. The only other time I'd ridden in a small plane was when I was in Boy Scouts, and it seemed like we were going to run out of asphalt before the pilot finally lifted it off the ground. Alan's plane seemed to just jump into the air and go straight up. I was pushed back into my seat and could barely lean forward to look out the window.

"Holy schmoly!" I yelled out. "What have you got in this thing? This is great!"

"This is just about the fastest single-prop in the air," Alan boasted. "Once we gain altitude, we'll be cruising at about three hundred plus miles an hour, depending on the headwind."

"You're kidding. What time do you figure we'll be in Miami?"

"Well," he said, checking his watch and his papers, "it's about ten-thirty right now. That should put us there by around . . . say, sixty-thirty eastern time."

I made a quick calculation in my head. "Six hours? All the way to Miami?"

"Non-stop," he added. "No gas stops. No potty breaks. I hope you're not too hungry, because I didn't bring anything to eat."

"We'll manage," Curtis answered. "I have some snacks in my bag."

My mind was busy working. "This is super. If we can find a boat without too much trouble, we could be underway before dark." I was starting to feel more optimistic. "That gives us all night to get there. We might actually be able to beat Clawson's deadline."

"Excuse me for asking," Curtis interrupted, "but just exactly where ARE we going?"

"To find Roshayne . . . and Clawson's yacht," I answered. "I told you all that last night in your room, remember?"

"No, I mean how are you going to find them? Do you know where they are?"

"Well, no. All I know is that they're somewhere out in the ocean east of Florida. I'm hoping Roshayne might know something, or be able to find out somehow."

Alan spoke up from the front. "If they have a GPS on board, it'd be a cinch. Most boats have them these days."

"Explain," I said, leaning over the seat.

He pointed to one of the instruments in the dash. "This is a GPS. Global Positioning System. It gets signals from satellites and can pinpoint our exact location, down to a couple of yards, practically anywhere in the world." He punched a couple of buttons. "See, here's our current position." He read off our latitude and longitude in degrees, minutes, seconds, and then some. "If I knew the position of this yacht of yours, I could fly you right over the top of it. No problem."

"That ought to be easy enough," Curtis piped in. "You could do that without your girlfriend's help, Bart. Just go . . . what do you call it . . . Inviz to the bridge on the yacht and have a look at the instruments. Piece of cake."

"Sounds too easy," I said. "What if they don't have one?"

"Well, they have to navigate somehow," Alan answered. "That's a big ocean out there. If it were me, I certainly wouldn't want to be floating around for days without knowing where I was."

"It's worth a try," I agreed. "I'm going to go check it out." I shifted around to get comfortable. Leaning close to Curtis' ear, I asked quietly, "Have you told Alan about my out-of-body stuff?"

"I briefed him on the phone last night," he whispered. "He didn't believe me at first, but I told him about how you saved that girl in the mountains and a little about your run-in with Mr. Clawson and the Indian. He seemed okay with it."

The seats in Alan's plane didn't tip back, so I had to use my backpack for a pillow and lean against the side. Fortunately, the seatbelts included shoulder straps, which kept me from falling over. It took longer than usual to get relaxed in that position, but after a few minutes of deep breathing and heavy concentration, I finally made it out.

I was surprised, when I floated out the side of the plane, at how high up we were. It seemed just about as high as flying in a jet. I let myself drift along above the wing for a few seconds, then focused my thoughts on Clawson and Derek. In the blink of an eye, I was transported at warp speed to my destination some two thousand miles away.

When I arrived back at the yacht, Derek was sitting next to Clawson on the foredeck. Hawk was sitting aft by himself, staring out at the ocean and meditating. Even though he was a hundred feet away, I drifted upward a ways, just to make sure.

"I've decided to head back to port," Clawson announced. "I can't wait out here much longer."

"What about the girl?" Derek asked.

"If we haven't found Bart by the time we reach the trench, we'll tie weights to her feet and dump her. Find Carlos and tell him to get underway immediately."

"Yes, sir." Derek left to find the captain.

This might be my only chance, I thought. *I need to see the bridge.*

Slowly and carefully, I drifted down lower and lower to the ship, watching Hawk closely for a reaction. When none came, I moved into the bridge and found Derek confronting Carlos and another crewman.

"The boss wants you to head back," Derek instructed.

"When?" Carlos asked.

"Immediately."

"Then we can turn on the panel now?" he asked in a heavy Spanish accent. I looked around the room and saw that all of the instruments, including radios and radar—and the GPS—were turned off.

"Yes," Derek answered. "Turn them on."

"Even without the Indian?" questioned Carlos nervously. "The boss man, he say no turn on nothing without the Indian say okay."

"I said turn them on! Start this thing up and get it moving!" roared Derek.

Carlos hesitated. "The boss man say he kill me if I turn them on without—"

"And I'll kill you first, if you don't," yelled Derek, leaning menacingly over the small captain.

Carlos backed up a step and stood trembling, debating which choice was the most dangerous. Derek definitely looked like he was going to rip something apart.

Derek stared at him hard for several seconds. "All right!" he yelled finally. "I'll get him."

Before Derek could take a step, Silver Hawk burst into the room. "He's here!" he shouted, pushing past Derek.

Clawson came in right behind him. "Are you sure?"

"Yes," Hawk said, almost reverently. "He has come." His lips formed a wicked smile as he looked around at the ceiling. "Where have you been, boy?"

With that, he rushed out of the room and disappeared. It didn't take much of a genius to figure out that he was heading for a place to lie down and jump out.

Back to body! I commanded myself. I figured I had about a sixty-second head start, if I was lucky.

"We've been had," I announced loudly as soon as I opened my eyes.

"What do you mean?" asked Curtis with a start.

"Hawk will be here any second," I warned. Leaning forward between the front seats, I asked, "Alan, can you turn off the GPS and all these instruments?"

"Well, sure, but—"

"Turn them off! Hurry!"

He looked at me funny, then flipped half a dozen switches.

"What about that compass?" I asked, pointing at the device attached to the windshield.

"It's not electric," responded Alan. "It's just a regular magnetic—"

"Wait!" Curtis said. "I know." He dug around in his backpack and came up with a refrigerator door magnet of the Denver Broncos.

"Where'd you get that?" I asked, taking it from him.

"At the convenience store," he answered. "You know . . . a souvenir of Colorado."

I handed the magnet to Candy. "Hold this against the side of the compass."

Candy pulled out the gum she had been chewing, stuck it to the back of the magnet, and pasted it to the side of the compass. The needles went haywire.

"Now turn right and head . . . that way for a while," I said to Alan, pointing somewhat south.

Alan banked the plane and was just leveling back up when I felt Hawk's repugnant presence fill the cabin.

"Shhh!" I said, holding both hands in the air. "We've got company."

Chapter 17

- Cruising -

The foreboding feeling lasted for several minutes, during which time I stayed absolutely silent. Curtis watched me intently as I stared into the air of the cabin, but he kept quiet. After a couple of minutes, Candy asked what was going on, but was hushed by a quick hand gesture from Curtis. Alan was too busy flying by the seat of his pants, without instruments or radio, to pay much attention.

A couple of times I felt Hawk's presence dissipate ever so slowly, then come back again. I figured he must have been moving around outside the plane, trying to figure out where we were.

Finally, after a long and grueling fifteen minutes, he left. I stayed quiet for a couple more minutes, just to make sure.

"He's gone," I said quietly.

"How do you know?" asked Alan.

"When he's here, it's like a bad spiritual smell to me," I answered. "Almost nauseating sometimes. There's no question about it."

"So, now what?" Curtis asked.

"I need to hear what he says to Clawson," I said. "I'm going to go Inviz again."

I settled back against the wall and the seat, and concentrated on getting out.

Clawson was pacing the deck again when I got there.

"In a WHAT?!" he demanded loudly.

"A small, bright red airplane, holding four people."

"Who's with him?"

"A pilot that I do not know, and his friend, Curtis, and the girl."

"His friend, Curtis?!" Clawson exploded. "From the funeral car?"

"Yes."

"Then he WAS in the casket, you imbecile!"

"But he was not dead," defended Silver Hawk, "and his spirit was not there. I still do not know where he hid himself."

Clawson fumed and paced. "So, where are they now?"

"As near as I can tell, they are over the central states somewhere and heading in this general direction. They have turned off all their instruments."

"Turned off—?!" Clawson swore profusely. "Well, did they say anything? Talk about their plans?"

"Bart has the same ability to feel my presence as I have to feel his. No one spoke while I was there." Hawk looked into the air briefly and smiled. "But he is here now . . . watching us."

Dang! I forgot to get up out of range.

Clawson swore again and stopped pacing, looking tentatively into the air over Hawk's head, then he took several deep breaths to compose himself.

"Well, Bart, you little fool. Come find me, if you can. I am amazed and impressed by your persistence, but it is for nothing. I had thought to dispose of your girlfriend later this afternoon, but now I think I'll wait for your arrival and let you watch the fun. That is, IF you still arrive." He glanced briefly at Derek, and they exchanged smiles.

I rose up into the air and waited.

Clawson continued, "Your airplane can't stay in the air forever, and when it comes down—"

Hawk raised his hand and signaled Clawson to stop.

"What? Did he leave already?" Clawson asked angrily.

"I'm not sure," Silver Hawk answered. He closed his eyes and concentrated. "I can still feel his presence, but not strong—like he has moved away."

He's catching on, I realized. I rose higher until I could barely see and hear them.

Hawk kept his eyes closed, his brow furrowed, concentrating. "Now he is gone," he announced finally.

Clawson turned to Hawk and spoke to him in a low whisper.

I was too far away to hear it clearly. All I heard were the words "make sure," then he turned to Derek and whispered something that I didn't catch at all.

They left Clawson, walking in opposite directions. Hawk was heading below deck.

He's going to check on me, I realized. *Back to body.*

As soon as I opened my eyes, Curtis asked, "What's going on?"

Candy and Alan both turned around to face me. Immediately Hawk's presence filled the cabin.

"I don't have a clue," I said for Hawk's benefit. "I was so far up, I couldn't hear them very well."

"Why didn't you go down closer?" Curtis asked.

"I didn't want Hawk to know I was there."

No sooner did I say that than Hawk left, apparently satisfied that I was back in the plane.

"I'll be right back," I said, lying right back down again.

"Oh, come on, Bart," Curtis said in exasperation. "This is getting ridiculous."

I ignored him and went right back out-of-body. *Derek!* I thought.

I was right. Derek had gone directly to the bridge to give Carlos instructions, and Carlos was at that very moment turning on his instruments. I scanned the panel quickly until I found what looked the most like Alan's GPS. When the display lit up, I quickly memorized the numbers, took a quick glance at the rest of the instruments, and shot back to my body as fast as possible, hoping I had come and gone quickly enough that Hawk wouldn't notice.

"Give me a piece of paper and a pencil," I said as I sat up. "I saw his GPS."

Alan handed back his clipboard, and I quickly jotted down the memorized coordinates and passed it back to him.

"North twenty-one degrees, forty-five minutes, twenty seconds," he deciphered from the numbers, "and west sixty-six degrees, fifty-nine minutes, five seconds. Hold this." He handed the clipboard to Candy and dug around in his briefcase until he found the air chart that covered the coordinates given. Then he spread the map out on his lap. While the plane cruised by itself, Alan made several notations with his pencil and ruler.

"That puts them right here," he said finally. He made a small black X on the map. "Did you happen to see what direction they were headed?"

I tried to re-create the images in my mind. "There were so many gauges . . ." I said, thinking hard. "There was one that had a big arrow pointing straight up, with a dial around it, like a compass."

"What number was it pointing at?" Alan asked.

"It was . . . seventy-five, I think."

"That'd be—"

"Or maybe one seventy-five."

He lifted his pencil from the paper and looked at me. "Well? Which is it?"

"Uh . . ."

"Was the boat pointing east or south?"

"South, I think."

"One seventy-five then. That'd put them . . . headed straight for Puerto Rico—about two hundred and fifty miles away."

"That close?" I asked, alarmed. "Only two hundred and fifty miles?" I took the map from him and studied it. "How long will it take them to get there?"

"Well, from what you've told us about the yacht, being as big and as old as it is, I'd say their top speed would be somewhere around twelve to fifteen knots. Not much faster. So . . . about a day, day and a half, tops."

I made some measurements with Alan's ruler. "They're nearly a thousand miles from Miami," I said in despair. "There's no way we could ever catch up, even with a real fast boat."

"So, let's fly to Puerto Rico instead," Alan suggested. "They're a U.S. territory. We don't need visas or anything."

"Puerto Rico?" My hopes started to rise again.

"We could be there by midnight tonight."

Curtis asked, "Then what? Wait for them to dock?"

"No way," I said. "That would be too dangerous. They won't dock without a million of their guys around. Can we rent a boat in Puerto Rico?" I asked Alan.

"Sure," he answered. "That's probably where they got theirs. When we land in Miami, I'll make some calls. I know some people."

"I'm not sure I want to land in Miami," I said.

"Why not?" asked Curtis.

"We can't go non-stop to Puerto Rico," Alan informed me. "We won't have enough fuel."

"I'm thinking that if we land in Miami, there'll be someone there watching for us. I mean, how many bright red little planes could be landing there? We'll be sitting ducks."

"Yellow," said Curtis.

"Huh?"

"Bright yellow," he said again. "The plane's yellow."

I looked out the windows at the wings. "No, it's red." Then I scratched my chin. "Wait a minute. It WAS yellow. I distinctly—"

"You're both right," interrupted Alan. We looked out the windows again. "It's temperature-sensitive paint," he said with a grin.

"You're kidding," Curtis said.

"When it's hot, like on the ground in the summer, it's bright yellow," Alan explained. "A good, easy-to-see color when you're taxiing around. But when it's cold, like up here at twenty-six thousand feet, it turns red. A good, easy-to-see color against a blue or white background."

"That's pretty neat," Candy spoke up.

"That's fantastic," I said. "Hawk specifically said 'bright red plane' to Clawson, so they'll be looking for a bright red plane—"

"And by the time we land," Curtis concluded, "we'll be yellow again. Cool."

"How would they know we're going to Miami, anyway?" Candy asked.

"That's easy," Alan said. "All they have to do is call around to a few airports, and they'll have my flight plan. You can't go anywhere without a flight plan. So, Bart, can I turn on the instruments now? Or do you want to keep heading to Texas?"

"Well . . ." I paused, glancing quickly up at the ceiling. "Go ahead and turn them on," I said with determination, "and let's just go to Miami as planned. Hopefully we can be in and out fast."

With the steady droning of the engine and the soft, gentle ride of the plane, the monotony of the flight soon set in, and for some time we were all quiet. I decided I had played spiritual cat-and-mouse long enough with Silver Hawk, and there was little else I could do except sit back and wait for Miami. In the meantime, I settled down to think about Roshayne's predicament and tried to come up with a workable plan for her rescue. So far, all we had going for us was that we could probably get to Puerto Rico ahead of them, maybe rent a boat if we were lucky, and with a little more luck, meet them somewhere in the middle of the ocean.

But is that really luck? I wondered. *What are we going to do once we find them? Clawson isn't going to just let us waltz in and take Roshayne off the boat. And we'll probably be meeting them in broad daylight, so there's no way we're going to sneak up on them. We don't have diving equipment—and wouldn't know how to use it, anyway. We don't have guns—*

"So, Bart," Alan interrupted, "how did you learn how to do this jumping out of your body stuff, anyway?"

"Well, it's not really something I learned. I was sort of born with it, I think. It just took me some time and practice to figure out how to do it."

I spent the next several minutes recapping for them my early experiences in grade school, and the accident and what I thought had been a near-death experience up Payson canyon. I told them how I had experimented with Paul and figured out how to get out on purpose, and how I had accidentally propelled myself into Roshayne's bedroom.

Candy had turned around to watch me, and she and Curtis hung on every word. Candy was especially intrigued by my ability to appear to people.

"Yeah, that's really cool," Curtis chipped in. "When he found that little girl, Becky, up by Silver Lake, he appeared to her, and she thought he was a real angel."

"So did Gary and Joe," I added. "Remember?" We both laughed and rehearsed for them the details of the rescue.

"Then he appeared to me last night," Curtis announced, "right in my bedroom. THAT was cool."

"So how do these guys on the yacht figure into all this?" Alan asked.

I explained how Paul and Tamara and Roshayne and I had witnessed Tiffany's murder—Clawson's own stepdaughter—and all the subsequent messes we had gotten ourselves into.

"What a trip," Candy said in awe when I had finished. "Do you jump out a lot? What else have you done?"

"I'm not a comic-book super-hero, if that's what you're asking," I said with a chuckle. "Most of the time when I go Inviz, it's pretty much just exploring and traveling. I've been to lots of places and seen lots of things, believe me."

"Sounds so exciting," Candy said in a hushed voice. "I wish I could travel anywhere I wanted."

"I did have one pretty weird experience a few days ago," I remembered, "just before this whole thing started." They looked at me expectantly. "I saved my sister . . . or at least I saw her get saved . . . or I dreamed she was saved . . . or . . . well . . ."

"What are you trying to say?" Curtis asked. "You talking about that fire at the skating rink that your sister was in?"

I nodded.

"I heard about that," Candy said. "It was all over the news." She got a dreamy look in her eyes. "I'd sure like to meet that handsome hero who carried her out." She sighed.

"That's just it," I said. "I thought I carried her out. He doesn't remember a single thing."

I recounted the whole experience for them, right down to the choking and burning hair, the tripping and falling, finding Charlene unconscious on the floor, and carrying her through the thick smoke to safety.

"Then I passed out . . . and woke up an hour later in my own bed. It was like I was never there."

I could almost see the gears turning in Candy's head. "Wait a minute. You said the guy was knocked out in the explosion?" she asked.

"That's what everybody thinks, since he can't remember anything after that."

"And then YOU were there . . . and found Charlene, and carried her out . . . ," she repeated the details slowly. "Then YOU passed out, and he woke up." Her eyes suddenly lit up. "I know!" she exclaimed. "You must have been in his body while he was unconscious."

"Don't be ridiculous," I said. "I can't get in somebody else's—" Before I could even finish the sentence, I knew it was true.

"Maybe he hit his head, and his spirit was knocked out of his body," she continued. "Maybe he was too shocked or too hurt to get himself back in. Maybe—"

As Candy proceeded to expound on her theory, I became lost in my own thoughts. *Someone else's body? Holy schmoly! I was inside his body! I was moving his body! Smelling with his nose. Coughing smoke from his lungs. Wearing his shirt. Of course! His shirt!*

"And your sister was also unconscious?" Candy asked.

"Huh? Yeah, she was," I answered, only half-listening.

"Then that explains why SHE thought it was YOU. Her spirit eyes saw your spirit, not the other guy's body."

"Incredible," I muttered under my breath.

"And if you hadn't gone in there when you did," Candy was saying, "he and Charlene would both have died in the fire. You saved them both, Bart."

She's right, I realized with a start. *I did save Charlene . . . and that guy Andy Riggins, too.*

"I think God put you there, just for that reason."

She's right again. God is giving me another way to use the gift.

Curtis and Alan joined in with their own theories, and soon the three of them were going the rounds. Meanwhile, I was off in never-never land. Candy's sudden revelation—that I could actually occupy someone else's body—and the ramifications of what it all meant were absolutely mind-boggling.

And I saved both their lives! Holy cow!

Then I remembered something from my visit to the entrance of paradise when I had first met the angel David. He had shown me scenes from my future. In one of them I had seen a young girl lying unconscious in the midst of a raging fire, and I remembered desperately wanting to reach in and pull her out.

That was Charlene all along, I realized. *And I did pull her out.*

Suddenly, the angel David's parting words from the chapel came blasting into my consciousness. "As you saved your sister from the fire, so shall you conquer those who seek to destroy you."

"YOU GUYS!" I yelled, jarring them into sudden silence. "That's it! I know how to do it! Holy cow!" My eyes grew bigger, and my mouth opened wider as the plan began to formulate in my mind.

"Do what, Bart?" Curtis asked.

"Rescue Roshayne, of course."

I quickly outlined my sketchy plan as fast as the ideas came to mind.

"You've got to be kidding," Candy exclaimed when I finished. "Totally awesome."

"One hundred percent cool," Curtis declared.

"Unbelievable," Alan added with a smile.

"I've got to talk to Roshayne right away," I said as I leaned back to get comfortable.

I'm out of here! To Roshayne!

Chapter 18

- Appearances -

As I separated from my body, I made it a point not to go directly to the yacht in the blink of an eye. Instead, I stopped a considerable distance away and approached it slowly. I was relieved to see that Hawk was on the foredeck, about as far away as he could be from Roshayne's room. He was basically just staring out at the ocean. Clawson was up on the sundeck getting a back rub from one of the bikinis. Derek was nowhere in sight.

I descended slowly about a hundred feet behind the boat until I was waist deep in the water, then I closed in and melted through the back end into the lower interior of the yacht. After a minute of exploration, I found Derek in his room surrounded by a complex-looking array of instruments, computers, phones, radios, and monitors. He was making some notations on a map similar to the one Alan had.

Looking at three small screens lined up side by side, I realized they were the monitors for Roshayne's bedroom—one looking at the empty bathroom, one aimed from the ceiling to the couch, and one with a full view of the bed. Even though it was early afternoon, the room was dark, with only a teeny bit of light filtering in around the closed porthole. Roshayne was lying on her side on the bed and appeared to be sleeping. I knew that if I materialized and appeared to her, Derek would surely see me on the monitors. I also knew that I couldn't talk to her unless I did.

Remembering what I had done with Tamara in the jail cell, I decided to try something a bit different. I passed through the wall from Derek's command center out into the hallway, then straight on through the other side into Roshayne's suite.

I was directly in front of the picture with the hidden camera, and was seeing her exactly the same way as on Derek's monitor. I floated over to her side, then sank down into the floor and under the bed. Next, I positioned myself so I was floating horizontal and face-up, like hiding under the bed. Finally, I rose up as slowly and carefully as I possibly could into the box spring and mattress. One nice thing about being out of my physical body was that I could see and focus on things right next to my eyes, so I knew I was in the right spot when I found myself looking at the right side of Roshayne's face. I maneuvered around until my mouth was directly under her ear.

Confident that I was totally immersed in the bed and hidden from the cameras' view, I willed myself to become visible. I could only hope that the bed would absorb the resulting light being emitted from my spirit body.

"Roshayne," I whispered so softly as to be almost inaudible. She didn't move. "Roshayne," I whispered again.

"Bart?" she said out loud, sitting up suddenly.

I quickly pulled my face further down inside the pillow. I didn't want Derek seeing my lips and nose sticking out through the pillowcase. I waited. After a few seconds, Roshayne lay back down.

Again, I maneuvered into the appropriate spot. "Roshayne, it's me," I whispered. "Don't move."

"Bart?" she said softly.

"Shhh," I cautioned, again in a whisper that was barely audible even to myself. "I'm inside the bed, under the pillow, talking right into your ear. Don't say anything yet, and keep your eyes closed like you're asleep."

I could sense her body stiffening in apprehension. I listened carefully for a few seconds, and with the assistance of my enhanced out-of-body hearing, detected Derek's door being opened and closed, and his footsteps moving quickly down the hallway. *He must have left,* I concluded after a few more seconds of silence.

"We need to talk," I whispered. "You can probably hear me crystal clear, since I'm basically inside your ear, but you need to answer back in the softest whisper you can manage. I'll be able to hear you, don't worry." I sensed some movement on the bed. "What are you doing?" I asked.

"Pulling my hair over my face," she whispered, louder than I liked, "so the cameras can't see my mouth."

"Good idea," I said, "but try whispering softer, if you can."

"Is this better?" she barely breathed.

"Perfect," I answered. "Are you all right, Rosh? Have they—?"

"I'm okay," she whispered. "I'm a little scared and nervous, but I'm okay, I guess. What's going on, Bart?"

"Clawson and his gang are determined they're going to kill me. They're afraid—"

"I know all about that," she interrupted. "I want to know what YOU'RE doing."

"I'm on my way to get you."

"How?"

"Right now, my body is on board an airplane with some friends of mine from Orem."

"Is Paul with you?"

"No. He and Tamara were with me for a couple of days, but we kept getting caught and sidetracked by Clawson, so I sent them back home and came on by myself. Harder for Hawk to track that way."

"What are you going to do?" she asked nervously.

"We're going to rent a boat when we get to Puerto Rico and come out here to meet you. Is that where Clawson got his boat?"

"Yeah, but Bart, you can't do that. That's exactly what they want you to do. As soon as you get close, they'll kill us both—and your friends, too."

"I don't plan on getting that close," I answered slowly. "They'll never even see us. I've got a plan, but I need your help."

"You do? What?"

"First, do you know how well armed they are?"

"I've only seen handguns, but I've heard they may have other stuff. Derek said something once about a high-powered something-or-other gun."

"I figured as much."

"Why don't you just look around and find it?" Roshayne asked.

"Because Hawk seems to know every time I'm here, and he hurries to jump out and catch me."

"What makes you think he's not watching and listening right now?" she said anxiously.

"Relax," I said, trying to sound unconcerned. "He's chanting and meditating up on deck. As long as I stay down, and we talk really soft, I don't think he'll know. Does anyone besides Derek have a key to that padlock on your door?"

"Clawson and Hawk each have one, too. They come and go a lot."

"How about the crew? Do they bring you food or anything?"

"No. Derek usually gets me and takes me up to the dining room to eat. He stands and watches me, like I'm going to run away or something. What do they think I'm going to do, jump off and swim?"

"How about their schedule?" I asked. "When do they eat? When do they go to bed?"

"They eat whenever they get hungry, which is all day, it seems like. They stay up pretty late, from what I can hear. Sometimes they're all in Derek's room for hours doing I don't know what."

"They're blackmailing people," I told her. "They've been doing that ever since we sent them to jail. Hawk is still spying and snooping around. Derek still has an army of bad guys doing their legwork, and Clawson coordinates and orchestrates one sting after another. They have millions stashed in foreign banks already. All they're doing right now is moving their office from the jail to some deserted island somewhere."

"My heck," she whispered. "No wonder—"

"What a sec," I said urgently. "Be quiet."

I detected footsteps moving down the hall again—more than one person it seemed. They stopped outside Roshayne's door briefly, but didn't say anything. Then Derek's door opened, and they went in.

"Sounds like they're all in Derek's room again," I said. "I'm sure they'll be watching, so be sure you don't move."

"Okay," she answered.

"What else can you tell me?" I asked. "When do they get up?"

"Well, usually Clawson and Derek spend forever playing around and partying with their girlfriends, so they don't get up until around nine or ten."

"That's good," I said.

"But Hawk goes to bed early and is up with the sun, I think.

He's really spooky. Sometimes he comes in and stands by my bed and watches me in the middle of the night."

"Why?"

"I don't know. I pretend to be asleep, and he just stands there . . . sometimes for ten or fifteen minutes. Then he leaves real quiet and locks the door."

"That's perfect," I said, working all the relevant information into my plan. "Couldn't be better. Wait a second."

There were voices in Derek's room. I focused my attention on the sounds and listened intently.

"You think he's in there?" It was Clawson's voice.

"I heard her say his name twice," answered Derek, "and she sat up the first time and looked all around the room."

"Then what?"

"She just lay back down. She hasn't moved since."

"If she thinks he's there, why doesn't she talk to him? Tell him stuff?"

"She probably suspects the room is bugged," Derek answered. "She definitely knows about the cameras. She stares holes in this one, and she covers herself with towels or blankets when she's in the bathroom."

They were quiet again, busy watching Roshayne on the monitors.

"I need to hurry," I whispered. "They're watching and listening. Here's my plan."

I outlined quickly what I had in mind for the next day.

Roshayne listened intently. "Are you sure you can do that?" she whispered when I had finished.

"Pretty sure."

"But how am I supposed to know—?"

"I'll find ways, don't worry."

Another voice spoke up in Derek's room. "Why is room not dark?" It was Silver Hawk. "Window is closed. Light is off."

"That's strange," Clawson added. "It looks like the bed is glowing."

"Rosh, I think they're on to me," I whispered.

"Then take off," she said urgently.

"He is inside the bed," Hawk said gravely. "It is Bart making the light. He is inside the bed."

"Why?" asked Derek.

"He's talking to her," Hawk replied. "Somehow, he is talking to her."

"They have me, Rosh," I said. "Make sure you have your things together and be ready. I'm not sure when it'll be."

"Zoom in on her face," Clawson ordered.

"I'm scared, Bart," Roshayne said with a slight whimper. "This sounds risky. What if we get caught? They could kill us."

"We won't get caught," I answered. "Don't worry."

"Her mouth is moving!" Clawson yelled. "You can see it through her hair right there!"

I heard sounds of feet shuffling, then Derek's door flew open.

"Gotta go," I said.

The padlock was rattling on Roshayne's door. I commanded myself to disappear.

"Be careful, Bart."

Roshayne's door flew open, and she bolted upright.

"What are you doing?" Clawson barked.

"What do you mean?" she answered lamely.

I stayed inside the mattress until I was one hundred percent sure I was invisible, then rose up over Roshayne's head.

"You know what I mean," he growled. "You're talking to Bart, aren't you?"

Roshayne made a feeble attempt at looking surprised, and glanced around at the ceiling. Clawson wasn't fooled. "What were you talking about?!" he yelled.

Roshayne looked down and said nothing. Derek rushed quickly to the side of the bed and grabbed Roshayne's wrists. Before she could even blink, he yanked her roughly off the bed to the floor and dragged her to where Clawson was standing.

"Stand up!" Clawson ordered.

Roshayne tried to get her legs under her, and Derek jerked her into the air and set her down roughly on her feet. Then he pinned her left arm painfully and awkwardly behind her back until she winced from the pain.

"Tell me what's going on!" Clawson demanded, "before Derek starts breaking bones!" Derek pushed her wrist up into her shoulder blades until she cried out.

Clawson stepped closer. "Well? Is he here?"

A tear formed at the corner of each eye and ran down her cheeks. "Yes," she answered through gritted teeth. "He's here."

Clawson looked at Hawk, who nodded in the affirmative.

"What kind of plans are you two scheming?"

Roshayne struggled helplessly against Derek's brute strength. "Nothing," she cried out. "He just wanted to know if I was okay. He was—"

"Liar!" he shouted, slapping her sharply across the face. "I don't know how you managed it," Clawson said, looking in the air off to my left, "but it won't happen again." He headed for the door. "Bring her," he said to Derek. "From now on, Bart, she will be with me. She will sit by my side, she will eat by my side, and she will do everything where I can see her . . . or better yet, where Hawk can see her. And tonight, Hawk will stay here in the room with her."

He headed out the door, with Derek and Hawk following. Roshayne tried to resist, but Derek tightened his grip on her arm, putting a stop to it immediately. I followed them down the hallway.

"Don't hang around here, Bart," Clawson said over his shoulder. "You won't learn anything, and you can't do anything. If you want your girlie friend, you'll have to come in person—physically. I have a good idea you've figured out where we are, so come and get her."

They climbed the stairs in single file and headed for the lounge chairs on deck. "And let me warn you right now, Bart," Clawson continued, "if I see any sign of Coast Guard or military or police anywhere—boats, planes, helicopters, whatever—there won't be any trace of her left on this boat. Nothing. She will cease to exist."

Derek pushed Roshayne roughly into a chair and sat down beside her. Clawson and Hawk settled down into their chairs, and the four of them just sat staring at each other. After a few minutes, Derek picked up a *Playboy* to read, and Clawson tipped his chair back and closed his eyes. One of the deck hands brought cold drinks, which he left on the small table. The bathing beauties came and sprawled out in the two remaining chairs to soak up some sunshine.

The whole time, Hawk sat rigidly with his hands palm-down on his legs, watching Roshayne. I was sure, from what I'd already seen of him, that he was capable of keeping that type of vigilance for hours.

There was nothing else I could do—nothing more to see. I had no choice but to continue with my plans as best I could, and hope that Clawson and Derek and especially Hawk would all be cooperative when the time came. I muttered a quick prayer to that effect and rose up into the sky.

Looking down from five hundred feet, the yacht looked like any other pleasure boat occupied by happy vacationers—three men and three women leisurely passing the time and enjoying the out-of-doors, their crew waiting on them hand and foot. How I hoped their numbers would not be diminished by one during the next twenty-four hours. If I could get there in time, it just might work, with a little luck.

No, a LOT of luck.

I'm not giving up until you're safe, Roshayne, I promised. *For now, back to body.*

When I re-entered my body, I opened my eyes and found Curtis and Candy sound asleep. Alan was dutifully flying the plane. Looking out the window, I saw nothing but clear blue sky above us and a solid sea of clouds down below. It felt like we were suspended and motionless in the middle of nowhere, and I concluded that we were as safe as we could possibly be for the time being. I decided to get some much-needed sleep while I had the chance.

It's going to be a long night.

Chapter 19

- Miami -

When I woke up, the sun was about an hour away from sinking into the clouds behind us. Candy was awake and talking quietly with Alan through the headsets and mikes. Curtis was still asleep and looked extremely uncomfortable, like he was going to have a very stiff neck when he woke up.

I leaned forward and asked quietly, "Where are we?"

Candy turned around to face me. "We're almost there. Alan says another twenty minutes or so."

"I've already started my descent," Alan said. "It takes a while to get down out of the stratosphere."

Our talking woke up Curtis. "Where are we?" he asked.

"Twenty minutes from Miami," I answered.

Alan became occupied by the necessary communications on the radio as we drew nearer to the airport.

"Did you talk with Roshayne?" Curtis asked me.

"Yes, but it was a little tricky. They figured out I was there and barged in on us."

"Did they see you?"

"No, I was hiding in the bed."

"Say what?"

I explained what had happened.

"Pretty sneaky," he said.

"One thing I noticed, though," I said thoughtfully. "I don't think Hawk knows how to show himself to people. From the way he talked, I don't think he's ever done that before."

"We're almost there," Alan informed us.

We occupied ourselves watching the landscape growing and

seemingly coming up to greet us. The thick, green everglades soon gave way to towns, which just as quickly turned into a major city.

"Welcome to Miami," Alan announced.

I became a little nervous as we neared ground level. I'd never watched an approach through the front window before, and it seemed like we were in a nosedive for the ground. The runway looked like a narrow stretch of sidewalk way out in front of us.

I was relieved that it kept growing as we got closer, and heaved a sigh of relief when Alan finally pulled back on his joystick at the last minute and saved us from what looked like certain death. We glided over half of the runway before we finally touched down.

"Otherwise, we have to taxi forever," Alan explained. "We don't use much of this international, jumbo-sized runway."

Jumbo-sized was right. It was cement on all sides, and it still took us a good five minutes before we reached the municipal side of the airport where we were directed to park the plane.

Alan completed another round of radio talk, then turned to face us. "That's funny," he said. "Ground control says our refueling truck is waiting for us. I don't remember asking for one."

"What do you usually do?" I asked.

"If I'm staying around, I just tie down and worry about fuel when I leave. They have pumps where you can just taxi in and fill up. It costs less than having a truck come out."

"Maybe that's their standard procedure here," Curtis offered.

"I guess so," Alan shrugged. "Oh, well. We're not staying around, so it doesn't matter anyway. I've already filed a continuation flight plan for Puerto Rico, so they know we're in a hurry."

Alan found the assigned area, and after pivoting the plane around ready for departure, we rolled to a stop. As the engine spun down he lifted open the door, and we were immediately assaulted by the heat and humidity.

"Great," Candy complained. "There went my hairdo."

In spite of the sweltering heat, it felt good to climb out on the pavement and stretch.

I was amused to see how bright yellow the plane was again, and wished I had paid attention to its changing as we came down. There wasn't a trace of red anywhere. Even so, I couldn't help looking around nervously, half expecting the goons from the gray sedan to come flying out from somewhere with their sawed-off shotgun.

"We better take care of potty breaks now," advised Alan, "before we take off again."

Candy was already heading for the closest building, and Curtis and I followed her. Alan stayed behind to give instructions to the fueling crew.

After a few minutes in the comfort of the air-conditioned building, my stomach reminded me that it had been a long time since our snacks on the freeway, and I began searching for something to eat. "Do you have any food here anywhere?" I asked a girl at a counter.

She pointed down a hallway. "There are vending machines in the break room at the end of the hall."

"Thanks."

I found the goodies in the back end of an L-shaped lunchroom, and was trying to decide between chocolate chip cookies and Twinkies when my attention was drawn to a hushed, one-sided conversation going on right around the corner from the machines.

"Sí, señor," a man said softly with a thick Spanish accent, "A little plane just landed that matches that description."

I dropped my quarters in the slot and punched F-7 for the chocolate-chip cookies.

"But it is yellow, señor, not red . . ."

My heart did a flip-flop, and I froze with my hand halfway in the machine.

"Sí, señor, that is correct. N8087G. Those are the numbers . . ."

Those are Alan's numbers! I realized. *They've found us after all!* I slowly withdrew my package of cookies and slid in between two vending machines, out of sight of the phones.

"That's right. Three guys and a pretty señorita. The pilot is buying gas, the rest are inside . . . one of them matches that description . . . name's Bart? . . ."

Beads of sweat popped out on my face, and I held my breath. *He's talking about me!*

"Okay, señor. No problem. I know what to do . . . of course . . . he is no problem, señor . . . you pay me same as always?"

I heard him hang up the phone and tried to make myself part

of the wall as the man behind the voice walked out of the break room. After taking a few deep breaths, I slowly poked my nose around the corner. The room was empty. At the door to the hallway I paused again, but the hall was also empty. To the right was a set of double doors, one of which was just closing, so I assumed he had gone that way. I beat a hasty retreat to the left down the hall.

Curtis was just coming out of the men's room when I got there. I pushed him back in and closed the door behind us.

"What's the matter?" he asked.

"They found us," I answered in a whisper. "I just heard a guy talking on the phone about us . . . probably to Clawson or Derek. They know we're here, and they're planning something to get rid of me. He even knew my name."

"Mercy queen," he said, his eyes wide. "What are you going to do?"

"I don't know. I've got to stay out of sight. If they see me, they could grab me and haul me off somewhere. Maybe shoot me in a dark alley or something."

"Maybe shoot you on the spot," he added, "with a high-power rifle or something."

The door swung open, hitting me in the elbow, and a man walked in. We both just about jumped out of our skins.

"Can't hide in here," Curtis whispered. "The door doesn't lock." He peeked out the door and looked both directions. "Park yourself in one of the stalls while I look around. I'll be right back."

"But . . ." I objected. He left before I could finish.

I stood rooted to the spot, too shocked to think straight, until the door opened again and a Latin-looking guy walked in. He glanced at me quickly, and I wasn't sure if he didn't sort of half smile as he went past.

No way I'm staying in here, I decided. *I've seen all the movies about what happens to guys in the men's room.* I opened the door and hurriedly followed Curtis down the hall. He stopped in front of a door and tried the knob. The door opened out, and he looked back down the hall, very surprised to see me coming.

"What—?"

"There's a guy in the bathroom that recognized me. He—"

"Get in," Curtis commanded, shoving me through the door.

I stumbled and fell into a storage closet of some kind as Curtis hurriedly closed the door. I was just standing up and brushing off my pants when the door flew open again, almost giving me a heart attack.

"Stay here until the plane's ready. When Alan has the props turning and has clearance, I'll come and get you, and we'll make a run for it."

The door slammed shut, plunging me back into total darkness. I hardly dared to even breathe. I stood fixed to the spot, sweating profusely and imagining all sorts of ways my life was about to end—barging in with knives, blasting through the door with shotguns, a garrote around the neck from someone already in the closet. That thought sent chills up and down my spine, and I froze like a statue.

After what seemed hours, but could only have been ten minutes or so, I finally dismissed the garrote idea, since I was still alive. Several times I heard footsteps in the hall, and I braced for the door to open, ready to mow down anybody in the way and run like heck.

Finally, I heard someone approach and stop right outside the door. For several seconds, he just stood there.

Is he waiting for the coast to clear? I wondered. *Hurry up and open the door and get it over with!*

Then I realized that the doorknob was turning very slowly.

Oh my heck! This is it!

The door slowly began to open until there was about a quarter of an inch gap. My shirt was soaked from perspiration, and my hands were trembling. *Here goes nothing.* The muscles in my legs were just starting to flex, ready to pounce, when I heard Curtis whisper, "Bart?" My knees went weak, and I just about collapsed to the floor. I had to reach out and find a shelf to steady myself.

"Bart?" he whispered again, opening the door another crack.

"Yeah, I'm here," I squeaked.

"We're just about ready. Alan and Candy are in the plane, and the engine's running."

"Have you seen anybody? I mean, does it look like—?"

"There are a couple of Mexicans or Cubans standing outside watching. They stared holes in Alan when he walked out to the plane."

"Oh my gosh! They'll shoot me dead if we walk out there!"

"Alan's going to taxi down a couple of buildings. I've found a back door that we can get out, then we'll run down the back and meet him there. Hang on."

The door closed, and I heard Curtis walk slowly down to the break room. Seconds later, he was back and opening the door wide. "Let's go," he said, grabbing my arm and leading me quickly down the hall. We hurried around a corner, down another impossibly long and vulnerable hall, then burst through a door into the bright sunlight. I had to shield my eyes to keep from being blinded.

"Come on!" Curtis coaxed. "Run!"

I didn't need much coaxing. We hit it at a dead run without looking back. Two buildings later, we turned the corner at close to a hundred miles an hour and raced for the front, where Alan's yellow plane was just coasting into view. We slowed down at the front of the building while Curtis scanned both directions, then beat it for the plane.

The door was open, and Alan leaned forward as far as he could while we climbed over. Candy was in the back, and Curtis joined her. I plopped down in the co-pilot seat as Alan gunned the engine. As we taxied away, I looked out the window and spotted two guys leaning against the front wall of the building, watching us intently. I expected them to run after us with machine guns or something, but they just stood there . . . smiling.

We were halfway to the end of the runway before Alan reached up and closed the door. My heart was pounding madly, and I could hardly breathe. An excruciating five minutes later, it was finally our turn, and we took the last corner so fast I thought the wings would hit the ground. Seconds later we were in a steep climb, and at a thousand feet I realized I had been holding my breath. I let out a big gush of air.

"That wasn't fun," Candy said, breaking the tension in the cabin. "What's going on?"

"Bart almost got himself killed," Curtis said. "Those guys figured out it was our plane and were planning to pick him off before he could get back."

"Well, I don't know that for sure," I clarified, "but I know they were planning something."

"Well, we got away, so they failed," Curtis said triumphantly.

"So . . ." I wondered half to myself. "Why were those guys smiling when we left?" The hair stood up on the back of my neck, and I sat up straight. "I've got to go find out." I glanced at Curtis and Candy in the back, both of them with the look of death on their faces. "Trade me places," I said to Candy.

We carefully maneuvered ourselves through the seats, trying hard not to bump Alan. As soon as I was in the back, I settled into the corner and closed my eyes. No one said a word in the plane, but I knew they were all watching me intently.

I left my body as the plane reached ten thousand feet. Then, concentrating on the faces of the two men I had seen at the airport, I transported myself instantly back to the hangar building where I had been hiding. They were with an Oriental man and two other guys in a small, dirty office.

". . . it was pretty funny," one of them said. "They ran like chickens with their heads cut off to get in that plane." They all laughed, and one of them took a long swig of something from a black bottle.

"They thought we were going to shoot them or something," the other one said. They laughed again, slapping their legs and rocking precariously back on their seats. I recognized the second voice as the one I had heard talking on the phone.

"So, when is it set to go off?" asked the Oriental, a bit less jovial than the others.

The first one glanced at his watch. "In about fifteen minutes," he answered. "They should be plenty far enough out by then that no one will even see it happen."

My blood turned cold. *They've put a bomb on the plane! Back to body!*

"They planted a bomb!" I yelled as I sat up. "There's a bomb in here that's set to go off in fifteen minutes!"

"Where?" demanded Alan.

"I don't know!" I said in panic. "Where could they put it?"

Curtis cried out, "In the engine! It's probably in the engine! What are we going to do?"

"No," Alan answered, more composed than the rest of us. "I was still out there when they checked the oil. I don't think they had a chance to put anything in there."

"How long were you away from the plane?" I asked.

"Only a couple of minutes to hit the john," he answered, "but Candy was on her way out when I walked in the building."

"Did you see anything?" I asked Candy.

"I wasn't watching them," she said tearfully.

"Think!" I yelled, making her jump.

"Well . . . I . . . they were putting gas in."

"Oh, no!" Curtis said. "Not the gas tanks! We're dead!"

"The opening's too small," Alan reasoned.

"Wait!" Candy said suddenly. "The baggage door was open! When I came back out to the plane, one of the guys was closing it. Come to think of it, he was in a big hurry to get it closed before I got here."

Curtis and I spun around, knelt on our seats, and started poking around carefully through Alan's mess in the back. I checked my backpack, which had my street clothes and the money. Curtis' backpack was nearly empty, except for some Hostess cupcakes. There was a first-aid kit, which I opened carefully. Only the usual Band-Aids and stuff. Also a small toolbox, with the usual things.

Then I saw an emergency blanket in the far back corner. I touched it carefully. "There's something hard inside!" I breathed to Curtis.

"Don't touch it!" he cautioned.

"We've got to get rid of it," I answered desperately. I turned around to Alan. "Can we open a window and throw it out?"

"The only thing that opens is this door and the baggage door. But we're pressurized. I can't open anything without getting down lower." I felt the plane drop into a steep dive even as he said it. "We're at twelve thousand right now, and going two hundred and fifty knots," he said. "I've got to slow down. Bring that thing up here and get ready."

I looked nervously at Curtis and reached over the seat. Cradling the bundle in both hands, I slowly brought it over the seat back. I could feel the plane leveling out and slowing down as I settled carefully into my seat.

"How much time?" I asked.

Curtis looked at his watch. "Three or four minutes. Maybe less."

"I'm down to a hundred and fifty," Alan informed us, "and at five thousand feet. I'm lowering the flaps." It felt like brakes being applied, and the plane's speed decreased dramatically.

"How slow can you go?" I asked.

"I stall at eighty-five," he answered.

"Eighty-five miles an hour is the slowest we can go?" Curtis asked with an edge of despair in his voice. "We'll rip the door right off!"

"No, we won't. It's about like freeway speeds. Lots of wind, but we'll be okay. Get ready."

I watched the needle on the airspeed indicator slowly come down to a hundred, then ninety-five, then ninety.

"Two minutes or less," Curtis said, studying his watch.

"Take hold of your stick," Alan said to Candy, pointing at her right armrest.

"What? I can't—"

"All you have to do is hold us straight and level for a few seconds," he said, "while I open the door."

The needle reached eighty-five.

"Okay," Alan said. "Take it." He slowly released his hold on his joystick as Candy squeezed hers stiff-armed. "Relax," Alan said. "It's like a video game." Candy flexed her fingers and took control of the plane.

Immediately, Alan turned and unlatched the door. The wind that came in was near hurricane force, and I had to close my eyes against it. Candy grabbed her hair with her left hand to keep it out of her face. Alan gripped the door solidly and slowly lifted it up about a foot. I passed the volatile package gingerly over into Curtis' hands, and he leaned carefully around the left side of Alan's seat.

"What if it hits the wing?" Curtis yelled over the noise of the wind.

"Throw it as far out as you can," Alan yelled back. "It's the tail I'm worried about."

Curtis half stood and leaned over as far as he could reach. Alan opened the door another six inches. Curtis cocked back his arms right against Alan's chest, then heaved outward with all the strength he had. I held my breath.

As soon as it was apparent that the bomb was out and hadn't hit any part of the plane, Alan quickly lowered the door and latched it shut. The blast of air stopped abruptly. Alan grabbed the stick and threw the plane into a steep left-hand dive, throwing Curtis over on top of me.

"There it is!" he yelled, pointing out the windshield. We were heading almost straight down and diving fast.

The blanket came unfurled and blew away like a failed parachute, while the bomb continued its fall, turning slowly over and over. Seconds later, just before it hit the water, it suddenly transformed itself into a brilliant orange ball of fire, maybe twenty feet in diameter. The flames burned brightly for all of two seconds, then disappeared. There wasn't enough left of the bomb to even make a splash. As Alan pulled us out of the dive, I saw the blanket settle onto the water, all folded out like it was being spread for a picnic on the grass. As we sped past and started our climb out, the blanket gradually became waterlogged and sank out of sight.

I took one last look back and heaved a great sigh of relief. Not a word was spoken for several minutes after that, until the plane was back at twelve thousand feet and cruising. We had all come within seconds of being blown to smithereens, and the emotional impact it had on us was dramatic.

"That was WAY too close," Alan finally breathed. Candy burst into tears and buried her face in her hands.

"It's okay," Curtis said, leaning forward and patting her on her shoulder. "It's over. We're okay."

I just lay back against the headrest and closed my eyes. *You're going to pay for this, Clawson,* I vowed. *Oh, you're going to pay!*

Chapter 20

- María -

It was seven o'clock p.m. eastern time in Miami when we left there, and by the time we crossed another time zone and came in sight of the island of Puerto Rico, it was nearly midnight. After the sun went down there was absolutely nothing to see, so I settled back and fine-tuned in my mind what I intended to do during the final leg of our quest.

Alan spent a good deal of time on the radio, arranging air-to-ground phone links looking for his several friends in the area. After dozens of calls, one of them referred him to a pleasure boat owner in Puerto Rico who had a craft available for our use. I was blown away by the cost.

"He charges four thousand dollars a day," Alan informed me.

"You mean four hundred, right?"

"No, I mean four thousand. Or fifteen thousand a week."

"You've got to be kidding! Is the deck paved with solid gold, or what?"

"That includes all the fuel, food and supplies, plus a crew of four," he explained. "You should be grateful he's even available. Usually it would take a couple of days to stock a boat and get it ready, but he had a last-minute cancellation late this afternoon."

"I guess I'm grateful, then," I said sarcastically. "At least it's not my money. How fast does it go?"

"He says he can do close to fifty knots if he opens it up all the way, but of course he would charge extra for the additional fuel consumption and wear and tear."

"How much?"

"Another thousand."

"Holy cow!" I swallowed hard. "Okay, go for it. I don't see that we have much choice." It was amazing how fast and easy I could spend someone else's money. "Tell him we'll want it for two days."

I decided it was time I checked Mr. Clawson's money. Up until then, I had been too preoccupied with other things to even think about it. I fished out Tamara's backpack from the baggage area and pulled my clothes out onto my lap. Then I extracted the ziplock baggies one at a time, for a total of six. Inside each one was a bundle of hundred-dollar bills about half an inch thick, wrapped with an official bank band. On the outside of each band, it read $10,000.

Curtis took one look and whistled. "Ten thousand dollars each. Mercy. That's sixty thousand dollars you've got sitting in your lap."

Candy and Alan both turned around to look. Nothing like the mention of cold, hard cash to turn heads.

"Now might be a good time to talk about MY expenses," Alan mentioned casually.

"I was wondering when you'd get around to it," I replied.

"Oh, I figured you were good for it," he answered. "And if you weren't, I would have beat it out of Curtis' hide."

"So what do we owe you?"

"Well, fuel for the round trip will be about three hundred fifty gallons," he calculated, "plus expenses. That's around . . . a thousand dollars. Then there's time off work, tie-down fees, all these phone calls . . . and if you want me to wait for you, there'll be food and lodging, and . . . well, you know."

"I know. Fun in the sun." I extracted thirty bills from one of the bundles and handed them to him. "Here's three thousand. That should cover things. If not, let me know."

"That should just about cover it," he said as he shoved the money in his shirt pocket. "It's not every day I fly to the Caribbean, you know," he added to his defense.

The rest of our flight and landing was uneventful. While Alan tied down his plane and arranged paperwork with the airport, Curtis and Candy and I looked in vain for a car rental agency.

"This place is the pits," I told Alan when he joined us. "Are you sure we landed in the right place?"

"Well," he confessed, "I made a last-minute adjustment to our flight plan about half an hour ago. I got thinking that maybe San

Juan might turn out to be another round of the fun we had in Miami, so I changed course. This is a small municipal airport in Bayamón."

"That was good thinking," I said. I had to admit I was relieved; I had also been worried about a welcoming committee. "Why didn't you tell us?"

"I thought the less I said, and the less you knew, the less your Silver what's-his-name friend would overhear."

I knew Silver Hawk had been assigned twenty-four hour coverage on Roshayne, but I was still nervous about him slipping out for a look-see. I was grateful for Alan's foresight.

"So, now where do we go?" asked Curtis.

"San Juan is about thirty minutes from here. We'll just have to take a taxi."

Finding a taxi and communicating to the driver in his broken English took over thirty minutes, and the ride to San Juan was over an hour. I was beginning to get real concerned about the timing. I knew my success depended entirely on being able to fit things into Clawson and Hawk's schedules on board the yacht.

Another half-hour was lost driving around the harbor in search of the right yacht. The directions given to Alan were less than accurate.

Finally, at a few minutes past two in the morning, we found the right place. The taxi driver milked us a hundred dollars for the ride, claiming he didn't have change, and I was in too much of a hurry to argue. He was already driving off when I realized Alan hadn't gone with him.

"Aw, what the heck," he said, "I wouldn't want to miss out on the grand finale, now would I? You don't mind if I tag along, do you?"

"Be my guest," I answered.

The owner and captain of our boat was a short, fat man by the name of Antonio Ramos, who spoke fluently in both English and Spanish without a trace of an accent.

"You can call me Tony," he said as he ushered us across the gangplank. "Welcome to the CHRISTINA DORITA MARIA. Named after my wife, my mother, and my mistress . . . in that order." He winked and bellowed out a hearty laugh. "I call her María for short." He laughed again.

The yacht was about sixty feet long and modern looking. As soon as we stepped on board, the plank and tie-downs were cast off.

"I presume you're anxious to make way. Am I right?" Tony asked.

"Yes," I replied. "The sooner the better."

"We're on our way. Let me show you to your rooms while my first mate clears the harbor. Then you can enlighten us on your destination."

As he led us across the deck and down the stairs, he pointed out the various features of his craft. "We are equipped with two comfortable suites, each with a king-sized bed, TV, VCR, the works." He glanced over his shoulder, apparently unsure about where Candy fit in. "Who's with who?"

Curtis spoke up. "Candy's my sister, so I guess we'll share. Alan and Bart can take the other one."

We sized up the rooms quickly, and Curtis dumped his backpack on the bed. Considering its contents, I decided to hang on to mine.

"We were told you might like something to eat, once you boarded. We are proud of our galley and selection, and my cook is standing by. Would you like to eat something?"

My stomach growled loudly at the mere mention of food. "That'd be great," I said. "I can't even remember when I ate last." Thinking back, I realized the last square meal I'd eaten had been Sunday dinner, after church—nearly three days earlier—just before I met Paul at the Spanish Fork cemetery. It seemed like weeks.

I couldn't help wondering how Paul and Tamara were doing. I felt a twinge of guilt for sending them back to face the police and everything without me.

Tony furnished us with impressively lengthy menus, and we placed our orders. Then he marched us up to the bridge, where he promptly sat down in his patent leather captain's chair, folded his arms, and said, "Now, let's discuss the fare."

"We were told four thousand a day, plus some extra for the hurry," I said. "What do you need? Half up front?"

Tony stroked his chin and studied me for a moment. "I'm afraid you might have been misinformed," he said. "My standard fare is six thousand per day. And I'll need two thousand for the rush."

"What?" we all said in unison.

"It's extremely risky to run engines at such high RPMs for extended periods. I'm sure you understand. I have to protect myself."

I could see why he had been in such a hurry to leave. It was pretty hard to bargain once we were already at sea and underway, and we certainly didn't have any other options. Of course, Tony knew all that.

"Okay," I said, my eyes furrowed to convey my displeasure. "Twelve thousand for the two days, plus two. That's fourteen—"

"My minimum is three days. That'll be twenty. Cash, of course."

"Twenty thousand—?!" I didn't dare object. I was stuck between the proverbial rock and a hard place. Tony was our only chance of saving Roshayne before Clawson and crew made land and disappeared again. I turned around so Tony couldn't see, and pulled a bundle of money from my backpack. "Here you go," I said, slapping the wad into his greedy hands.

He leafed through the bills quickly. "That's only ten," he said, frowning at me.

"Half of twenty," I clarified.

"I'll need at least another five. I've had my share of shysters rent this boat, then disappear without settling their accounts. I just can't take the chance. Nothing personal, you understand."

I peeled off another fifty bills inside my backpack and handed them to him. The money disappeared into his deep pockets, and suddenly he was all smiles. "Now, where are we going?" he said, standing up and leading us to his table of charts.

We all leaned over the maps, and Alan asked if he could use the instruments. "We are meeting another yacht," he said. "The last time we spoke to them, they were right about here and traveling at about twelve knots towards San Juan. By now, that'd put them in this area." He made some pencil marks.

"It's important that we meet up with them as soon as possible," I added. "We have some . . . deadlines that need to be met."

"Hey," Tony said, raising his hand and backing off. "You're not doing anything illegal here, are you? I won't be involved in anything—"

"No. Nothing like that," I assured him. "We're just . . . anxious, that's all." *He's one to talk about illegal,* I thought. *He's just performed the highway robbery of the century.*

Alan continued plotting. "You say your boat can do around fifty knots?"

"If I push it REAL hard," responded Tony, making sure we understood the great strain and sacrifice he was going through.

Alan ignored him. After a few more measurements and calculations, he made a mark on the chart. "We should be able to find them right about here."

There was a red X printed on the chart already, right next to Alan's mark. "What does that X mean?" I asked, pointing it out for Tony.

He put his face down real close to the chart and muttered something under his breath. When he straightened up, he had a new look in his eyes that bordered on fear. "That," he said gravely, "is the Puerto Rico Trench." He let that sink in, as though we should all know its significance. "The deepest known point in the Atlantic Ocean," he stated for our benefit. "Almost nine thousand feet."

"And?" I prompted.

"And coincidentally the most notorious, most dangerous, most feared point in the Bermuda Triangle."

"Bermuda Triangle?" laughed Alan. "That's a bunch of bunk. Hollywood hype. Don't tell me you believe that stuff."

"Many more have disappeared in the Triangle than have been reported, I assure you. My crew can attest to that. I, for one, do not intend to become a statistic."

"Oh, come on," I said. "What could possibly happen?"

"Yeah," echoed Alan. "What's the problem? The weather report calls for clear skies and calm seas for the next several days. I've already checked."

"Weather reports have nothing to do with the Triangle. In there, the weather does what it wants, when it wants, to whomever it wants. I'm very sorry. I will not place María and my crew at risk. I can't take you there." Tony sat in his chair and defiantly crossed his arms. For several seconds we held a staring contest.

I pulled the backpack off my shoulder and dug out the other five thousand. "At least not for seventy-five percent up front, you can't take us there. Is that right?" I offered him the stack of greenbacks.

Captain Tony's eyebrows rose, and for a fraction of a second, he hesitated. Then, like a frog zapping a fly, the money disappeared into his pocket, and he swung around to the control panel. "Ahead full!" he bellowed, pushing his first mate aside. "Course three four eight degrees."

We were practically knocked off our feet as he gunned the engines, and had to grab each other for support. The intercom buzzed, and Tony picked up a handset from the counter and spoke quickly to a crewmember. Turning to us, he announced, all smiles, "Dinner is served."

After parting with a third of Clawson's money, I wasn't sure I still had an appetite, but the pleasant aromas that drifted up to us, as we made our way to the dining room, soon confirmed the need. To the utter amazement of my companions, I wolfed down two dinner rolls, a salad, and three full plates of food, accompanied by three tall glasses of ice-cold milk and two servings of chocolate cake before I came up for air.

When I finally pushed my chair back and wiped my mouth, Tony, the perfect host, stepped up to the table and asked politely, "Is there anything else we can get for you?"

"Yes, as a matter of fact, there is," I said with a smile. "I need some strong ropes, some blankets or cushions, and if you have one, a big roll of duct tape."

Everyone looked at me as if I'd lost my marbles.

"I have a bad habit of falling out of bed when I'm out at sea," I explained.

Chapter 21

- Possessed -

After shedding the tux and changing back into my street clothes, I gathered Curtis, Alan, and Candy around me in my suite and gave them instructions.

"Okay, here's what we're going to do. I'm going to lie on the bed, and you guys are going to tie me down."

"We are?" Candy asked. "Why?"

"Because sometime in the next few hours, I think I'm going to try to kill myself. It's going to be you guys' job to see that I don't."

"You're crazy," scoffed Curtis. "Why would you want to do a thing like that?"

"It has nothing to do with wanting to," I explained. "I have a strong suspicion that I'm going to become possessed before the night's through."

They all looked at me kind of funny, but carried out my instructions as I gave them. I had them wrap pillows and blankets around my ankles and wrists, and then wrap two loops of rope around each before tying them down securely to the legs on the bed. The pillows helped protect my skin from rope burns and from cutting off my circulation. Then I had more pillows and blankets added to my thighs, arms, chest and waist, and the process was repeated.

"You need to make sure I can't hurt myself, no matter how hard I try," I warned them. "I'm likely to try everything I can physically do to kill myself."

Candy was smiling at the absurdity of my suggestions and the humor of the sight I presented.

"I'm not kidding," I said to her and the rest. "It could get ugly."

When they were ready, I strained every muscle I could, twisting and arching my back, testing the bonds, and making sure I was secure. After I was satisfied that my body was totally immobilized, I told them to run several layers of duct tape over my forehead and all the way around the bed so I wouldn't even be able to move my head. "You might as well add duct tape to my arms and legs, too," I added. "I don't want to take any chances."

When they were completely done, and I was totally constrained, I asked, "Now think hard. Is there anything in the world you guys can think of that I might still be able to do that would kill me? If there is, we need to fix it."

Curtis ventured, "Well, you could try to suffocate yourself by holding your breath."

"That won't work," Candy said. "He'll just pass out for a few seconds, then come right back."

"Short of putting you in a straight jacket," Alan said, "you're probably better protected right now than most loonies in the loony bin. I think you're safe."

"Okay," I said. "Until I get done with this, at least one of you needs to stay here at all times and watch . . . just in case. And someone needs to be on the bridge."

"How long do you think it'll take?" Candy asked.

"Probably several hours, but I'm not sure. It'll depend a lot on what's happening on board their yacht."

"How will we know when you're through?" Curtis inquired.

"Let's work out a code right now," I suggested. "If I say anything else but the code, don't let me up, okay?"

"What if that Indian guy is listening right now?" Curtis asked. "He'll know the code."

"Good thinking," I said. I thought for a minute. "I'll have to tell you things that Hawk wouldn't know. I'll come up with something. You'll know, don't worry."

"I'm not worried. You're the one who should be worried."

"I'm not worried," I said confidently. "What time is it?"

Candy glanced quickly at her watch. "It's almost four o'clock in the morning."

"Perfect. Well, I guess I'm ready. Wish me luck."

"Good luck," they chanted in unison.

I closed my eyes and relaxed. The vibrational state came almost before my eyelids even hit bottom, and I rose effortlessly out of my body. I looked down for a moment at my still form on the bed, all wrapped up and tied. It really was a sight.

Well, here goes, I thought. *To the yacht.*

I stopped in the middle of Roshayne's room. I saw immediately that the lights were on, and Silver Hawk was present. He was sitting on the floor at the foot of the bed, his back straight and his legs crossed. His hands were resting on his knees, and he was staring intently at a spot on the opposite wall, which had nothing on it that I could detect. There were some odd things on the floor in front of him, like a couple of small bones and a leather pouch with beadwork on it. He looked like a wax figure in a museum. I had to watch for a long time before he even blinked.

Is it possible he could jump out in that position? I wondered. That thought alarmed me. If Hawk was already out, he could be waiting to spring an attack that I might not be able to avoid.

I don't think he is, I decided after looking around. *But I can't believe he doesn't know I'm here.* I floated down directly in front of him. I needed to get his attention, but I didn't dare materialize for fear of Derek or Clawson spotting me on the cameras. I thought about checking out the rest of the yacht, but decided against it. I absolutely had to be by Hawk and ready whenever he decided to jump out.

Come on. Get out, I urged, trying somehow to direct my thoughts at him. *I'm ready for you.*

Still no movement.

I took another look around the room. Roshayne was in the bed, deep under the covers with her eyes closed. I hoped she was asleep, although I found it difficult to believe she could be, with Hawk sitting at her feet. I shuddered to think what it must have been like for her, being locked up for almost a week already, with microphones listening and cameras watching her every move, and then having Hawk stuck to her like glue for the last several hours.

I moved over again to where Hawk was sitting and hovered right in front of his face. He didn't move a muscle.

"Come on, Hawk," I coaxed mentally. *"You must know I'm here."*

"I know you're here," he said suddenly, catching me totally off guard. His eyes remained fixed on the far wall. "What do you intend to do now, boy?"

He can hear my thoughts, I thought out of sheer reflex.

"Only if you try very hard," he said. "You are not skilled at mind-talking. I have been sending you the talk for some time."

I concentrated hard, trying to pick up an impression mentally from him, but was not able to hear anything.

"Why don't you show yourself to me, boy? Talk to me, like you did to the girl. That is a skill you seem to have perfected very well. Show me how it is done, and I will teach you the mind-talk."

"I was right," I thought. *"You DON'T know how."*

"I can learn," he said, perceiving my thoughts again. "You can learn. We can teach each other. We can benefit from each other's skills."

"Why don't you just get out of your body and talk to me in spirit?" I challenged.

I thought I was starting to get the feel of how thoughts got transmitted, but I was concerned that I might think something that would give away my real intentions. I had to force myself not to think about them. I had to push all thoughts of my plans from my mind.

"I have tried before," he answered evenly. "Every time I do, you disappear back to your body. What are you afraid of?"

"You know darn well what I'm afraid of. You tried to kill me the last time we met spiritually."

"No harm was intended. No harm was done."

"Yeah, right."

He sat staring at the wall for a few moments. I thought maybe he was trying to send telepathic thoughts again, but I still didn't hear anything.

"Very well," he said at length. "I will learn the skill on my own. Now that I know it is possible, it is only a matter of practice and patience." Carefully he gathered his artifacts into his bag, rose to his feet, and headed for the couch. "I will join you now."

He lay down on his back, crossed his hands over his chest, and closed his eyes. Within a matter of mere seconds, I perceived his spirit form rising out of his body, the same way I had seen him do it before. He rose into the air, and we hovered face to face over Roshayne's bed.

"So, here we are, boy," he said, glaring at me. *"Just you and me. Tell me what you intend to do."*

"I intend to see to it that you and Mr. Clawson and Derek serve your time in prison. I intend to expose you to the world. And I intend to take Roshayne back home."

Hawk laughed loudly and looked at me with furrowed eyebrows. *"You should have learned by now that you have no power over me. Showing yourself and talking to her has not gained you anything."*

"Maybe not, but I have other abilities that you don't have. And I have goodness and righteousness on my side. And by the time I get done with you, you'll be begging for mercy."

"What other abilities?"

I decided I had stalled long enough. During the course of the conversation, I had drifted slowly around the room until I was directly over Hawk's inert body on the couch. Without another word, I dived for the couch.

"What are you doing?" he demanded.

I assumed a horizontal position over the couch.

"Is this your ability?" he mocked.

I quickly aligned myself with his body and settled into it.

"You think you can use my body?" He laughed loudly.

I wiggled around, carefully placing my hands and feet in the exact places that his were in. I expected to feel a bonding of some sort, but nothing happened.

"You are far more stupid than I thought, boy" he said in a taunting tone. *"I am disappointed. I thought you might actually know something."*

Embarrassed and humiliated, I rose back out into the air.

"You are a fool."

"It should have worked," I thought mostly to myself. I was so sure after talking about Charlene's rescue with Candy and Curtis, and remembering what the angel David had said, that it would work.

"You, of all people, should know that only through the silver cord can you enter your body. Mine is attached to me, and yours is attached to you."

Something he said caught my ear. I had always thought about returning to my body in terms of WITH the cord, or BY the cord, or BECAUSE of the cord. Was it possible that I might be able to do it THROUGH the cord?

Without warning, I lunged at Silver Hawk, focusing my entire concentration on entering or inhabiting his spirit body. Instead of banging into him, as I fully expected, or passing through him, like I would have with a physical body, we merged. There was a gigantic discharge of some kind of energy, like an electrical surge, that flooded my being and sent strange sensations all up and down, inside and out. It was like two highly charged wires being touched together. The effect was so dramatic that I almost forgot my purpose.

Hawk was equally distracted and surprised. I couldn't see him because we had effectively blended into one being. But because of the blend, I felt his shock . . . and fear.

I've got to hurry, I remembered, *before it stops.*

With energy coursing wildly through our beings, and our joined spirits pulsing madly, I concentrated on my objective. *To Hawk's body!* I commanded.

I felt as though a giant vacuum had caught hold of my head, and I was suddenly sucked through a tight and restricted space and slammed into something hard.

"What have you done?!" Hawk screamed. *"You can't—!"*

I opened my eyes and lifted my head, and his voice abruptly disappeared. I seemed to be somewhere near the couch. Hawk was nowhere to be seen. I looked around the room in all directions, but there was no trace of him. I commanded myself to float upward over the bed, but I was stuck in place.

Then it occurred to me. *Did I—?* I lifted my arm and was shocked to see a brown, wrinkled hand adorned with silver and turquoise rings rise up in front of my face.

"Holy mackerel!" I said out loud. "I did it!" My voice was low and throaty-sounding. Like . . . Hawk's.

I jumped up and rushed to the bathroom. Looking into the mirror, I gasped audibly and backed away. Hawk was staring at me from the glass. Even knowing what had happened, I was stunned at the sight. I stared and stared for several minutes before the goose bumps and creepy-crawlies finally subsided. I opened and closed my mouth, blinked my eyes, stuck out my tongue, turned my . . . his head. It was the weirdest feeling I had ever experienced in my entire life. I stroked the hair, felt the wrinkles, and examined the chin and ears. I felt like I had been made up for Halloween or something.

After a few more facial exercises, I finally came to accept the fact that I was actually inhabiting Hawk's body. I was moving him around as though I was in my own body. I smiled at myself in the mirror, an expression I had never seen on Hawk's face before. The sight of the image made me laugh, which was even more out of character for Hawk than the smile. I took great pleasure in knowing that Hawk was hovering spiritually nearby, watching his body moving around without him. I would have loved to see the expression on his spirit face right about then.

Finally, I turned to leave the bathroom and was brought to a halt by the sight of Roshayne sitting up in the bed and staring at me.

Chapter 22

- Codes -

Her face portrayed a mixture of fear, anxiety, and anger. For several seconds we just stared at each other, not knowing what to say.

"Rosh?" I finally managed. The sound of her nickname combined with Hawk's throaty voice was a strange, unfamiliar blend, and Roshayne grew immediately suspicious.

"Rosh, it's me. Bart," I said, trying in vain to make Hawk's vocal cords sound friendly and light. The effect was almost comical, and Roshayne crab-walked backwards off the bed and shrank into the corner.

"I did it, Rosh," I said excitedly, giving up on changing the voice. "I got in his body! It's me!" I took a step forward, and she put up both hands.

"Don't . . . ," she started. "I . . . you . . . don't come any closer . . . please."

"But Rosh, I told you I was going to do this, remember? Under the bed?"

"I don't know," she stammered. "I . . . just don't know. You . . . you look . . ."

"I know," I said, realizing what she was facing. "This looks very suspicious. But you have to trust me. It's the only way we're going to get you off this boat."

The mention of escape softened her, and she started chewing on a fingernail.

"Okay, let me prove it's me," I offered. "I'll tell you some things that Hawk couldn't possibly know. Things from before Tiffany's murder. Will that do it?"

"How do I know what you've heard or learned since then? You jump out . . . I mean Hawk jumps out as much as Bart does . . . you do."

She wanted to believe, I could tell.

"Okay," I said, "you ask me questions. Anything you can think of that I, Bart, would know that Hawk wouldn't."

She thought for a moment. "When's Bart's birthday? . . . no, too easy. When's my birthday? . . . no." She thought harder. "Name the people in the car when we had that accident up the canyon."

"You, me, Scott Norton, Tammy Edmonds, Neil McBride, Jill Frampton, and Paul Bishop." I rattled off the names quickly so she could tell I didn't have to think about it.

"Where were we going for our date the night Tiffany was killed?"

"Homecoming dance," I said before she even finished.

"Very good. Now, what's the name of the nurse at Payson High School?"

"Oh, come on, Rosh. How do you expect me to remember something like that?"

"If you're Bart, you'll remember," she answered, her eyes narrowing.

I thought back. The only time I had anything to do with the school nurse was the day my body fell off in English class—the first time I realized I was going Inviz rather than just having a near-death experience. I had banged my head hard on the desk and needed a big Band-Aid and some Tylenol. *What was her name? It was like somebody else's name that I know. Come on. Think.*

"Sharla!" I blurted out. "Like Charlene. I don't remember her last name, though."

Roshayne raised an eyebrow. "I'm impressed. Now tell me the first time we kissed—Bart and I."

"The last day of tenth grade. Yearbook day." I had to smile just thinking about it.

"This is all very strange, you know," Roshayne said. "I'm looking at Silver Hawk, but the smile is out of place. The voice is Hawk's, the smell is Hawk's." She wrinkled her nose.

I hadn't noticed until then that he ready did have a peculiar odor. Yuck.

"But the facts convince me that you're Bart in there somewhere. Mostly it's the eyes. The hatred is gone. They actually almost sparkle." She stared long and hard at the eyes. MY eyes. Trusting, smiling, loving eyes . . . I hoped. "So, now what?"

I took a step toward her.

"No, please . . . Bart. It's Hawk's hand. Please don't touch me with it. I don't know how you can stand being in there."

"It's difficult, believe me." I walked over and stood by the couch. "Okay, the first thing I need to do is find out what Clawson and Derek are doing. Hopefully, they're shacked up with their babes and sleeping."

"I heard them making a lot of noise in the hall, but that was over two hours ago," she said. "I don't know if they're in their rooms or not."

"I'll have to check. Then I need to get you off this boat as soon as possible. After that, I'll figure out where we are and let the guys know. The hard part is that now I can't sneak around invisible, so I'll have to convince anyone I run into that I'm Hawk."

"Then, whatever you do, don't smile."

I smiled. "Oops, sorry," I said, struggling to keep a straight face.

"I'm serious," she said. "Clawson will kill you if he finds out."

"I thought about that," I answered just as serious. "If he does, he'll actually be killing Hawk, you know. Then I can just leave his dead body and go back to mine."

"You wouldn't!" she said, shocked.

"I'm not going to intentionally get Hawk killed, no. The point is, I'm not in danger here. YOU are."

"You're right," she said. "Get going."

I headed out the door.

"Lock it," she added. "It wouldn't do to have Clawson find me unlocked right now."

Fishing around in the pockets of Hawk's jeans, I found a key ring with four keys. One of them fit the padlock, so I snapped it shut.

The hallway had three other doors besides the one leading up the stairs. I knew the one directly across the hall was Derek's. I put my ear to the door and listened. No sounds. Slowly and carefully, I twisted the doorknob. It was unlocked. When I had turned it as far as it would go, I cautiously pushed the door open a crack, ready to run if necessary. The lights were on in the room, so I stopped and waited, holding my breath. Nobody came, so I opened it another half-inch and was able to see Derek on the bed. As expected, his girl was with him, and to my relief they were at least semi-covered by the sheets. Both were sleeping soundly. I eased the door closed and spent forever turning the knob back to avoid any clicking noises.

I was starting to sweat. *How can anybody stand having this much hair?* I wondered.

At the next door down, I repeated the same procedure. The room was dark, and I was suddenly worried that anyone inside would surely see the crack of light coming from around the door. I listened, but heard nothing. Pushing the door a little more, I was able to see an unoccupied bed, queen size, and a couch with some clothes scattered on it. Jeans, and plaid shirts.

Hawk's room, I realized. *I'll come back here later.*

The last door, right across the hall, had to be Clawson's. I was especially careful opening it up. It, too, was dark, but the sound of deep snoring was audible even before I got the door opened. I couldn't tell if the other girl was with him or not, but since there weren't any other guest rooms, I assumed she was. I closed the door and hurried back to Roshayne's room.

"We're in luck," I said, once back inside. "They're all sleeping and probably will be for a while. Let's go."

"Wait. What do I need?" she asked.

"Do you have a hat?"

She nodded.

"Get it. Sunscreen?"

She shook her head.

"Bring the sheet from the bed." As we were leaving, I noticed the small refrigerator by the TV. There was a six-pack of Sprite, as well as various cans and bottles of liquors. I grabbed the Sprite. "Do you have any food in here?" I asked.

"No. Why do I need food?"

"I don't know how long you'll be out there. I just want to make sure you'll be all right."

"I'll make it," she said bravely. "Let's hurry." She wrapped the soda and her hat, shoes, and purse in the sheet, and we made our exit into the hallway.

In contrast to the well-lit lower deck, it was almost pitch-black topside—perfect conditions for what we were doing. I wanted to take Roshayne's hand to lead her, but she withdrew, reminding me whose body I was using. Quietly, we made our way around to the side where the motorboat was hanging in its cradle. It was a nice-sized water-skiing boat, with plenty of horsepower hanging on the back. The problem was, the hoist was electrically operated and probably very noisy.

"Stay right here," I said. Roshayne hugged the wall in the dark.

After crawling all around the base of the hoist, I finally found what I was looking for. "There's an emergency release here," I whispered in Roshayne's direction. With some effort, I managed to pull the lever to release the boom from the motor. It made a heavy clanging sound when it snapped back, causing us both to freeze for several seconds. Finally, when I was sure no one was coming, I pushed on the side of the boat, causing the boat and boom to slowly swing out over the water. I was pleasantly surprised at how easily it moved and realized that Hawk was in pretty good shape physically, especially for his age. It was nice having such fine-tuned muscles at my disposal. I had to climb up on the railing and balance out over the water to get the boat clear of the side.

"Okay," I whispered. "Come on."

Roshayne came towards me, nervous and apprehensive. "I'm not sure about this," she said, eyeing the boat and the dark water below. "Are you sure—?"

"It's the only way," I said urgently. Then, guessing that her hesitation might still stem from doubts about my presence in Hawk's body, I added, "This is one of those things you told me about in my yearbook, remember? Saving lives? Inspiring people? Using the gift? I'm sure God is behind us, Rosh. Have faith."

She smiled a thin smile, took a deep breath, and climbed up the ladder on the side of the hoist. I was a little nervous for a minute as she crawled out and lowered herself into the boat, but she managed it without incident.

"What am I supposed to do?" she whispered from the darkness.

"Just stay comfortable and float around. This yacht is moving fast enough that we'll leave you behind pretty fast. By the time it gets light, you'll be long out of sight."

"Then what? Start the engine and head somewhere?"

"No! Don't do that. They might still hear it. Besides, we need you to stay in one place so we can find you and pick you up."

"Hurry, okay?" she said with a pleading tone. "Don't leave me out here."

"Say a long prayer, Rosh, and we'll be there when you finish."

With that, I released the locking mechanism and began turning the hand crank to lower the boat into the water. In spite of Hawk's superior muscles, the effort sapped a tremendous amount of energy, and I wondered a couple of times if I had the strength to do the job.

Finally, I heard the boat splash softly into the water, and the strain eased on the cables. After a few more cranks to create some slack, I whispered over the railing, "Turn it loose." I could barely make out Roshayne's shape moving around in the dark boat as she fumbled with the hook on the cable. The cables swung free a moment later, and fearing they might bang against the hull of the yacht, I cranked them back in quickly and pulled the boom back into place. It would be obvious to anyone looking that the boat was missing, but there was nothing I could do about that.

By the time I had finished and looked back down, the boat had already slipped several yards behind the yacht and was rapidly disappearing from view.

"I love you, Rosh," I whispered into the night sky. "Please, Lord, watch over her."

I remained at the rear railing for several minutes, straining to see into the darkness, until I was sure she had completely disappeared. I looked around again at the night, breathing a silent prayer of thanks for the calm seas and the clear sky.

Then I suddenly remembered the final part of the job. *I've got to find out where we are, before she gets too far away!*

In a panic, I headed for the bridge. The door was open, and one of Carlos' men was slumped down in the captain's chair, snoring away. I waited a minute, then cleared my throat. He came awake with a jerk, instant fear in his eyes at the sight of me.

"Sí, señor. I'm terribly sorry, señor. I was not really sleeping, I was only—"

"No matter," I said, assuming the meanest face and demeanor I could muster. "Tell me where we are."

He glanced nervously at the darkened control panel. "I don't know, señor. We are traveling in the blind, without instruments, as you said."

"Then turn them on," I commanded.

He started to sweat and fidget. "I can't do that, señor. Carlos, he kill me for sure. He say only he turns on the panel."

"Then go get him," I barked angrily.

"Sí, señor." He took two steps backward, glanced again at the controls, then turned and hurried off to the crew's quarters. Minutes later, Carlos and his man came storming onto the bridge. Carlos was swearing a steady stream in Spanish, which stopped abruptly in mid-sentence when he saw me.

"What do you need, señor?" he asked nervously. I simply glanced at the panel and stared him down. He succumbed quickly and started lighting up the instruments. I watched carefully as each of them came on, paying particular attention to the GPS, speed indicator, and compass. When he was finished, he backed away, waiting for more instructions.

"I need to use the radio," I said with authority. I was about to invent a bogus reason, but decided Hawk would not have needed to explain himself to the crew.

Carlos quickly handed me the portable mike, and I told him which frequency I needed. He made the adjustments. "Just push the button to talk," he said.

Glaring at him, I said menacingly, "I know how."

"Sí, señor."

I pushed the button and looked out through the windows into the night. "Guardian? Puppet," I said, then released the button. Twenty seconds passed with no response. "Guardian? Puppet. Do you hear me, Guardian?"

"Guardian here," came Alan's voice over the speaker, a little too loud for my comfort.

"Eleven. Three. Seven. One," I spoke slowly and precisely into the mike. "Twenty-two. Fifty-four. Sixty-six. Nineteen. Forty-one. Two-zero. Fifteen."

There was a prolonged silence when I finished. I knew Alan was busy working on the chart on Tony's table, and making calculations. The numbers were a code that Alan and Curtis and I had worked out during supper. Eleven represented our current speed in knots. Three-seven-one meant one hundred seventy-three degrees, our heading. The rest was the longitude and latitude shown on the GPS, given backwards, except for the last number, which told them that it had been fifteen minutes since I set Roshayne free in the motorboat.

"Forty-five. Six," blared the speaker, causing us all to jump.

"Four," I answered, short for the well known Ten-Four acknowledgment. I handed the mike back to Carlos. "Turn it all back off," I instructed, "and maintain your present course and speed until I . . . until we instruct you otherwise." I realized that my vocabulary had been a little off from what Hawk would have said, and could only hope Carlos would pay more attention to the face and the voice than he did the words.

"Sí, señor," he answered.

As the instruments blinked off one by one, I made a hasty exit from the bridge and went directly to the guest suites, where I barricaded myself in Hawk's room. With the door locked, I finally breathed a big sigh of relief, turned on the lights, and dropped exhausted onto the soft, overstuffed couch.

I made it, I congratulated myself. *I did it!*

Of course, I was a long way from finished. I knew only too well that Hawk himself had been watching and listening and following my every move the whole time. Alan's last coded message told me that it would be six hours and forty-five minutes before he would be in position. After getting our coordinates, he would have worked out a course with Tony where they would steer around us, either on the east or the west, just over the horizon, then come around the back and pick up Roshayne. An extra half-hour was added in case he needed time to do some looking for the boat. So that meant I had to stay put in Hawk's body for almost seven more hours, to prevent him from spilling the beans.

I decided the best thing to do was to just stay in Hawk's room for as long as possible while the rest slept off their party. Whatever came after that, I would just have to take a step at a time.

Chapter 23

- Suspense -

My biggest problem for the first while was staying awake. I didn't dare sleep; I had no idea whether or not I could stay in Hawk's body if I allowed it to lose consciousness. So I paced the floor for a while and worried. Then I decided to check out Hawk's room, to keep me busy. I opened and closed drawers and doors, careful not to make any noise, but didn't find anything of any significance. Just clothes, Indian jewelry, and more of his medicine-man paraphernalia.

What a boring existence.

At six-thirty, I crept up the stairs and peeked out at the aft deck. It was already light out. Finding the deck deserted, I took the chance and walked to the rear railing. I searched the horizon for a full minute and was greatly relieved to see that there was no sign of Roshayne or the boat, although I worried about how she was doing, dealing with that wide expanse of endless ocean.

At around seven o'clock, it suddenly occurred to me that Hawk was supposed to be watching Roshayne in her room, and everybody on board expected him to be there. I shut off the lights in Hawk's room and quickly made my way back to her empty suite. I was relieved to see that the room still looked the same. As far as I could tell, no one had been there.

What am I going to say when they come in? It's obvious she's not here, and they can easily verify that on the cameras anyway.

I stepped back into the hall and listened quietly at Derek's door. I had to know if he was watching the monitors. I slowly opened the door a crack and checked in again. He and the girl were still lying motionless on the bed.

Back in Roshayne's room, I set about arranging the bed with clothing from her suitcase and cushions from the couch to make it look like she was asleep under the covers. I wished I had a wig or something, but had to settle for just pulling the sheets up high over the pillow. Then I sat on the couch and waited—stiff-backed and stiff-armed, like Hawk would do.

I didn't have long to wait. At ten minutes past eight, there came a soft knock at the door, causing me to jump to my feet. I tried desperately to come up with what to say to Mr. Clawson or Derek, whichever it was.

Here goes, I thought as I opened the door quickly. One of Carlos' crew was standing nervously at the door, and I tried to conceal my relief. "Buenos días, señor," he said politely. "It is past your usual time, and we want to know if you are going to have breakfast on the sundeck, or do we bring it to your room? Or perhaps here in the señorita's room?"

"Yes, bring it here," I said. "I cannot leave the girl alone."

"And what would you like for breakfast this morning?" he asked.

My mind went blank. I had not prepared an answer for that question. I had no idea what Hawk ate and what he didn't eat. I could only assume it would be unusual.

"You don't know my tastes, after so many days?" I snarled.

"I . . . well . . . ," he stammered.

"Same as yesterday," I barked, "or the day before. Whatever. Doesn't matter."

"Sí, señor," he said agreeably. I shut the door in his face before he could say any more and heard him hurry off down the hall.

Ten minutes later he was back, knocking softly on the door. I opened it, and he and a mate carried in several silver platters and arranged them carefully on the small table.

"Would the señorita want to eat now?" he whispered, looking in the direction of Roshayne's bed.

"No," I said sternly but quietly. "She will eat later." I pushed them out into the hall and closed the door.

Breakfast was pretty much what I expected. A huge piece of meat—what kind I had no idea—covered with a sour, bitter sauce, a dish of black, mushy, disgusting-looking beans, a hard-as-a-rock piece of dark bread with seeds in it, some scrambled eggs full of onions and red peppers, and a steaming mug of black coffee. I picked at the eggs, but the taste was wild and spicy. Nothing else attracted my attention. *I can't leave it all on the plate, though,* I thought, *or it'll attract attention.* I tried to find a container of some sort that I could put the food in, but the room was pretty bare. The only things left in the room were some of Roshayne's clothes and her suitcase. Finally I settled for a couple of videotape cases, leaving the videos sitting loose on the TV. Carefully, I scooped all the food off the plates and stuck the cases in the fridge.

I never did drink coffee, and I decided against drinking his, especially after smelling it. The coffee went right down the drain in the bathroom.

Twenty minutes later, the crewmen came and retrieved the dishes. I had rearranged the bed after they left the first time so it would appear that Roshayne had turned over in her sleep. They both glanced suspiciously at the bed, but said nothing.

After they left, I started pacing. I was way too nervous to sit anymore. At around nine o'clock, I thought I heard a door being opened and closed, but I couldn't hear any footsteps or talking. Nine-thirty rolled around, and I was starting to get worried. I had expected Clawson and Derek to be up and around by then. By ten, my nerves were starting to wear thin. The whole yacht was as quiet as a morgue. No one seemed to be moving around at all. I debated checking Derek's room again, but decided against it. Too risky. By ten-fifteen I was like a fish in a blender, just waiting for someone to flip the switch.

According to my calculations, the María would be finding Roshayne by eleven. I was supposed to give them a radio update at ten-thirty, to be sure we were far away before they moved in for the rescue. After that, I would be done and could return to the María and leave Hawk and Clawson behind.

At ten twenty-five, sweating profusely and having a hard time keeping my hands from shaking, I carefully opened the door and checked the hall. No sign of anyone. Clawson and Derek's doors were still closed. I had an uneasy feeling that something was not right. *This is too easy,* I thought. *I can't believe Clawson's not worried about Roshayne yet. He should have been checking on her and Hawk long before now. Maybe he's waiting for a report from Hawk.*

A report was out of the question, of course. I quietly climbed the stairs and made my way to the bridge. Another crewman I'd never seen before was manning the controls—or at least he wanted to be. They were all turned off, as usual.

"Good morning, señor," he said, jumping to his feet and smiling broadly.

"Turn on the instruments," I barked. I expected the same reluctance as the night before, but the man immediately spun around and began switching things on. *Maybe he's more afraid of Hawk than he is of Carlos,* I concluded.

I watched intently as things came to life. The radio lit up, along with several other things I didn't recognize. The GPS came on, and I committed the numbers to memory. The speed indicator was registering thirteen and a half knots. *Good,* I thought. *Just that much farther away from Roshayne.*

Then the electronic compass came to life, and I stood there in shock. Instead of the heading from the night before of one seventy-three, it was pointed at three-fifty. I spun around and looked out the window.

The sun is on the wrong side, I thought in panic. *We're going back north!*

"Hand me the radio," I demanded angrily. He gave me the mike. I was about to give him the appropriate frequency when I noticed on the read-out that it was already set there. *Must have been left from last night,* I realized. *I should have been more careful.* "Guardian? Puppet," I spoke into the mike.

"This is Guardian," came the immediate answer. Alan was obviously waiting for my call.

"Thirteen. Zero. Five. Three," I said, giving him speed and course backwards.

"Repeat?" came Alan's surprised voice.

"Thirteen. Zero. Five. Three," I repeated, then proceeded to the GPS coordinates. "Twenty-two—"

"HAWK!" came a booming voice from behind me.

Chapter 24

- The Race -

I almost dropped the mike in my surprise. Spinning around, I found myself face to face with Mr. Clawson. He was not a happy camper. Derek came in and stood at Clawson's right, his arms folded and muscles bulging. Carlos came and stood on the left, wringing his hands and searching the floor like he'd lost his last contact lens or something.

"What are you doing?" Clawson demanded.

I struggled to keep my composure. Hawk would have just stood calmly and answered simply.

"I am . . . checking our course," I answered. I showed them the mike, then pulled it to my chest, holding down the button.

Clawson moved in closer until his face was only inches away from mine . . . or Hawk's.

"What business do you have checking our course?" he demanded. His eyes were on fire, and I was sure he was seeing an abundance of fear in mine. "That's Derek's business. Your job is to watch the girl and watch for Bart."

"The girl is—"

"Shut up!" he screamed in my face. "Thanks to you . . . BART . . . the girl is gone!"

I reacted poorly to the unexpected mention of my name, and Clawson saw it immediately.

"Hold him!" he signaled to his bodyguard. Derek stepped behind me and grabbed my arms in a painful, viselike grip. I didn't even try to resist. I knew it would be futile. Besides, I knew it wasn't my body he was hurting.

"You must be mistaken," I said, trying to cover up.

"Oh, no. There's no mistake," he said. "The second you left her room, we checked it out. A bed full of clothes and pillows!" I remained silent. "How did you get in Hawk's body, Bart?"

"I'm not Bart. I am Hawk. Don't you see Silver Hawk standing in front of you?"

"Oh, I see Hawk, all right. And I hear Hawk. But you are not Hawk. He came to me in my room earlier this morning and explained the whole situation."

My adrenaline increased with that piece of information. "What do you mean, he came to you?"

"He appeared to me. Just like Bart did . . . like YOU did to your girlfriend under the bed. I didn't believe him at first, since he's never done that before. I assumed it must be Bart appearing in Hawk's form to deceive me."

"That is exactly what happened," I defended. "It WAS Bart, and he HAS deceived you. I am Hawk."

Clawson laughed. "A pitiful performance, Bart. He learned the skill from watching you. And I had only to observe you in the girl's room for a short time, and I knew. I tuned in just in time to watch you dispose of your breakfast. You've paced holes in the carpet since then."

My eyes were distracted by a shimmering motion to the right of Carlos, like a reflection of light off water. As I turned and stared at it, Clawson and the rest saw it also. After a few uncertain moments, Hawk's form began to stabilize, although not solidly.

Carlos and the other crewman shrank back in fear and crossed themselves. "Ave María," Carlos said under his breath. "El diablo del triángulo!" Everyone took a step or two backward to distance themselves.

"You are dead, boy!" screamed Hawk as soon as he was visible enough to be seen and heard. His eyes were burning with hatred. "You are dead! The instant you leave my body, you are dead!"

I began to sweat. *Is it possible he's managed to kill me? Is my body lying strangled and bleeding on the María?*

He zoomed in on me, and even I took a step backward, pressing myself hard against Derek's chest.

"I will not rest until I have crushed your filthy bones into the dust!"

I relaxed. For the moment, I was still alive.

Clawson drew some courage, more confident than ever now that he knew who was who. "He is right, Bart," he said, eyes narrowed. "You are a dead man. Once we find your girlfriend, she will be promptly disposed of, and you will be hunted down and caught. And I will personally rip you apart limb by limb for the trouble you have caused us."

"I'm not afraid of you," I said, using Hawk's deep, gravelly voice to my best advantage. "Anyway, you're too late. Roshayne's only minutes away from being picked up right now . . . and there's nothing you can do about it."

"Oh, is that right?" Clawson chuckled, raising his eyebrows. "Carlos?" he said, motioning toward the controls. Carlos moved to the instrument panel and punched some buttons on the GPS.

"We know exactly where she is . . . Bart." He emphasized my name every time he said it, to reinforce to whom he was really talking . . . for himself and everyone else. "Before Carlos shut down the system last night, after your little midnight walk, he recorded the location in memory." He pointed at the GPS. "Take a look for yourself."

I saw the heading "Memory 1" on the top of the screen, and underneath were the coordinates I had given to Alan, plus or minus a second. My confidence started to wane.

"You'll never get there in time," I said. "My friends have been on their way all night. They're almost there already."

"Oh, so are we, Bart. We've been heading back since early this morning. As soon as Hawk appeared to me in my room, I reversed course. We expect to find her within minutes."

I was devastated.

"And there's nothing YOU can do about it," he spat the words at me sharply, one at a time. "Get him out of here!"

I've got to get out of here, I agreed. *I've got to warn Rosh.*

I wasn't at all sure of how to do that. If I needed to lie down and relax, I was in trouble because it was obvious Derek and Clawson weren't going to give me a chance. Before Derek could take a step, I closed my eyes, let my head tip forward, and relaxed all the muscles in Hawk's body. Derek had to catch me to keep me from slumping to the ground.

Out! I screamed at myself. *Get out!*

There weren't any vibrations, and the exit happened so fast that I hardly felt it.

Hawk saw his body go limp, took one look at me spiritually hovering over it, and dived in immediately. He straightened up, letting loose with a long string of profanities and struggling fiercely against Derek's hold on him.

"You think using that kind of vocabulary is going to convince me that you're Hawk all of a sudden, Bart?" he said, his face still in Hawk's face. He glanced around to see Hawk's spirit for confirmation and was momentarily caught off guard by not finding it.

"I AM Hawk!" Hawk yelled. "He left! I'm back! Let me go!"

"I can't do that, Bart. Take him down and lock him in the girl's room," Clawson said to Derek.

Hawk yelled out something that I didn't understand, but apparently Clawson did. He looked puzzled, unsure of how to deal with what he'd heard. I could only assume it was something that I wouldn't know . . . in a language I wouldn't know. Hawk's face became contorted with impatient rage as he awaited Clawson's reply.

"Take him away," Clawson directed, turning his back on Hawk. "I can't take the chance. Either way, he's of little use to me now."

Derek literally picked Hawk up off the floor and carried him out the door. The air was thick with obscenities from both of them.

Just when things were settling down, another crewman came running onto the bridge. "I've found her!" he yelled, pointing frantically toward the north. "On the horizon!"

Clawson and his crew dashed out the door and up the stairs to the sundeck. Clawson was handed a large pair of binoculars and shown the general direction to look. He scanned the horizon briefly, then stopped and stared through the glasses for several seconds. His mouth curved into a tight smile. "It's her, all right!" he said, handing back the binoculars. "Let's get ready."

I didn't wait around for any more. I headed straight to Roshayne.

At first I thought the boat was empty, just floating peacefully by itself. Then I realized Roshayne was lying part way under the dash and was covered with the sheet to keep the sun off.

I materialized immediately. "Roshayne, get up!" I yelled. "Hurry!"

She was so startled that she stumbled madly to her feet and clawed her way desperately out from under the sheet, eventually sending it overboard. Her face was a mask of sheer terror.

"Bart!" she said, suddenly smiling from ear to ear. "You're here!" Her smile faded quickly when she saw the look in my eyes. "What's wrong?"

"They're on their way back! They've already spotted you." I pointed to the south, and we could both see the outline of Clawson's yacht on the horizon.

"No!" she cried, slumping down onto one of the seats. "Where's YOUR boat?" she pleaded. "Where are your friends?"

"I don't know. I've got to find them. See if you can get the motor started, and I'll be right back."

"I don't know how," she said desperately. "I've never been on a boat before."

"Pull the cord. Turn the key," I said impatiently. "I don't know. Figure it out. I've got to find out where Curtis is."

"Bart, I—"

Curtis! I commanded myself.

The bridge on board the María was crowded with people. Curtis, Candy, and Alan were all huddled around the control panel and staring intently out the window. Tony and his crew were watching anxiously over their shoulders.

I planted myself directly in front of them, in the middle of the window, and made myself visible.

You'd have thought I'd dropped a dozen stink bombs on the floor by the way they all shot backward against the walls and tried to melt through the paneling. Eyes and mouths were wide open everywhere. Four of the seamen started making dozens of crosses in the air.

Curtis recovered first. "Bart! It's . . . it's you! Holy schnykies!"

"Oh my goodness!" Candy said slowly. She looked like she was about to faint.

"Roshayne's in trouble," I said, skipping the pleasantries. "Clawson found out I let her go, and they're on their way back to get her."

"We know," Alan cut in. "We heard the whole thing on the radio. That was brilliant, by the way, holding down the mike button."

"How close are you?" I asked.

"She's right there," Curtis said, pointing around me. "We'll be there in a few minutes."

I spun around and looked out across the water. We were heading basically west, and I could barely make out the outline of the motorboat on the horizon.

"Clawson's closer," I said. "We'll never make it."

"He's only doing thirteen knots," Alan stated emphatically. "We're doing nearly forty."

"Forty?" I floated over near Tony, and he about had a coronary. "I thought you said this thing would do fifty!"

"I lied," he said, trying to summon up some courage.

"You owe me a refund."

"Anything you say."

"There he is!" yelled Curtis. Off to our left, barely showing over the water, we caught sight of Clawson's yacht's sundeck. "It'll be a race to the finish."

"I'm going back to see Roshayne," I said. "Goose this thing as hard as you can, and let's get her out of that boat."

Roshayne!

She was frantically pulling on the cord of the outboard motor, but it wasn't starting. I materialized.

"What's wrong?" I asked in desperation. "It won't start?" I moved over to the dash. "There's a key! Turn the key!"

"I did," she answered, shaking out her tired arms. "I ran the battery down."

"Great!" I mumbled. I scanned the controls. "Oh, great. You never opened the throttle, Rosh! No wonder!"

She wearily staggered over to the driver's seat, and I pointed to the throttle. "I didn't know," she said, near tears. "I didn't know."

"Pull it back and forth a couple of times," I instructed, "then leave it halfway and try the cord again."

Roshayne primed the engine and yanked on the cord again several times until her strength gave out. She collapsed onto the nearest seat, panting for breath.

"Hurry, Rosh! They're coming!" I pointed at Clawson's boat, growing bigger by the minute. "And there comes ours!" I said excitedly, pointing to the east.

Roshayne looked back and forth at the two boats. "Clawson's closer," she cried. She hurriedly jumped up and yanked on the cord again. On the third pull, the engine coughed. On the fourth pull, it sputtered for three seconds. She pulled again with every ounce of strength she had left, and the engine abruptly roared to life. The boat also shot forward, nearly knocking Roshayne overboard, and heading directly for Clawson's yacht.

"Holy cow," I muttered, helpless to do anything. I felt the panic rising as she struggled to gain a handhold and finally pulled herself back into the boat.

Crawling on all fours, she made her way back to the driver's seat, pulled herself up, and yanked hard left on the wheel. The boat nearly capsized from the sharp bank, but she somehow managed to keep it upright. As soon as she leveled out, heading straight east towards the María, she pushed the throttle to the stops. The engine roared, and the boat fairly jumped into the air.

Then the engine coughed once, twice . . . and died.

"NO!" screamed Roshayne, banging on the wheel. "NO, NO, NO!"

The boat slowly coasted to a stop and rocked gently back and forth.

"Start it again!" I yelled, still hovering in the air over the boat. "Try again!"

Roshayne pumped the throttle again, and went back to pull the cord. Several exhausting attempts yielded nothing, and I was afraid she had flooded the engine.

"What's that noise?" she asked, standing straight up.

I listened. "It's an outboard engine!" I said excitedly.

"From your boat?" she said, peering into the distance toward the María.

I didn't remember Tony having a boat. I listened again and turned to face Clawson's yacht. To my horror, I discovered two jet skis skimming across the water and closing in. "Jet skis!" I yelled in panic.

Roshayne took one look and started pulling afresh on the cord like there was no tomorrow. Tears streaming down her face, and wet, sweaty hair plastered to her forehead, she cursed and pulled over and over, crying helplessly until she couldn't stand it anymore. Totally exhausted, she collapsed in a heap on the floor of the boat just as Derek and Carlos pulled up on either side.

Derek grabbed the handhold and vaulted effortlessly into the boat. Carlos climbed over the opposite side. Roshayne was totally helpless to resist them and could do nothing but sob and shed streams of tears as Derek threw her over his shoulder.

I made myself visible. "Put her down!" I yelled.

Carlos fell all over himself, but Derek merely looked at me and smiled. I decided to try another tactic. Remembering the image I had used on Tamara in the jail, I promptly turned myself into an ugly, raging, fire-breathing monster. Carlos took one wide-eyed look and promptly leaped out of the boat.

"I demand that you put her down this instant, or I'll—"

"Or you'll what?" Derek yelled, spinning around to face me.

It was hopeless. There was absolutely nothing I could do, and I literally withered and faded under his stare, becoming invisible again. He laughed loudly and threw Roshayne overboard. Then he jumped in the water himself, climbed back on his jet ski, and pulled Roshayne choking and coughing from the water into his lap. Seconds later, he was racing back across the calm seas, with Carlos bringing up the rear.

The roar of their engines gradually faded and yielded to the sound of the María steaming up from the east. Tony cut the engines and brought his craft to a gradual stop only a dozen feet from the abandoned motorboat.

We'd lost the race. After everything we'd been through. After all our careful planning. After dodging repeated attempts on our lives. After all the prayers. After Roshayne's hours of sitting out by herself in the middle of nowhere, waiting.

We got there two minutes too late.

All was lost.

Chapter 25

- The Chase -

"Hurry downstairs and turn me loose," I said after materializing again to Curtis. "I'm getting back in my body."

It took several minutes for the three of them to undo all the tape and ropes, then I stretched and eased myself off the bed. My legs were so weak, I nearly fell down. "Whoa," I said. "What happened to me?"

"You were right about being possessed, Bart. You freaked us out good," Curtis explained. "Or at least Hawk did. Right after you radioed Clawson's position, you started squirming around like crazy. Your eyes practically bugged right out of your head, and you swore at us something terrible, demanding that we let you go."

"That was Hawk, not me," I clarified, shaking my legs and rubbing my shoulders.

"We know that. We told him to jump off a cliff. He calmed down, closed his eyes like he was asleep for a few seconds, then started talking real softly to us, trying to convince us he was you, and that you managed to get back in right after he jumped out. It was your tone of voice and everything, but we still didn't believe him. Then he started telling us things about you and Roshayne . . . you know, personal things that he probably made up . . . and I was almost fooled."

"At the last minute," Candy said, "he got confused and called us Paul and Cindy."

"Alan grabbed some duct tape and stuck a big piece over your mouth," Curtis continued. "Then he really went berserk. He arched his . . . your back, strained your neck, and twisted all around. He was a monster."

"We were afraid for a minute that you . . . he might get loose," Alan added. "He nearly broke the bed. Then, all of a sudden he quit, and your body went totally limp again."

"If he'd been in his own body instead of mine, he probably would have gotten free," I said, leading them back up on deck. "He's a whole lot stronger than I thought he was."

"So, what did you do in HIS body?" Alan asked.

"I'll tell you all about it once we get done with this thing. Right now, all I'm thinking about is Roshayne."

We arrived back on the bridge and found Tony and crew anxiously looking out the window. "What's going on?" I asked.

"They've turned around and headed back toward Puerto Rico," Tony answered after examining me from head to toe. "I'm trying to follow at a discreet distance without losing sight of them."

"I thought they'd head out to sea," Curtis said. "Why would they head for land with us following them?"

"Maybe they're low on fuel," Tony said. "If they are, they don't have much choice."

"What I'm worried about is what they're doing to Roshayne," I said. "They threatened to kill her once they picked her up."

"I don't think they'll do that . . . yet," Tony said. "She's a valuable hostage right now, and they're going to need all the bargaining power they can muster before they get done."

"Why don't you go Inviz and go back there and find out?" Candy asked.

"I want to, believe me, but I don't dare. Hawk's lost his clout with Clawson and needs to do something to make it up. Now that he's seen what I did to him, he'll jump at the chance to come back here, in case I'm untied, and throw my body right off the boat to drown. Maybe take a couple of you with me."

"That's scary," agreed Candy.

"We're just going to have to be patient until we reach port, then see what we can do."

"Maybe we can radio ahead and have the police waiting," Curtis offered.

"Too risky," I said. "Who knows what he'll do with cops all around. He already warned me about that."

Tony cleared his throat and looked nervously out the window.

"What's wrong?" I asked him.

"Nothing," he said. "Just clearing my throat, that's all."

For the next three hours we followed Clawson's yacht, staying close enough that we could see them through Tony's high-powered binoculars, but far enough away that we weren't an immediate threat to them.

While Alan stayed down on the bridge to keep an eye on our course, I spent most of the time topside with Curtis and Candy watching. After a while, the binoculars practically became part of my eyes. I was worried about Clawson dumping Roshayne overboard, and swept the glasses back and forth constantly, looking for anything floating in the water. I was relieved after about three hours to see Derek parade her around the rear of the boat, looking in our direction, as if to let us know she was safe, but reminding us she was being held captive and in their power.

Another half-hour later, Tony suddenly cut power. I had been so busy watching through the glasses, I hadn't even noticed that Clawson had stopped. We were practically on top of them before Tony noticed and stopped also.

I raced back down to the bridge. "What happened?"

"I don't know," he said nervously. "They just stopped."

"Why'd you get so close? Why didn't you stop?"

"I was . . . talking . . . you know."

His eyes got real shifty, like he was hiding something. That made me nervous.

"So, now what? We just sit here?" I asked. "Back up."

"No, we just sit here," he answered simply, staring straight ahead through the glass. "We wait." His fingers were twitching.

"Ave María, pues hombre!" cried one of the mates, pointing fearfully at the chart.

"What's the matter?" asked the captain gruffly without turning.

"The trench! We're right over the trench!"

"So what?" barked Tony.

"El triángulo," he whispered hoarsely. "The devil's triangle. This is the worst place—"

"Don't be stupid!" Tony yelled, spinning around and grabbing his mate by the collar. "It's a stupid fairy tale. Shut up and get back to work."

A violent argument ensued, ending with the mate running out to warn the rest of his superstitious comrades of their impending doom. Tony shot a menacing look at us and returned to the window.

I slowly left the bridge and signaled the guys to follow me back up top.

"What's going on?" Alan asked when we were out of earshot.

"I don't know," I answered. "Tony's suddenly acting very weird, and Clawson's stopped in the middle of nowhere."

"You think Tony is planning something?" Curtis whispered. "You think he's in cahoots with Clawson?"

"Maybe Clawson offered him a ton of money to change sides all of a sudden," Candy offered fearfully.

"If he did, we're in big, big trouble," I agreed.

"How are we going to find out?" asked Alan.

"Have any of you seen him on the radio?" I asked.

"Well, no. Not when we were there," Alan answered. "But there were a couple of times when we weren't."

"When?" I asked.

"Like when Hawk got in your body. Curtis came up yelling for me, and I went down to help for about twenty minutes."

"And then when we turned you loose," Candy added. "That's about it."

"I was right by the radio the rest of the time," Alan said.

"Could have been either of those times," I observed.

"Wait!" Alan cut in. "I made a quick trip to the rest room about a half hour ago. Maybe he called him then."

Candy started shifting from one foot to the other and wringing her hands. "What are we going to do? They could kill us all."

"That they could," I agreed.

Curtis had been half listening and half watching Clawson's yacht in the distance. "You guys! Look!" he said suddenly, pointing at Clawson's yacht.

"What?" I asked, rushing to the railing.

"There's something going on, up on the sundeck."

I lifted my glasses and focused. "It looks like Derek, with Roshayne again," I said. "He has her hands tied behind her back, and he's just standing there holding her. Wait! Now Clawson's coming up. He's got his girlfriend with him. She's tied up, too."

"Why would he—?"

"Now Hawk's coming up, with Derek's girlfriend," I cut in. "Why would they have all three of them tied up?"

"We're moving," Curtis said quietly. "Look. We're going around them—real slow. They're almost straight east from us already."

"You're right," I said. "I thought they had turned sideways." *What's Tony up to?* I wondered.

"What are they doing now?" Candy asked.

"That's funny," I said, looking through the glasses again. "They're not even looking at us. They're facing the other way and just staring out to sea."

"No, they're not," Curtis said, pointing south. "Somebody's coming."

We all turned and stared in disbelief as a black shape slowly took form on the south horizon.

"That's a really big boat," Alan said after several minutes, "and Clawson's waiting for it."

"Now we're REALLY in trouble," Candy said.

"We should have kept that motorboat," I said. "Maybe we could have made a run for it."

"Tony has one!" Curtis said, smiling broadly. "It's hanging from a sling on the back!"

"You're kidding." My mind raced, reliving my boat-napping experience from just hours earlier. "I know exactly what to do," I said excitedly. "If you guys can keep Tony and crew distracted for about ten minutes, I think I can get it in the water."

"Then what?" Candy asked nervously.

"When you hear me start the motor, you all run across the deck and jump overboard and start swimming. I'll pick you up."

"What if they shoot at us?" Candy said, near panic.

"I haven't seen any guns," Alan said, "but that doesn't mean anything. Tony doesn't look like the type, though."

"He's the type that likes money," Curtis said. "He'd probably sell his own mother if the price was right."

"Look at it this way," I said. "We're dead, one way or the other. Clawson has three boats ganging up on us. That new one probably has a dozen of Derek's bad guys, with all kinds of guns and things. When it gets here, they storm our boat, Tony pretends to resist, then turns us over to Clawson. Tony's rich, we're dead, and Clawson's home free. At least this way, we have a chance. We can make a dash for Puerto Rico and hope we can find a ship along the way somewhere."

"Or we can radio for help from the motorboat," Alan said.

"Exactly," I agreed. "Let's get going. We don't have much time."

"What about Roshayne?" Candy asked.

"She's safer if we're still alive," I said. "Clawson will just keep chasing us. If we let them take us now, she'll be just as dead as us."

Chapter 26

- Guardians -

When we arrived back down on the bridge, Tony and his crew were busy watching the approaching ship through the windows. I let Alan, Curtis, and Candy wander on in, while I hung back in the doorway. After I'd made sure Tony had acknowledged my presence and turned back to the window, I slipped back out and headed aft.

Tony's motorboat was smaller than the one Roshayne had been in, but still plenty big enough for four people, and with a hefty motor on the back. The winch was similar, too, but I couldn't find a manual release anywhere.

Looking up and down the deck, I pulled the electric control out of its slot and pushed the Up button for a split second. The boat rose a quarter of an inch, and the electric motor was almost noiseless. Gathering courage, I pushed and held the Down button. Quietly the motor began to descend. Satisfied that no one inside would hear the ultra-quiet machine, I worked the controls to swing the boat out over the back.

One of the disadvantages to the quiet motor was that it moved at a snail's pace, and I was getting desperate by the time it cleared the rail. I was pushing the Down button and had the boat within a couple feet of the water when Candy suddenly came running out on the deck.

"Bart!" she yelled loudly.

"Quiet," I whispered. "They'll hear you."

"Never mind," she said. "Forget the boat. Come here quick. It's the Coast Guard!"

"The Coast Guard?" I said stupidly.

"The big boat's the Coast Guard!"

"You're kidding."

"Tony called them last night while Hawk was in your body. He was on the radio, just like you thought, only he was calling the GOOD guys."

"Then why was he—"

"He got scared after what you said about calling the police and getting everyone killed. He's still worried sick that we're all going to get shot to pieces."

It took me a few seconds to register the significance of what she was telling me, then I took off at a dead run back inside the bridge. Tony and crew, as well as Curtis and Alan, were crowded around the window, watching the drama that was unfolding. I raced up to the observation deck for a better view.

Sure enough, there was a monster-sized Coast Guard cutter closing in on Clawson's yacht, the deck of which was crowded with uniforms and bristling with big guns. There was even a helicopter parked on board.

Clawson, Derek, and Hawk were still on the sundeck with the three girls. We were close enough that I could see Clawson and Derek holding guns to Roshayne's and the one girl's heads. Carlos was standing behind Clawson holding a portable megaphone. His crew had disappeared.

The cutter slowed as it got nearer and came to a full stop at a distance of about three hundred yards. "This is the United States Coast Guard," blared an enormous speaker. "Put down your weapons and prepare to be boarded."

A motor surfboat and a rigid-hull inflatable were being lowered over the sides with half a dozen guardsmen in each. Carlos lifted the megaphone to Clawson's mouth. "Call off your dogs, or I'll kill one of these girls right here on the spot," came his tinny-sounding voice from the small horn.

The boats and crews had hit the water and were preparing to approach the yacht. When the cables were thrown free, they fired up their motors and waited by the side of the cutter for instructions. There was an anxious wait.

"We're sending over one boat," came the captain's voice from the cutter. "Release your hostages, and you'll be free to go."

An officer on deck motioned at one of the crafts, and it started slowly toward the yacht.

Clawson was yelling something at Derek. Derek grabbed the girl Clawson had been holding, and held both her and Roshayne tightly around their waists. Clawson grabbed the megaphone from Carlos. "I said BACK OFF, or I'll start dropping bodies in the water!" He waved his gun over his head menacingly. "I'm not stupid!"

The boat continued its approach, and the cutter's speaker remained silent.

"I warned you!" Clawson yelled. The guardsmen were halfway between the two ships. He dropped the megaphone on the deck and grabbed Carlos by his shirt, jerking him around and out in front against the rail.

Without any hesitation at all, he shot his terrified captain point-blank in the chest, sending him toppling backward over the side. His body hit the water with a sickening thud and disappeared from sight.

The small boat stopped immediately, and for a couple of seconds everybody's eyes were riveted on the spot where Carlos had gone under. One of the guardsmen rose to jump over, but was restrained by his superior. Finally Carlos floated to the surface and bobbed up and down in the tide, face down.

No one spoke and no one moved. The tension in the air was thick.

The quiet was suddenly interrupted by a loud banging sound that seemed to be coming from our boat. I looked around to see what was happening. Running to the back of the deck, I saw that the boat I had left dangling from the hoist was swinging in and out, knocking against the hull of our yacht.

Looking around at the sky, I was surprised to find that it was nearly overcast with thick, dark clouds. A storm had formed out of nowhere without anyone even noticing. The wind was picking up, and the seas were becoming very rough.

I raced back to the front. The first boat had returned to the side of the cutter, and both of them were having a hard time keeping their positions due to the sudden weather change.

"State your demands," came the voice from the cutter.

Clawson and Derek talked to each other for several seconds, then Clawson lifted the megaphone. "We want your fastest boat and a dinghy brought to our yacht. Full tanks. Then we want clear sailing south. When we can no longer see you on the horizon, we'll leave the girls in the dinghy, and you can pick them up."

The wind became very gusty and picked up quickly to forty or fifty miles per hour. Clawson and group were having a hard time keeping their footing. At one sharp pitch of the boat, Hawk stumbled and had to let his girl go to keep his balance. The girl promptly tore away and ran down the stairs, her hands still tied. Seeing her escape, the other one took advantage of the next dip and roll to squirm free, also. She ran down the stairs.

Personally, I figured Clawson had let them go, but wanted to make a scene for the Coast Guard. There was no way anyone was going to break loose from Derek if he didn't want them to. Proving that theory, Roshayne tried to break free and was restrained effortlessly.

Clawson yelled some commands to his two minions, and Hawk took over control of Roshayne. Derek ran downstairs. I thought maybe he was after the girls, but to my relief, they appeared moments later, racing away from the other side of the yacht on the two jet skis. They made a wide arc, then came back around behind us and headed for the cutter, eventually disappearing around the other side.

Shortly after that, Derek appeared on the main deck. He had a large pack on his back with an antenna sticking out the top. Several other bags and pouches hung from his shoulders and waist. In his arms he was carrying what looked like a couple of M-16s and another very large rifle or bazooka or something. One of the M-16s he tossed up to Clawson, who handed it to Hawk.

"You've got five minutes, or your men start getting sprayed with lead," Clawson barked over the megaphone. He promptly led Roshayne down the stairs, gun to her head, and joined Derek by the side ladder.

A black bundle was thrown over the side of the Coast Guard cutter, which immediately blossomed into a small rubber dinghy. The two boats were dispatched toward Clawson's yacht, with the dinghy in tow.

"If you try to follow us, we'll blast your helicopter out of the air," warned Clawson. "Boats, too. We're armed with rocket launchers."

The guardsmen were having a very difficult time tying up to the yacht with the seas picking up. A light rain started to mix in with the wind, making it difficult to see. Finally the first boat was cleared, and the guardsmen returned to the cutter in the second one. Derek climbed halfway down the ladder and dropped in his bags and pouches, then he climbed back up on deck and headed below for more. The whole time, Clawson and Hawk kept firm grips on the rail, with Roshayne sandwiched in between the rail and Hawk. I could sense more than see the terror in her eyes. The rain suddenly came down with a fury, and it became impossible to keep the binoculars dry enough to see clearly.

Then, out of nowhere came an ear splitting, crackling, hissing sound, followed by a roaring boom of thunder. Out of the low, black clouds directly overhead fell a brilliant white ball of fire, which landed with a tremendous explosion in the water right between Clawson's yacht and the cutter. The guardsmen's boat nearly capsized from the resulting turbulence. The air was suddenly hot and full of static electricity—just like after the lightning we had experienced at camp.

Derek re-appeared and started making his way down the ladder again. When he was just about to jump in the boat, the heavens let loose with a volley of fireballs, one right after the other. I'd never seen anything like it. They were at least fifteen or twenty feet in diameter and blindingly white—like cannonballs of lightning.

"Saint Elmo's fire!" yelled one of Tony's deckhands.

The first one hit a hundred yards south of the cluster of boats, with the second and third striking much closer. The fourth one struck the back end of the cutter, making a terrible sizzling, burning sound. Men on board raced immediately to survey the damage.

Clawson and his group remained frozen in place, tentatively watching the hailstorm of lightning balls and trying to decide whether to board the boat or stay on the yacht. Before they could make up their minds, the next ball of lightning blasted down out of the black clouds and struck Clawson's yacht dead center on the sundeck, instantly disintegrating it. The whole boat reeled from the hit. Derek was knocked off the ladder and bounced roughly off the side of the small boat and into the water, then disappeared in the high seas. Clawson, Hawk, and Roshayne were thrown against the rails, then knocked back against the bulkhead and onto the deck. Carlos' crew appeared from below and made a run for it, diving off the bow as fast as they could clear the railings, and trying unsuccessfully to swim toward the cutter.

Seconds later, just as Clawson and Hawk were coming to their feet again, another bolt of lightning struck the foredeck, and the entire yacht exploded in a shower of splintered wood. Clawson, Hawk, and Roshayne were all thrown head over heels high into the air, right over the top of the damaged yacht, and came down like broken crash dummies into the water.

By that time, I was clinging to the rail for dear life myself, my feet having gone out from under me several times already on the wet deck. At the sight of Roshayne hitting the water, I cried out in angry desperation, reaching out with one hand as though I could catch her and save her. Clawson and Hawk swam strongly but unsuccessfully against the rough seas, trying to make their way around the yacht to the Coast Guard's small boat. Roshayne and Derek were nowhere to be seen. I held my breath. Finally, Roshayne shot to the surface, gulped for air, and went back under.

"Her hands are tied!" I screamed into the wind. "Help her!" No one heard. She came up again, gasping for air, and was pulled right back under. "Somebody help her!"

A big wave hit the side of our yacht, throwing me off balance and causing me to bang my head on the railing. Losing my handhold, I was promptly swept off the observation deck and sent tumbling down the rain-drenched stairs. I grabbed at every rail and bar that came close, but was unsuccessful in stopping the fall.

When I landed upside down on the main deck, Curtis was making his way toward me from the bridge. He grabbed me under the arms and pulled me several feet along the deck until he could wrestle me into the bridge area. Alan slammed the door shut behind us, and the roar of the wind and rain subsided slightly.

"We've got to save her!" I yelled frantically, struggling to my feet. "She's in the water! Roshayne—!"

"I know," Curtis yelled back, "but we can't see her anymore."

I rushed to the windows and tried to make sense of the distorted images through the rain-swept glass.

"We've got to do something!" I yelled again. I headed for the door, determined to jump over and find her myself. Alan pulled me back, and he and Curtis held me tightly while I kicked and struggled for a few seconds.

Cooler heads prevailed. I realized eventually that any effort on my part to save anyone in that storm would have been sure suicide. If it hadn't been for my friends, I would surely have drowned myself trying. I slumped into a chair in shock.

"We've been caught in a current!" one of Tony's men called out. He was studying the control panel. "We're being pulled backwards on a heading of about ten degrees."

"We'll fight it!" Tony yelled, gunning the engines.

Looking out the window, I could vaguely make out that we were moving away from the other ships. Clawson's yacht was several hundred yards away to our left and listing badly—more than likely taking on water. The cutter was turning and heading toward it.

"We're showing thirty knots speed," yelled the first mate, "but the GPS says we're still going backward."

"Full ahead!" yelled Tony.

"What's going on?" I asked, still numb.

"I don't know," Tony answered. "We're caught in a current of some kind."

"Our heading has changed to twenty degrees," yelled the mate. "Now twenty-five . . . thirty."

The rain eased up somewhat, and we were able to see through the windows that the cutter was drawing quickly away from us and was almost directly west. What was left of Clawson's yacht was straight south.

"We're being pulled in a circle," said the astonished mate. "Heading is now forty-five degrees."

"What the—" Tony cursed. He made a dash out the door and headed topside. Curtis and I followed. The rain had nearly stopped, and the clouds were slightly less ominous than before, but the wind was still ferocious. "We're caught in a hurricane or something," Curtis yelled.

Tony looked all around. "I don't think so," he said.

The three boats became more spread out than ever, but it became evident that all three were being swept by the same tide. The yacht, being smaller and half-submerged, was going much faster than us, especially since it wasn't fighting back. The cutter, being much larger and more powerful, had given up on Clawson's yacht and was trying to maintain its original position.

In a matter of minutes we were heading east, then southeast, then south. The cutter was becoming smaller and smaller to the north, nearly a mile away from us, but still following us around.

"It's like we're caught in a whirlpool," Curtis said, almost under his breath.

"Nonsense," Tony said gruffly. "There's no such thing in the ocean."

Still, the effect was exactly that. No matter how much power the crew applied to the engines, we were being swept helplessly backward in a wide circle, about six miles in circumference. The cutter was following us, but in a wider arc, while the remains of Clawson's yacht were much nearer the center and nearly submerged.

As we stood grasping the railing and surveying the wide ocean, a truly remarkable thing happened. The flat ocean surface began to sink about two miles away from us. It was like some giant had pushed a mile-wide glass bowl against the ocean, causing a huge depression in what should have been level water. The depression got deeper and deeper, and wider and wider. Clawson's yacht was soon sucked to the very edge of it.

"Impossible!" yelled Curtis.

"It IS a whirlpool!" I yelled.

"We've got to get out of this circle!" Tony said, suddenly struck with fear. He ran back down to the bridge.

The center of the huge depression suddenly collapsed downward, as though someone had pulled the plug on the bottom of the ocean. Clawson's yacht was quickly sucked in and disappeared over the edge into what looked like a liquid tornado.

Soon, Tony came back up on the sundeck with a hand-held walkie-talkie and shouted instructions to his crew below. Using the center of the whirlpool as his reference, he started the ship on a slight outward spiral, trying to distance us a little at a time from the center and the pull of the current.

Trying to steer with the instruments had become a hopeless cause.

As we struggled against the relentless current, we saw one of the Coast Guard's small boats come into view some distance away. We strained our eyes, trying to make out who was in it. "That's the boat Roshayne was supposed to be in!" I yelled frantically.

Curtis just nodded his head, thinking the same thing I was. If she hadn't managed to get in that boat, where was she? Swimming helplessly by herself on her own? Not with her hands tied! Saved by the other Coast Guard boat? I could only hope.

I grabbed Tony's binoculars and hurriedly focused on the boat. I expected to at least see Hawk and Clawson, maybe Derek. But it was completely empty.

"No!" I yelled. "NO!!" I shook my fists at the heavens. What kind of God would let this happen after so much effort? What happened to the angel's promise? What happened to faith and prayers? I collapsed to my knees in despair.

After three complete trips around the shrinking spiral, we were again on the west side where we had first started. Tony was sweating profusely, still yelling into his radio. Curtis and I stared trance-like at the gaping hole in the ocean.

We were losing headway. As hard as he tried, Tony could not get his boat out of the whirlpool's grasp. As we approached the north point of the circle, we came so close we could see a hundred feet down the far wall of the funnel. Second by second, yard by yard, we were drawn closer and closer until we were on the very edge. The yacht started tipping sideways, being pulled mercilessly into the abyss. There was nothing left to do except hang on tight and prepare ourselves for certain death.

Just at that moment we heard a loud, rushing sound and saw a huge column of spray being belched from the funnel high into the air. It was followed immediately by tons and tons of water, like Old Faithful, only a hundred times higher.

Whatever demon of the sea had pulled the plug had finally decided to put it back. The sucking effect was stopped. The sea rose up under us like a fast elevator, causing a sinking feeling in my stomach as the funnel collapsed on itself and inverted into the sky. Salt water came down on us in torrents, flooding the deck and sweeping anything loose off the sides.

We hung on for dear life. After lifting us nearly fifty feet in the air, the ocean sank again, leaving us momentarily airborne. Then we followed it down with a vengeance. It was nothing short of a miracle that the boat didn't burst at the seams, but the sturdy hull took the shock, and we rolled and pitched crazily from side to side for several minutes.

Ultimately, the surging water found its level, as it always does. Within minutes, the clouds thinned, the wind died, and the waves subsided. It was as if nothing had ever happened. The whole ocean, from horizon to horizon, settled into an eerie calm.

Amazingly, we were still afloat. And still alive.

Chapter 27

- In Shock -

As a lot, we survived fairly well. One of the crewmembers had broken a leg, which the others braced in a makeshift splint. There were also several cuts and bruises, which Candy attended to from the first-aid kit on board. Other than that, we were whole.

The numbness in my own bruised and battered limbs did not compare to the numbness that settled over my mind as I struggled to accept Roshayne's horrible fate. I slowly went into shock, and the events of the next several hours went by in a barely recognizable semi-blur.

The María had not faired as well as was originally thought. There were several cracks in the hull, and it was taking on water quickly. After only half an hour, she had settled two feet deeper than usual in the water. Tony found some flares in the emergency trunk and fired several into the air. A few minutes later, the Coast Guard cutter was spotted heading in our direction.

The motorboat I had left dangling off the back was long gone, and there was only a small raft on board, plus several life jackets. We all put on the vests and watched as the yacht sank lower and lower. The crew tried their best to breathe life back into the abused engines, but they refused to cooperate.

Finally, seeing that the cutter was not going to arrive in time, we inflated the raft and abandoned ship. We looked on in silent reverence as the María gurgled her way into the sea, rolling over on her side like a wounded whale, and pitched nose-first into the deep. Several bursts of bubbles came back to the surface, then there were only faint ripples left marking her grave.

For another thirty minutes, we floated gently but helplessly on the nearly glass-smooth surface of the Bermuda Triangle, the sun burning down from a clear blue sky. The events of the preceding hours seemed like a bad dream, and I began to drift in and out of consciousness.

If only I could just wake up, I thought, *I'll find myself in my nice warm, dry bed at home. This entire thing is just a horrible nightmare. I'll get up in a few minutes and take a hot shower and put on some clean clothes. Then I'll go downstairs to the kitchen and have some of Mom's famous Elderberry Casserole and a tall glass of ice-cold milk. Later on this afternoon, I'll call Paul in Payson, and we'll take Tamara and Roshayne out to eat—maybe to the same restaurant where we went on our first date. That'd be nice. Maybe—*

I was brought somewhat back to reality when two pairs of hands lifted me up by my armpits and passed me bodily up a ladder. Other hands reached down and pulled me in over the side, where still more hands covered me with blankets and carried me into a cool, air-conditioned room somewhere. My wet clothes were stripped away and replaced with dry ones. A cold rag was placed on my forehead, and the lights turned down.

I imagined at one point that Paul was looking down at me. I saw his mouth moving, as though he was talking to me, but I didn't register the sounds. Then Tamara's face came slowly into focus alongside Paul's. Then Candy and Alan and Curtis. I closed my eyes and pinched them tight. *I'm hallucinating,* I thought.

Even with my eyes closed, I saw images of people. Lots of people gathering around and looking down on me. Then the crowd parted, and I saw Roshayne leaning over me and smiling. *Bart,* she said, *wake up. It's time to wake up.*

Her smile was beautiful, her hair glistening and smooth, her lips perfectly formed. There was a sparkle in her dark brown eyes, and she leaned over and kissed me on the cheek. *Come on, Bart,* she whispered in my ear. *Please wake up. You need to wake up now.*

She backed away, and her smile faded. I tried to reach for her, but couldn't raise my arms. They were so, so heavy.

Bart, wake up . . .

Don't go! I pleaded, but she backed away and was lost in the crowd. *Roshayne, don't go! I love you! Please, don't leave me!*

Bart . . . Bart . . .

"BART!"

My eyes flew open as my name came resonating through my groggy mind. There was Paul again, with Tamara, smiling down. "Come on, Bart," he said. "You can do it."

"Paul?" I said shakily. "Tammy?"

"We're here," Tamara said, smiling. She bent down and gave me a kiss on the cheek.

"You can't get rid of us that easily," Paul said, placing his hand on my shoulder.

I struggled to sit up, and hands and arms came from everywhere to help me.

"Where am I?" I asked, rubbing my eyes to clear the cobwebs.

"The infirmary on the Coast Guard cutter," Curtis said, coming around into view.

"We thought we'd lost you there," Candy said, coming around the other side. "You slipped off into la-la land in the raft. Are you okay?"

All at once, the full recollection of the day's events came flooding back. Clawson. The María. Hawk. The Coast Guard. Whirlpool. The storm. Roshayne.

"Roshayne!" I cried out. "Where's Roshayne?!"

All eyes went to the floor, and silence reigned supreme in the room. I looked from one face to the next, hoping against hope.

"No!" I groaned. "Don't tell me—"

"She's gone, Bart," Tamara said softly, kneeling in front of me and taking my hand in hers. "We've looked everywhere. She . . . she—" Her voice cracked, and tears flowed.

"Oh, please," I cried, my own tears bathing my cheeks. "No. Please, no."

I fell back down on the bed and cried like I had never cried before. My chest heaved, and my lungs seemed to burst from the agony. "Why?!!" I screamed at the ceiling.

No one spoke for several minutes, allowing me to vent my anguish. Finally the tears stopped, and I sat up. Not daring to make eye contact with anyone, I rose to my feet and stumbled out of the infirmary, looking for some open air. I could hear them all following. Several men in uniform passed us, but none of them said anything to me, as if they knew. They all knew.

Why didn't they save her? I cried inside. *That's their job. Where were they?*

At the rear of the boat, I ran out of places to go and stopped at the railing. I gazed blindly out over the sea, while the gentle breeze slowly dried my tears. The sun was about to set in the west. Apparently, I'd been out for several hours. Too many hours. Too long to still have any hope, I knew. Still, I couldn't accept that she was gone.

Behind me, my friends waited patiently.

They're hurting, too, I realized, feeling selfish. *We've all lost a friend.* When I was finally able to trust myself to speak, I turned to face them. "Tell me what's going on," I said quietly.

Curtis began. "We were picked up by the Guard without any problem, after the María sank. As soon as they had us on board, they began a search pattern. They knew exactly where the center of the whirlpool had been, so they plotted a grid covering a seven-mile radius around that."

"We've been steaming back and forth ever since," Paul added. "They've had their one remaining boat out looking everywhere, and the helicopter has been in the air constantly all afternoon."

"They haven't found a thing," Candy said with a tone of absolute finality.

I leaned against the rail for a minute and let that register. "What about the two girls?" I asked, "and Carlos' crew?"

"They're all here," Curtis answered. "They're fine. Of course, Carlos is—" He couldn't bring himself to say the word.

"What about all the other guys from the boats?" I asked, avoiding the real question. "I saw some of them—"

"All fine," said Curtis.

"And Tony?"

"Mad as heck, but fine," Alan said. "If you hadn't been out cold in the raft, he would have killed you for losing his boat."

I managed a thin smile.

"I'm sure it's insured," Paul said.

"So . . . what about . . . Clawson? And Derek? And . . ." I didn't know what to hope for.

"They're gone, Bart," Paul said, putting his hand on my arm. "There's no sign of any of them."

"Are you sure?" I asked, searching his eyes for any clues of insincerity.

"Positive."

I closed my eyes, leaned my head back, and let out a long breath. "I want to be alone for a while," I said at length, "if you don't mind." I heard footsteps receding. When I was sure I was alone, I opened my eyes and stared into the darkening sky.

"Why, Lord?" I prayed out loud. "Didn't I do everything I could? Didn't I make every effort I could possibly make?" Tears began to flow again. "Why did she have to die?" I lowered my chin to my chest and sobbed. "I've tried to use the gift the way the angel said. I've tried. I wasn't out for revenge. Honest. All I wanted was to get Roshayne back." My lip quivered, and I lost my voice to emotion.

"It's not fair," I whispered hoarsely. "It should have been me. I'm the one they wanted. Take me and bring her back. Please, God. Bring her back." I sank to my knees and sat back heavily on my heels.

Alone in an open sea, with the heavens looking down and earth holding its breath, I cried. I cried and cried until tears wouldn't come anymore. Then I cried without them. My chest heaved and ached from the excruciating pain in my heart.

I stood up and stretched my arms upward, my fingers extended and my hands and arms shaking.

"WHY?!!" I screamed at the top of my lungs.

All strength left me, and I collapsed to the deck and wept a fresh batch of tears.

Chapter 28

- Angels -

After an undetermined length of time, I heard footsteps around me on the metal deck again. Slowly I opened my eyes, and found Paul and Tamara standing in front of me. They had anguished looks, concerned looks on their faces. I realized I was being unfair. They had a right to mourn, too.

"So, how did you guys get here anyway?" I asked, before they could say anything. I wasn't ready to talk about it yet.

"We got as far as the Eisenhower Tunnel," Paul said, "and Tammy convinced me we had made a big mistake, leaving you to face Clawson by yourself. She wasn't going to give me a minute's peace until we turned around and went back. We parked my truck at the airport and flew to Miami. We maxed out her credit card."

"We decided it was time for bigger help," Tamara added, "so we found the Coast Guard office and told them what was going on."

"We told them we knew all about Clawson, and how he was wanted for murder, and had escaped from prison and everything," Paul said. "They just laughed at us. They didn't believe us at all. We just kept harping on them until they finally pulled up the warrants on the fax. But then we couldn't tell them where they were, and they told us finding them out there was hopeless. They kicked us out."

"We were flabbergasted," Tamara said. "We walked down the sidewalk a few feet, feeling sorry for ourselves. Then Paul turned around and said, 'They're not going to get rid of me that easy,' and he stomped back into their front office. He forced his way right past the front desk and into that captain's office . . . or admiral, or whatever he was . . . and said, 'We're wanted, too. There are warrants out for our arrest. We're criminals, and if you don't take us into custody right now, you'll never see us again.' It was really something."

"So he arrested us," Paul said with a smile. "They pulled up our warrants from Utah and threw us in the brig. We spent most of the night in jail again."

"Two nights in a row, Bart," Tamara said, making an attempt at some humor. "How am I ever going to live this down? An innocent thing like me."

I chuckled.

"Early in the morning, when we had finally fallen asleep on those hard-as-a-rock cots, they came and got us," Paul continued. "The admiral said they had received a call from some ship describing the same guys we had talked about . . . must have been that Tony guy . . . and their cutter had been dispatched.

"They rushed us to an airfield somewhere, put us on a Lear jet, and flew us to some base in Puerto Rico. Then they put us on a helicopter, and we flew out and landed on the cutter. We got here barely a half hour before they caught up with Clawson."

"And you know the rest of the story," Tamara said, regretting it immediately.

"Yeah," I muttered.

"Bart?" Paul said tentatively after a moment of awkward silence.

"What?"

"Tammy and I have been talking and . . . well . . . we wanted to ask you something."

"Okay."

"You remember how you visited Jill after the accident? When she was in a coma in the hospital?"

"Yeah," I said cautiously.

"And you saw her spirit and talked to her?"

I nodded.

"Is there? . . . I mean . . . do you think . . .?"

Tamara took over. "We want to know if you can project to dead . . . deceased people."

"What . . . ?" I stammered. "I don't . . ." I suddenly realized what they were asking. "To Roshayne?" I blurted out. My eyes opened wide. "Do you think—?"

"Can you?" Tamara asked urgently. "If you could just talk to her for a minute, you could tell her goodbye . . . for all of us." A single tear escaped and trickled down her cheek. "We all loved her, Bart."

I was in shock. Why hadn't I thought of that? *Of course. Why not?* "I've got to try," I said, heading for the nearest door.

Paul and Tamara hurried to keep up. "We can go back to the infirmary," Paul suggested. "There are beds there, and nobody's in there right now."

I got more excited by the minute. *Is it possible I could find her in the spirit world? Will they even let me in?* I remembered hearing that dead people hang around the earth for a while, before they're taken to their place in heaven. *If I hurry, I might still find her there!* I picked up my pace. *Please be there, Rosh!*

Once in the seclusion of the infirmary, I threw myself on the nearest bed and straightened out, placing my hands on my chest and closing my eyes. Paul and Tamara huddled over me, smiling hopefully. "Tell her I'll miss her," Tamara said, getting misty-eyed.

"Me, too," Paul added, wiping away a tear of his own.

I concentrated on relaxing for a minute or two and tried to slow down my breathing. Then, at the last minute, I remembered that I had sworn not to jump out again for fear of Hawk getting in my body. I opened my eyes and bolted upright. "What if Hawk gets in my body?" I cried out.

"He's dead, Bart."

"So?"

"So, he's not going into anybody's body. Not his, not yours, not anybody's ever again."

"What if I run into him or Clawson up there?" That thought scared me to death.

"Believe me, Bart," Paul said seriously, "they're NOT going to be 'up there' in the same place as Roshayne. You can count on that."

My fears quelled somewhat, I lay down again and closed my eyes. I breathed deeply and flexed my fingers. *Roshayne,* I thought. *Where are you? Let me find you.*

I thought back to the last time I had seen her and envisioned her swirling around in the water, hands tied behind her back, gasping for air. I pictured her being sucked under and kicking her way to the surface again.

Then I imagined her being pulled down by the force of the whirlpool, her eyes bulging in fear, her cheeks bloated, her lungs starving for air. I pictured her squirming and fighting until she lost consciousness, then floating helplessly, lifelessly to the bottom of the ocean, burying herself in the mud.

I sprang up on the bed again. "I can't!" I yelled out.

"Why not, Bart?" Tamara asked, surprised.

"All I can see is her drowning and struggling and . . . she's at the bottom of the ocean and . . . the sharks . . ."

"Bart," Tamara said sweetly, "Roshayne is NOT at the bottom of the ocean. You, of all people, should know that. She left her body, just like you do. She went . . . Inviz. Think about it . . . she's floating around up there somewhere, waiting for you." She waved her hand at the ceiling. "Go find her." She held my hand in hers and gave me a big smile of encouragement.

"Of course," I said, feeling stupid.

I lay down again and tried to relax. I tried to picture Roshayne out-of-body and waiting somewhere for me. It brought to mind the scene I had witnessed during my near-death experience at the entrance to the spirit world. I was immediately calmed by the feelings of love and serenity I had felt there. I smiled. *She's going to love it there,* I thought. *It's so beautiful.*

I finally relaxed enough to get myself in a state of trance, and concentrated on bringing on the vibrations. They finally came, and at last I separated from my body and hovered over the bed. I could see Paul and Tamara holding hands and looking down at my body. *They'd make a good couple,* I thought for no reason at all. *Well, let's see if this works.*

Roshayne! I commanded myself. *Wherever you are!*

There was the customary blur of light, and I was filled with the thrill and expectation of finding her clothed in white, surrounded by family and friends, waiting to rush up and hug me and kiss me. It would be a glorious reunion!

A split second later, I stopped. But I was not in heaven—not even close. I was still out in the middle of the ocean. I looked around in all directions. Nothing but water as far as the eye could see. No Coast Guard, no yacht, no nothing. I looked up, thinking maybe she might be waiting over the site of her death.

Nothing. No one. No lights, no angels. No Roshayne.

I was devastated. What went wrong?

Suddenly, I heard a creaking sound directly beneath me. Looking down, I discovered that I was hovering about thirty feet over a small motorboat that was drifting alone on the water. It was Tony's lost boat. And there was someone in it!

"Roshayne!" I yelled. *"Holy cow, Roshayne!"*

I rushed down for a closer look. She was lying in a really odd position on her back, with her head tipped slightly to one side. Her arms and legs were submerged in several inches of water, but her hands were no longer tied. Her hair floated lazily back and forth with the rocking motion of the sea. Her eyes were closed, and her mouth was just millimeters above the water.

Please be alive! I begged.

It seemed like she was breathing, but I wasn't sure. I made myself visible immediately.

"Roshayne!" I yelled right next to her ear. She made a faint moaning sound. "She's alive!" I yelled to the whole world. "She's alive! Oh, thank you, God! Thank you! Thank you!" I yelled in her ear again. "Wake up, Rosh! I'm here!"

She didn't move. I rose up into the air to try and determine where we were. Establishing my directions by the remnants of the setting sun, I scanned the horizon. Only water. I rose higher into the air, scanning fervently in all directions.

Finally, at about a thousand feet, I spotted the mast of the cutter way to the north on the edge of the horizon. Roshayne was miles south of where the whirlpool had taken place. Miles south of the entire search grid.

How on earth did she get way down here? I wondered.

BACK TO BODY!

"She's alive!" I yelled, flying off the bed like I was spring-loaded. Paul and Tamara just about died of heart attacks.

"What . . .?" Paul stammered.

"She's alive, Paul! I found her! She's in a boat! Tammy, she's—" I ran out of the room, leaving them gasping for breath, and raced as fast as I could to the bridge to tell the captain. "She's alive!" I yelled to everybody I saw. "Glory hallelujah, she's alive!!"

Minutes later I was on board the helicopter, adjusting my ear protectors and strapping myself in. I hardly dared breathe during the swift flight out over the water. It was almost dark. *An hour later and we might never have found her,* I realized.

When the tiny boat came into view, I saw that Roshayne was awake and sitting up. She stood to greet us, waving both arms high over her head, and nearly capsized the boat. Hovering a mere ten feet above the water, two frogmen jumped out of the open sliding door into the water. They pulled themselves simultaneously into opposite sides of the boat. Before they could even think about removing their masks, Roshayne was smothering them with hugs and kisses.

A boom was swung out the side and a cable lowered. The frogmen carefully fitted her into the swing-like harness and signaled the operator. As she came up, my face erupted in tears of joy, and my heart caught in my throat. I motioned to the guardsman in front of me, and he moved over, allowing me the privilege. I almost fell out in my anxiety.

Her hand stretched out to meet mine, and we clasped each other firmly by the wrists. I swung her eagerly inside the cabin and wrapped her up in a ferocious bear hug, harness and all. We both started blubbering at once.

"Oh, Bart, you came . . ."

"I thought I'd never see you again . . ."

"I was so scared . . ."

"I was terrified. I thought you'd . . ."

"Thank you, thank you . . ."

We hugged some more, totally oblivious to the dozens of stares boring in on us.

"Bartholomew Elderberry, I love you so much," she said between breaths.

"And I love you, Roshayne Pennini." We hugged again.

Roshayne laughed and tried to dry one eye with the back of her hand. "I think they want to take this thing off me," she said, glancing around.

"Not a chance," I said, pulling her back. "I'm not ever letting go of you again. They're going to have to use crowbars and blow-torches to get us apart."

"That's okay," one of the men said. "Hug away. We're only burning fuel here at the rate of about a hundred bucks a minute."

We both laughed, and with great reluctance I let her go while they got her out of the straps. Then we sat together in the back of the helicopter and held hands and smiled at each other. I put my arm around her, and she nestled her head against my shoulder. The noise was too loud to talk over, so we just cuddled and enjoyed.

I had never been so happy in my entire life.

When we landed, the gang was there, anxiously waiting. Tamara climbed right in, and they hugged and cried 'til the cows came home. Paul was next, and got more than his fair share, in my selfish opinion. As we stepped out of the chopper, Paul introduced Roshayne to Curtis, Candy, and Alan. They all extended eager hands, but Roshayne gathered them all in a group hug.

Then she hugged the helicopter crew, and the pilot, and the mechanics, and the admiral . . . or whatever he was . . . and every willing male on board, of which there were dozens. I'd never seen so many hugs.

Finally, a young woman in uniform escorted Roshayne to the ladies' quarters for some dry clothes and a quick medical exam. I paced a trail in the floor waiting for her, exchanging laughs and high-fives with my friends. No sooner did she emerge than we were all swept away into a dining room, where an impromptu party was thrown in her honor.

It was a giddy affair. We drank gallons of Sprite and ate barrels of cookies. I couldn't believe our good fortune. God had smiled down on us after all. Roshayne was safe and sound, and the bad guys were history. I was suddenly ashamed that nearly three hours had passed since the rescue, and I hadn't bothered to thank the One responsible.

Dear Lord, I prayed mentally amid the noise and commotion, *I thank thee from the bottom of my heart. I thank thee for the gift that made this possible, for my life, for my good friends, for everything. I am eternally and sincerely grateful.*

It was well into the morning before Roshayne and I finally had a chance to get away by ourselves and compare notes.

"They're really gone?" she said, referring to Clawson, Derek, and Hawk.

"They're totally toast," I said without a single bit of remorse. "They got what was coming to them."

"And they got it from the one person they deserved most to get it from," she said, her eyes staring deep into space.

"Wait a minute," I defended. "I didn't kill them. I never—"

"I'm not talking about you, Bart."

I looked at her in total confusion.

"Who then? God?"

She smiled sweetly. "Bart, aren't you even the least bit curious about how I managed not to drown?"

"Of course I am. We just haven't had a chance—"

"Come here," she ordered, taking me by the hand. She led me to the rear of the ship, to the same place where I had questioned God only hours before. It was quite dark, lit only by a couple of running lights on the ship. The sky was studded with stars, and a full moon was just making its way out of the eastern sea.

"I've got something very special to tell you," she said.

"Okay," I said hesitantly.

We leaned against the railing, facing each other.

"Do you have any idea what it's like to drown, Bart?"

I swallowed hard. "I can imagine—"

"No, you can't. Not in your wildest dreams or worst nightmares." She paused and gathered her thoughts, staring over my shoulder into the night. "My whole life flashed before my eyes, Bart. I saw everything I had ever done. Everything I had ever said. I knew I was going to die." She looked me dead in the eye. "But not without a fight," she said firmly. "I fought hard. I kicked and kicked with my legs, trying to get back to the surface. Every time I did, I swallowed more water than air. My lungs ached, and I tried to cough it back out. Then more water came in. It was . . . it was . . ."

I put a hand on her arm. "I know," I said sympathetically.

"My hands were tied," she said, her voice faltering, "and I couldn't get them loose." She looked down at her wrists, still red and swollen from the abuse of the ropes. "My whole chest felt like it was going to explode." She sniffed loudly and choked on her words. "I started to see stars and colors, then everything started spinning around, and I was being sucked down. I looked up at the surface, shining and sparkling, mimicking me."

Her whole body began to tremble, and I clutched her shoulders firmly to steady her.

"It was so horrible," she cried, covering her face with one hand. "I kept going down and down, and my ears hurt, and my head felt like something was squeezing it so hard. I was totally desperate. I panicked and tried to scream, then I choked, and the whole ocean came inside me . . . then I passed out, I guess."

She stopped.

"You passed out?" I asked, wondering why she was standing in front of me and not lying on the bottom of the ocean. "So how—?"

"An angel saved me," she said, straightening up and grabbing my hands. She smiled, and her moist eyes sparkled in the moonlight.

"An angel?" I choked.

Thoughts of the angel David came to mind, along with a complete recollection of my own near-death experience. "An angel?" I repeated, getting more and more excited. "David?"

"Who's David? No, Bart, it was a girl."

"Oh, of course. Your guardian angel would be a—"

"She wasn't my guardian angel."

"Then?"

"Well . . ." Her eyes took on a faraway, glossy look. "I was sinking and sinking, and I heard someone calling my name, very softly. I thought I must have died, and they were calling me. You know . . . the angels. I opened my eyes, and there she was—so beautiful, shining white, her long, golden hair floating around in the air . . . or the water . . . I'm not sure. She touched my lips with her finger . . . and my chest suddenly quit hurting. I was breathing. Under water, I was breathing.

"Then she reached out to me. The ropes fell off my wrists, and I reached back. She took me by the hands and pulled me through the water. I can distinctly remember feeling the water flowing very fast around me. After a long, long time I broke through the surface, sputtering and coughing."

She paused. "The next thing I remember, I was lying in that boat, and the helicopter was coming."

My mouth was hanging wide open, my mind absorbing the story. It was so much like things I had seen and experienced myself—no one else could possibly have understood better.

"Did she say anything to you?" I asked breathlessly. "Did she tell you her name or anything?"

"She didn't say anything . . . but she didn't have to tell me her name." Roshayne smiled. "I already knew."

I waited expectantly.

"It was Tiffany," she said in a hushed voice, her eyes watering again. "That beautiful angel . . . was Tiffany."

The revelation hit me like a brick, and my vision blurred beyond repair. Neither of us said another word for several minutes. We both just stood gazing into the night, holding hands, and sharing in the sacredness of that special moment.

They got their just due, all right, I thought. *And so did she.*

CHAPTER 29

- Suntans -

We arrived in port about mid-morning. Between the Coast Guard and the police, we were run ragged by the end of the day. We filled out a mountain of forms, reports, and statements, being shuffled from office to office and from building to building. By the time we got done, I wasn't sure which was worse, facing Clawson or dealing with the government.

In the evening, it finally began to dawn on us that we were finished with the whole mess, free to do whatever we wanted to do, stranded on a Caribbean island—and wealthy. Candy, bless her heart, had had the good sense to wear Tamara's backpack around from the moment I left my body on the yacht, so we had a grundle of money. I gave Tony what he needed to cover the deductible for his insurance, and he promptly began the process of buying a bigger, better yacht. By the bulges in his pockets, it was evident that he still had the original money we had given him, so he wasn't hurting by any means. Once he realized that he was in for a nice upgrade, he became our instant best friend. In fact, he arranged with a friend of his to take us all deep-sea fishing later in the week and insisted that we stay.

Well, we couldn't pass up the chance at an instant vacation, so we all got on the phones, called home, and bought airline tickets for nearly everybody. My parents were floored. Once they finally got over their shock and realized that I was still alive and breathing, and that the bad guys were out of our lives forever, they jumped up and down at the vacation idea. The girls screamed so loud that I could hardly hear. I was worried about how Charlene was doing, but Mom told me she had recovered miraculously and in record time, and by Monday morning she was in perfect health, like nothing had happened. The doctors had no choice but to let her go home.

They all flew to San Juan the very next day: Mom, Dad, Darin, Charlene, and Cynthia. Roshayne's parents came with them, plus Paul's whole family and Tamara's mom.

Curtis' folks couldn't make it because of a funeral they were doing at the mortuary. Curtis, Candy, and Alan only spent a couple of days with us, swimming and snorkeling, then took off for Wyoming again in Alan's Lancair IV-P.

I also bought a ticket for George. Mom informed me that the police had hounded him incessantly after Curtis disappeared, but that he had defended himself and us valiantly.

I had almost forgotten that he had been in the car with us during the search. It never occurred to me that he would be a suspect. I felt guilty about how I had treated him earlier, and made a special effort to befriend him during our instant vacation.

With Roshayne's signed testimony, along with those of Clawson and Derek's girlfriends and Carlos' crew, the police were able to put together a pretty complete story. They talked with the police in Utah and Colorado, sent them copies of everything, and convinced them that we were innocent victims.

A couple of days later, we learned that the Orem police had managed to extract some fingerprints from the money found in Dad's car, and traced them to a two-bit thief in Sandy. He was arrested, spilled his guts, got all his buddies arrested along with him, and got us all off the hook for good.

I couldn't begin to put into words the relief that came with knowing we were no longer "wanted."

We rented a huge beach house, complete with a water-skiing boat, jet skis, scuba gear, and all the modern conveniences and toys imaginable, and had a regular riot.

Ten days later, on our last day on the island, Tony's friend came through with the fishing trip. It took some talking to get Roshayne on board—she was bound and determined that she would never set foot on a boat again—but she finally buckled to the pressure and came along.

"Hey, Bart! Top this!"

I looked across the deck at the sound of my name and saw Paul grinning from ear to ear. He was proudly displaying his latest catch—a huge Marlin that had to be at least six feet long.

"Shoot," I cussed under my breath as I started reeling in my line.

"Guess that about does it," Tamara said from the comfort of a padded lounge chair. "Time's up."

"Sure is," added George. He was posing next to his own catch for pictures. "And it looks like Bart drew the short straw."

The "short straw" meant I got to treat everybody to supper, admittedly not a difficult job, especially since I still held all the purse strings.

I climbed down from the fishing chair, gathered up my stuff, and retrieved my one and only two-and-a-half foot catch of the day.

"Hey, Bart," Roshayne teased, sipping at an ice-cold glass of tropical fruit punch. "Is that the seven-foot tuna fish you promised us? I thought you were good at this stuff."

"Yeah, yeah, yeah," I grimaced. "Go ahead, rub it in."

Epilogue

Well, another year has melted away. I've had a lot of time during my senior year to contemplate everything that happened. It's amazing, looking back, what crazy things people will do. I still can't believe I actually ran from the police.

What was I thinking?

It's also pretty incredible how much good people will do for the sake of love and honor. I'm deeply humbled whenever I remember that I was ready to sacrifice my own life to save Roshayne's. I'm convinced I'd do it again, though, in a heartbeat.

I'm also humbled whenever I think about the tremendous responsibility God has placed on my shoulders by granting me this wonderful/terrible gift. I'm not sure I'm up to another life-and-death adventure like the two I've been through already, but it's an awesome feeling knowing He's on my side and that He will always follow through with his end of the bargain.

I have a pretty good idea that I'm not done yet. Evil men, like Samuel Clawson, Derek Monroe, and Silver Hawk, will always be around.

There is still SO much to do.

About the Author

Brent "BJ" Rowley is a man of varied interests who describes himself as an enterprising entrepreneur—someone determined to experience life to its fullest. He has a diverse background in such things as residential painting, Indian dancing, commodities trading, and heavy equipment operator, to mention only a few. BJ currently works fulltime as a network engineer.

Writing young-adult fiction is a relatively new interest recently added to his list.

"It never occurred to me to write anything before," he says. "In fact, one of my worst classes in high school was twelfth-grade creative writing. I hated writing, and could never come up with ANYTHING creative at all."

With the success of his first novel, *My Body Fell Off!* (also published as *Light Traveler: The Adventure Begins*) and the subsequent creation of its sequel, *Silver Hawk's Revenge*, he has developed a new passion for the written word.

BJ also enjoys computer games, traveling, playing the guitar, and spending time with his family. He lives with his wife and the youngest three of his five children in Orem, Utah.

BJ would love to hear from his readers. You can write to him via e-mail at: fanmail@bjrowley.com

Or visit his website: http://www.bjrowley.com

He may also be contacted by writing in care of Golden Wings Enterprises: P.O. Box 468, Orem, Utah 84059-0468

Author's Note

Since the original publication of this adventure series (under two different titles), I have received varying degrees of criticism from a few individuals and organizations about the implications of depicting Astral Projection as a "Gift from God." And many have wondered about my incentive and motivation to write these stories the way I did. I would therefore like to explain the hows and whys . . . for anyone who's interested.

The original idea for this book came from reading a book many years ago entitled *Stranger With My Face* by Lois Duncan. Prior to that time, I had never heard of the term "Astral Projection" nor had I ever heard of anyone having, or claiming to have, the ability to leave their bodies at will. I was particularly surprised to learn that certain groups of people, notably Indians in the Southwest, claimed to be able to teach and learn the art.

The idea stuck with me, and I pondered it on and off over the ensuing years. After all, who hasn't wondered sometime during their life what it would be like to be "a fly on the wall" and to be able to observe things otherwise not possible or permissible?

When I first entertained the idea of writing a novel, my goal and objective was to write a book that would be uplifting and enlightening to my readers—one that would inspire them to live betters lives as a result thereof.

Yet, at the same time, I wanted a book that would be captivating and interesting and fun to read. I refer to this type of wholesome entertainment as a "page-turning good time." And, in fact, the most common response I hear from my readers now is the phrase, "I just couldn't put it down." So I must have done something right along the way.

When I began searching for a topic, I was reminded of this unusual phenomenon of Astral Projection and decided to make it my central theme. My original outline for the first book was simple: 1) The protagonist discovers that he has the ability to leave his body at will, and 2) he uses his newfound ability to solve some sort of major crime. From there, the book just fell together, almost as fast as I could type.

But the fact remained that I really didn't know anything about Astral Projection beyond what I had read those many years ago in one solitary youth novel.

I realized that I needed to do some homework.

As I undertook my research, I made a number of startling discoveries. One was that there actually ARE many real people in the world who CAN leave their bodies at will. And many of them have already written books on the subject. I was fascinated to read of their out-of-body experiences and to learn about the things they saw and did in the spirit realms.

At first it was somewhat confusing. They all used their own phrases and terminology to describe their experiences, and I had a difficult time following them. But gradually I came to realize that they were all essentially saying the same thing. And when I overlaid their terminology with words that felt comfortable to me—from concepts that I had learned in my own religious upbringing—things became startlingly clear. It was like a revelation to me. I was truly entranced, and I yearned to know more.

Once I started visiting libraries, I discovered that nearly all books on the subject of Astral Projection were to be found on the same shelf as books about Palm Reading, ESP, Occultism, Shamanism, Black Magic, and various other paranormal topics. In fact, some of the Astral Projection books themselves mentioned or treated similar topics within their pages. This bothered me at first, because I had always related most of those sorts of things with Satan worship or other such bad doings. I certainly didn't want my books to portray "things evil." That would have defeated my entire purpose.

I thought a great deal on the subject, and finally concluded that perhaps none of those things were, in and of themselves, evil or bad. As I took a good long look around, I realized that virtually everything God has given us—be they talents and abilities, wisdom and intelligence, wealth and material possessions, or even inventions and technology—can all be used for either good or evil purposes, depending on the intentions of the individual. For instance, there's nothing inherently wrong with money—in and of itself. Yet MUCH good and MUCH evil have been accomplished with its use. The same can be said of virtually everything.

So I expanded my original goal and determined that I would portray the good that could come of someone endowed with this unusual ability. I deliberately avoided the use of any familiar terminology that might be interpreted as evil, and went to great lengths to depict my protagonist as a good person. I made it very clear, from the very beginning, that his ability WAS God given, and that it was intended to be used only for good.

Naturally I included a villain—a necessary element for a good book to achieve its end—and decided that he would be the exact opposite of my protagonist: someone who had learned or acquired the same ability, but had applied it to evil. The first two books in this series consist largely of the conflict between the two. In the end, the good wins.

And that's as it should be.

I have been richly rewarded with dozens and hundreds of fan letters and emails from people who had been "enlightened and uplifted, captivated and entertained" by my books. I've read many exuberant letters thanking me and sharing with me how my stories have inspired them or someone in their family—most notably teenagers and young adults who previously didn't have much of a desire to even read a book. I've been quite touched many times by tearful and emotional accounts of readers who have pledged to make their own lives better and to use their own gifts—whatever they might be—to the betterment of society.

And yet, still, there are some who would accuse me of advocating Satanism, promoting occultism, and dabbling in the forbidden and prohibited. I'm very sorry to have left that impression. It certainly was not my intention. I can only assume that their reasoning stems from a lack of understanding on their part concerning things spiritual, i.e. things beyond what we can see, hear, and touch in this limited, mortal existence.

Indeed, there is MUCH that we don't know. But there is much that we can learn. I would encourage those individuals to do some research of their own, and they will inevitably find what I have found: that the ability to leave one's body is a marvelous gift—one that almost always results in enhanced understanding, deeper wisdom, increased knowledge, and a clearer, more humble outlook on life—one that holds great potential for good, depending, of course, on the disposition of the gifted individual.

One final thought: It wasn't until later, after my books became widely distributed, that I made my most rewarding discovery. It turns out that there are actually people out there—people who have the gift—who don't know that it is, or can be, a good thing. They think they've been cursed. They live from day to day, minute to minute, ashamed of what they have, hiding it from their friends and family, or even trying to ignore or "undo" the gift. They didn't ask for it. It's just something they have, and they can't understand why they have it or what to do with it.

What a joy and a relief it is for them to discover and finally understand, through reading my books and others, that they aren't evil or condemned—to learn that what they have is really not bad at all. It's just a gift—like so many others enjoyed by the so-called "gifted and talented." It's how they use it that will ultimately determine its real worth.

I don't expect people to become super-spirit crime-solvers. That's the stuff good fiction is made of. But to hear of their resolve to share their gift and use it for good has brought me more fulfillment than I ever thought possible when I undertook this project.

And that's why I will continue the series, in spite of the criticism from the many "do-gooders" trying to "bring me to the light." I have seen too much good come of these books. And as it says in the scriptures, " . . . for every thing which inviteth to do good, and to persuade to believe in Christ, is sent forth by the power and gift of Christ: wherefore ye may know with a perfect knowledge it is of God."

My very ability to write is just such a gift, and I'm very grateful for it.

—Brent J. Rowley

Order Form

"The Perfect Gifts for Family and Friends"

To order additional, **autographed** copies of *Light Traveler Adventure Series,* send this form with a check or money order to:

Golden Wings Enterprises
P.O. Box 468
Orem, UT 84059-0468

Amount of Book 1 ordered (ISBN 0-9700103-1-1)	______ x	$11.95 =	$________
Amount of Book 2 ordered (ISBN 0-9700103-2-X)	______ x	$12.95 =	$________
Amount of Book 3 ordered (ISBN 0-9700103-3-8)	______ x	$13.95 =	$________
Sales Tax (add 6.25% for Utah addresses)			$________
Plus shipping and handling			$ 2.00
Total			$________

Ship to:

Name ____________________________________

Address __________________________________

City ____________________ State_______ ZIP______

E-mail Address ____________________________

Sending copies of this form is acceptable. Please allow three weeks for delivery. Prices good through December 31, 2001.

For fundraising, corporate, or reading club discounts, write to Golden Wings Enterprises, P.O. Box 468, Orem, UT 84059-0468